Henry and Rachel

Henry and Rachel

Laurel Saville

lake union publishing

The characters and events portrayed in this book are fictitious. Any similarity to real persons, living or dead, is coincidental and not intended by the author.

Printed in the United States of America.

Published by Lake Union Publishing
PO Box 400818
Las Vegas, NV 89140

ISBN-13: 9781611099669
ISBN-10: 1611099668
Library of Congress Control Number: 2013903608

This book was inspired by real people, specifically, my maternal great-grandparents, Henry Benjamin Ford and Rachel Gilks Ford. It includes some facts about their lives and partial transcripts of actual documents; it also includes stories and anecdotes that have been passed to me by family members and which may or may not be true. However, the book is purely a product of my imagination, making this a work of fiction.

Table of Contents

HENRY

Every morning, I wake up feeling older by so much more than a mere twenty-four hours. I open my eyes and everything seems blurry, as if I am encased in a dense fog. I find my first thoughts are absurd reminders to myself of who and where I am, as if I have been captured by an enemy and am reciting rank and standing: I am Henry Ford, tangled in the linens of my bed, in the small, south-facing bedroom of my home just outside Royalton in this blasted island in the West Indies. The month is January or February or whatever day and date happens to be in front of me, and the year is 1922. My enemy in this case is only time itself, the inexorable passing of the years that has turned me inexplicably into an old man. How, I wonder, is it possible that I am looking down the barrel of my approaching seventieth year?

It takes so much longer than seems possible to unfold my legs from beneath the sheets. My knees crack and I have pains that shoot down into my twisted feet, like a small bolt of lightning trying to find its way to the floor. When I look at my face in the glass, I am shocked to find a grizzled man looking back at me, his hair more salt than pepper and his cheeks full of ravines made by the rushing waters of years and experience. When I take my morning walk up the road, my heart pounds in my chest and my shoulders are so bound into my back that my arms hardly swing from my sides anymore. No matter how clear the sky, to me the sun looks forever shrouded in mists as it rises above the banana and palm trees. The frogs' croaking sounds like they are singing to me from the valley below instead of from the puddles that form after a downpour just a few yards away from the steps that lead to my veranda. The forest is encroaching, like my age, into the garden I beat out of this patch of jungle so many years ago.

No one tells you of the indignities of old age. They speak of the wisdom, the self-assuredness that supposedly comes from being free from the petty concerns of youth. My experiences have, yes, piled up around me, but it seems these days they are more like potato peelings in the kitchen, something to be discarded or fed to the pigs. Wisdom. Bah. I have more questions, more worry, I am more pensive now than I have ever been in all my life. I would give up almost any of these troublesome body parts to inhabit for just a week, hell, just a night, the virile, hopeful, ready-to-laugh and disposed-to-flirt young man I used to be.

I know I used to be that man. This is not mere nostalgia speaking. I remember that man, that earlier version of myself, so well.

As my body fails me, my memories grow sharper, more crystalline, teasing me with their unattainable clarity, torturing me with their brilliant distance. It is not vanity, but simple observation to say that women once flocked to me. And I to them. I was the center of lively discussions in the best drawing rooms. I remember the rich, oaky taste of fine cognac, the pungency of cigar smoke, the smell of the ladies' perfumes, the texture of a rich pudding on the tongue, the feel of a plump silk pillow behind my head. These constrained limbs once hauled up sails, these stiffened legs once maneuvered polo ponies, this sensitive stomach used to feast on meals that went on for hours. I dream of these things still, and in that brief, delicious morning moment when wakefulness is not yet full upon me, I believe my dreams are real. Until, of course, I am struck full in the face by the morning sunshine. Then, as I try to stretch my unwilling limbs in this silent house that has been emptied of life, I am painfully reminded just how far gone are those days of my fullest glories.

These flaccid loins have even fathered children. Who should be, by all rights, along with their own children, clustered around me now. Instead, I am fussed over not by chubby-cheeked and golden-ringleted grandchildren, but only an old black woman. Not as old as me, not as decrepit as me, but plenty creaky nonetheless.

And this heart. This heart whose beat flutters and sputters like a float on a tossing sea, well, it once loved. I can say that, at least, can I not? I loved my first wife deeply, as one does another with whom you have true friendship. My second wife, I loved desperately, as one does another with whom you have little sympathy but some blasted and unreasonable attraction. My children I loved as simply, straightforwardly, completely, and unquestioningly as a father does.

These past years have caused my heart to become untethered. There are no more scraped knees to kiss, soft curls to smooth back, hungry minds to feed with an opened book, a discovery in the forest, a speck of water on a piece of glass under the microscope. And there is no warm flesh to reach for in the middle of the night when the light of the full moon breaking in through the window causes one's eyelids to flutter open.

I do not understand, no matter how much I tug at my beard and rack my brain, how I came to be in this place. Not this place, this island. But this place in my life, this situation. Everything I did in my life was an effort to land someplace distinctly different. And yet here I am: an old man, alone, on an island I both love and despise, in the middle of the Caribbean, picking at old wounds with only their dull pain for company.

Oh, old man, stop this boring bellyaching. It is time to cheer up and cease this dull prattle. At least, and this is no small thing, there is Vea. I hear her now in the kitchen, moving plates. From my fog-filled distance of age, I can still smell the bite of the cardamom and the dankness of the coffee she is making, hear the sharp sizzle of eggs in the pan. She has managed to keep a few chickens in the yard. She coaxed them back from the forest and set them up in a henhouse she has slapped together from spare wood and rusty fencing so they will not be devoured by some sharp-toothed beast. This house, even though the paint is peeling and the floorboards are cupping and a few cupboard doors are hanging from broken hinges, is still standing, miraculously enough, not completely destroyed by nature's ugly rot or her foul moods that bring earthquakes and hurricanes. This roof keeps the rain off my old head. Which, I might note, still sports a vigorous mane, regardless of its color. There is the veranda with its broken railing, yes, but also its rocking chair and hammock, the stub of a leftover cigar in the ashtray. As is increasingly common, a patient came in needing dental work but had no hard currency to pay me, so he proffered a box of cigars instead. While they are cheap, their thick smoke provides some satisfaction. More satisfaction, no doubt, than the few coins I would have charged to yank out his yellowed teeth. There is a small view of the distant sea, even though it is growing more obscured each year as the bougainvillea thickens around the posts, and the trees spread their pestilential growth farther and farther up into the sky.

The sun comes through my somewhat tattered curtains now. It is time to throw off the covers, let my feet hit the floor, try to uncurl my stubborn, arthritic toes, shake off sleep and this dark mood. Vea is humming her low, soothing singsong—there's a comfort. There will be cream for the coffee, as her relations keep a cow or two. There will be the papers, filled with chitchat about who is arriving on what boats and whom they will visit and when the polo matches and croquet tournaments are to be held. Now that the Great War is over, and the world is crazy with music and dancing instead of with blowing each other to bits, this nonsense is what passes for news. Who wants to discuss the teetering economies of Europe, the tearing apart of the no-longer-aptly-named United Kingdom, the wave of poor scratch farmers who have come down from the hills and are wandering the streets here, looking for nonexistent work, when we can discuss how short hemlines and hairstyles will go instead?

At least there will be the post. I will write to James today and I will wish, again, that there is news from him. Again, I will cling to my Janus-faced hope that he sends me news also of his mother, while I simultaneously wish to never hear another word of that damned woman for whatever time I have remaining.

Ah, here is Vea, gently knocking, a tray of steaming, fragrant breakfast in her hands. Ah, Vea. At least she has not left me. She and the chickens. An old man could do far worse.

MR. GEORGE

Henry. He was the most maddening of men. Brilliant. And a bumbler. Sensitive and selfish, charming and conceited. And he drew women to him like moths to a flame. It was remarkable to me. I don't know what they saw in him. He was handsome, I suppose, in an avuncular sort of way. He was broad in the body, robust, full of himself mostly, but to me he seemed to be lacking a certain virility and raw strength I thought women coveted. He was not a financial success, something I thought most women found essential in a man. He was a good talker, though. I have little patience for conversation of almost any kind, but especially that of women. I suppose they enjoyed his stories and the way he always noticed a new hair ribbon, a fresh hairstyle, something about their dress. Or the way he asked after whatever their latest little interest was. Novels or orchid growing or a lapdog or something.

Women love that sort of thing, chitchat and small talk.

I think they also saw him as someone who could be made over, improved upon. Women are always susceptible to men they believe they can shape to their own liking. Men who are almost good enough, but not quite. Someone they are convinced they can mold into their picture of an ideal man. Which of course never works. Not that it stops them from trying. And then there was all that sympathy for his wife and child who died together in childbirth in some undeveloped backwater. Guyana, was it? Someplace Britain was trying to civilize by sending yet more colonials there. No matter how many boatloads of gentlemen arrive, it seems the jungles, the natives, the very earth itself in these parts refuse the constraints so essential to civilization. Why he would bring a pregnant woman to a place like that is impossible for me to understand. But the women who fawned over him didn't know and didn't ask. They were too happy to have some pitiful story and sympathetic history they could tut, and tsk, and chatter over.

Not Rachel, of course. She was never one for chatter. Preternaturally quiet, that one. When she came to live with us, what was she? Maybe eight, maybe ten? She always seemed so much older than her years. Her birth, of course, never recorded, the years sliding into one another. Her parents hoping we'd raise her in such a way that she could become a governess or teacher. Give her some civilization for a few years and then they'd come and claim her back. Not thinking she might not want to go back to them. Not thinking their fortunes might not go in the direction they were hoping.

In any case, she was not much for civilizing, as it turned out. She played the role assigned to her with as little affect as possible; she remained apart, separate from all the stuff of what we called polite society. Watching everything from some dim corner, taking it all in, but keeping her own counsel. Some days a nod was all you'd get out of her. However, she was not one to be underestimated. For one, she had great and unexpected raw physical strength. She was a wisp of a thing—well into her teenage years, she stayed small and skinny—but I myself saw her pull apart two fighting dogs and another time subdue a frantic horse. She also had stamina. She liked to work. She preferred the kitchen to the parlor, the barn to the dining room. I overheard the kitchen girls marveling at her capacity for long hours of hard work. They said they'd never seen a woman who wasn't black work like that. Even Vea, who was not normally impressed by much, took note of her, respected her. Even, I daresay, grew quite fond of her. There was vigor in that girl's body and steel in that girl's spine. Of course, it was more than that, really. Her true strength, her most breath-taking power, was not of the physical kind. There was also cold water in her veins and brutal pragmatism in her spirit. She took any and all of the abuses that life tossed at her and let them fall to the ground and writhe in their own pain. None of it touched her. Or if it did, she simply turned it into another layer of personal fortitude.

RACHEL

HENRY HAD A VOICE THAT TRAVELED. I ALWAYS KNEW WHEN HE was in the house. He came often. Sometimes just for dinner so he could try and get Mr. George to invest in one of his schemes, sometimes for the parties that the Georges used to hold regularly. There were a lot of gatherings back then, when things were prosperous and peaceful. Plantation owners like Mr. George, but also soldiers, officers, businessmen, young ladies sent over from England to live with an aunt and try to find a husband, dowagers tasked with matchmaking—they all mixed together in drawing rooms, at the hotel in town, and in the stands at the polo grounds. Henry was a man who liked to be in a group. He was one for company and conversation.

His voice was not loud so much as powerful. It was full of its own energy. Like a cart coming noisily down the road, Henry's voice rumbled through the rooms and along the halls and seemed to find me, made me take notice of it, whether I was busy in the kitchen chopping vegetables, in my room sewing, or in the yard plucking a chicken. He was filled with conviction. He was enthusiastic about everything. The sound of him made my lips curl upward of their own accord, no matter how much I tried to focus on the task in front of me. *Gusto* is the word I heard someone use once when describing Henry. That person was snickering when he said it. Some friend of Mr. George's. But in spite of the snicker, I liked the sound of the word so much I asked someone what it meant. It seemed to fit.

I did not care much for the parties and gatherings that were a regular part of life at the George house. Too many people saying things about too many other people. And all those raised eyebrows, knowing looks, and hissing whispers that passed between people. Of course, that was all before Mrs. George started to get sick and the people stopped coming. Before even Mr. George began to avoid the place, always in town or the fields. Or away somewhere "on business." That catchall phrase men use to cover a multitude of activities, a multitude of things they want to keep from women. A multitude of sins, some might say. I don't think of things that way, though. I don't think that things fall so easily into one bucket or another—this thing a sin, that thing not—as if you were cleaning vegetables and cutting away the bruised and dirty bits from the solid flesh.

Before Mrs. George started to keep to her room, with her graying skin, ugly rashes, and strange odor, she was lively, those blue eyes of hers flashing and glinting at people like sunlight hitting something shiny. She flitted from one person to the next, like a butterfly on flowers. Only she was not so pretty or so nice as a butterfly. There was something nervous about her, something that made other folks a little uncomfortable, I thought. All the high-society folks came and dined and gave her the time of day because back then the Georges were important people, rich people with a fine cane plantation. But there was always something greedy about her. Back before all the darkness began to surround her and she entertained regularly, I would try to occupy myself when guests were due to arrive with some rearranging of linens in the cupboards or some preparations in the kitchen or fussing with the settings in the dining room. I was supposed to join in, to act like a relation, a poor relation who had come to live with them. But I wasn't one of those. I wasn't very good at pretending. I preferred to work. I wanted to avoid all the people, all those sorts of people the George house attracted, to avoid that which made me uncomfortable: conversation, questions, knowing looks. I didn't care what anyone thought of me—I just didn't want them thinking of me at all. Of course, all those chores needed doing anyway—there always is more work than time in this world, even for those like me who actually like work, who enjoy the satisfaction of finishing tasks large or small. At the George house, I did every little piece of labor I could find because, well, the tasks needed to be done. Mrs. George was not much of a housekeeper, and I was not much for social life. I suppose in that way we were a good match. She found the company of others, lots of others, necessary; I found it a burden. I had no gift for what they called small talk. It all seemed like nothing more than gossip to me.

However, the Georges liked me to make an appearance. I was to be living, breathing evidence of their charity, their generosity. I never heard anyone ask outright who I was or how I was related. Or why I was living with them. Well, I never heard anyone ask the Georges directly. I caught many a pair asking each other who I was, discussing their notions about me in hushed tones over brandy in the drawing room or as they bent over to inspect an orchid in the conservatory. All I had to do to shut them up quick was step out from whatever corner I had crawled into and clear my throat.

It's not that I cared if they gossiped about me, but I didn't want them gossiping about the Georges, and they couldn't do one without the other. The Georges were always vague about who I was, why I was there. I heard them tell people on many occasions that I was a "comfort" now that their girls were gone to England for school. They told people I was "like a daughter" to them. Of course, their real daughters would never have been expected to work in the garden or the kitchen or among the animals. There was a whole world of distance and difference in that word *like*. But no matter. I wasn't their daughter, wasn't even like their daughters in any way, shape, form, or inclination, and further, had no desire to be.

We made a fair trade, for the most part, the Georges and I. They gave me many things in this life that truly are necessary, such as food and shelter, and many things that others seem to think are necessary, such as social life and what I heard them refer to as "exposure to an elevated class of people." Implication being that I had been born into a bottom-dwelling class of people. In their estimation, I suppose this was true. This was another thing I didn't see that way. Seemed to me most "elevated" people were judgmental, lazy, bigoted, opinionated, and arrogant. Sure, they were rich and educated, but if that's what money and education got you, I think I was better off without them.

The Georges were not warm people, but they also abused me little. There were those few incidents, but I can't color all the days and months and years of quiet living I had with them by a few incidents. And Mr. George tried hard to make it up to me. He knew when he was wrong, that man did, and he tried to set things right. Warmth was not something I had a lot of need of, in any case. If that was because of a twist or more likely a knot in my own character or because I never had much warmth to begin with and so just never got in the habit of it, I don't know. I don't see how it matters much either way. I had little experience of the softer things in life and little need of them. Never saw those softer things do anyone much good.

Henry, now he was a warm person. I noticed it. He didn't have that coldheartedness, that selfishness that leads people to scrutinize and slander others. There was warmth in his voice. It was this warmth that seemed to seep through the house and find me, wherever I was, no matter what I was trying to do to stay out of the way. This warmth of his always made manifest in me a small chill deep inside my body that I otherwise didn't recognize in the usual rounds of my day-to-day life. His laugh would roll toward me like a distant storm, a promise of refreshment from a hot, dry summer day. His voice would coax me from whatever cubby I was trying to hide in—the pantry, the closet, a tight corner of my small room—and draw me outward, to a rocking chair on the veranda, a window seat in the drawing room, or a cushion half hidden behind a palm in the conservatory, someplace where I could sit, as unobtrusive as possible, and listen. Sometimes I was close enough for the smoke from his cigar to find my nose and make it itch in a ticklish, soothing sort of way. I suppose the stories he told did the same to the rest of me.

He spoke often of his family. He was the eldest of something like ten children, and his younger brothers and sisters were scattered all over the world, finding their ways in all those many places Britain had set its flag and its sights. He had visited many of these places and these siblings himself, and he related his adventures in jungles, deserts, muddy backwaters, and cities starting to boom. England had her fingers in pots all over the globe, and it seemed he and his brothers and brothers-in-law wanted a taste from every one. Each of them was trying to find adventure and money, and his tales made it clear that they usually found plenty of the former and much less of the latter.

He made fun of himself easily. Preferring that, I suppose, to having others do it for him. Having no relations of my own, I was, I guess, somewhat enthralled with wondering what it would be like to be at the center of such a bustling, boisterous, deeply connected crowd. He seemed proud of his brothers and sisters, pleased by them, almost as if they were of his own creation instead of that of his parents.

Sometimes he spoke of himself. He'd been to England for education in dentistry. He'd worked with some eccentric person who seemed as much an inventor as a caretaker of teeth. The two of them, in his telling, got up to all kinds of nonsense in a small building out behind the practice. They made many things, blew up a few by accident; nothing, it seemed, ever came to much. Other than providing excellent fodder for his rapt and bemused audience in the drawing room. He'd also been to America. That sounded like a grand place. He described flat fields that stretched to the horizon and cities so full of buildings they almost blotted out the sky. He told tales of New York, where ladies and beggars mingled equally in the streets. Where people came from all over the world to find work. This was a place where it mattered not what you came from, only what you made of yourself. That one country could have such diversity and opportunity astounded me, someone who'd never left the island. Before we even knew each other, before we'd even spoken, he put New York in my mind. He was the one who made me want to go.

He spoke also of his parents. His father a solid man, a much-respected, self-made banker of some sort. His mother quite beloved, warm, gregarious—it was from her he must have received his own nature. Certainly, I never knew him to be one who was good with money, as his father apparently was. Together, his parents had started a school where his mother taught. I loved listening as he described her dark good looks, how she was always surrounded by her children, or visitors, or other people's children, or all of this at once. Once, I heard someone make a snide remark under his breath about her.

"Spanish. Jewish," this man said. "No wonder she had all those children," he finished up knowingly before being hushed by his companion.

I think I glared at him, too. Even though I didn't understand the implications of his comment, I knew its spirit was mean.

I wanted to know where Spain was, so I found it on the globe Mr. George kept in his office. I wasn't sure what Jewish meant. I knew it was a people and a culture. I knew it was a religion, but I knew nothing specific. I had no use for religion of any sort, in any case. Seemed to me like not much more than a cover and an excuse. A way to control people and fill them with false hope. Of course this was nothing I would say out loud. I had spent plenty of time in church and I didn't think most people filling the pews on Sundays believed anything the preacher or the Bible said. For them, as far as I could tell, it was just another place to show up and be seen by others. Another reason to buy fancy clothes, another way to fill a few hours, another social obligation for idle people to tick off on their calendar. Prayer is no different than *obeah* in my mind. One is white man's magic, the other black woman's magic. A means to try and fix something you have no control over. At least obeah worked sometimes. I never saw prayer do anything much except give the praying person a convenient excuse for why things went the way they did, good or bad.

Anyway, Henry's mother was dead and so was his father. They'd died one after another, the husband first and then the wife soon after. Malaria took his father, I think. Heartbreak, Henry made clear, took his mother. A woman so in love with a man so exceptional, she couldn't stand life without him. I wished I'd known this woman, Henry's mother. A smart, strong, solid, educated woman—I never did meet any of those. A woman who knew how to make her way in the world, who knew how to draw love to her. I never did meet any women like that, either. She seemed a woman who might have helped me become some other kind of woman, or at least a better woman, than what I was. Than what I was able to turn myself into.

HENRY

Rachel was not beautiful. No, no one would accuse her of that. There was nothing in her physical bearing or the composition of her features that was particularly engaging. But engaging she was, for I heard many men speak of her strange attractions. They did so quietly, a few words hidden behind a suck on a pipe or a swig of bourbon, firmly out of earshot of the other women. This was the only way any of us could speak of her, this mystery among us, who was, in so many ways and for so many reasons, not simply unavailable to us, but not of us. I have known many beautiful women, women with quick wits, sharp minds, cascades of hair, overflowing bosoms, conversation that challenged and flattered you at the same time. These women drew you in, hand over hand. It was a skill learned at the knees of their mothers, aunts, nannies, governesses. It was a skill as essential to their survival in the world as learning a trade or acquiring a profession is to a man not born into land or wealth. As for Rachel? She was completely lacking in the expected feminine graces and arts. Stubbornly shy and yet completely self-possessed. More ready to help the staff than engage with the guests. More interested in chores than in conversation. Unadorned and unconcerned about her lack of adornment.

Maybe that was, in fact, the rub. With these other women, their beauty was an artifice, a skillful fly placed at the end of a pole and dangled teasingly into the waters filled with men, its sole purpose to hook a fat fish that would feed the entire family for weeks, months, a lifetime, generations perhaps. In stark contrast, Rachel seemed to me to be a whisper in a noisy room. Among the rustling skirts, fine silks, delicate laces, hair ribbons, perfume, chortles, giggles, and superficial chatter, she was a still object, sitting in quiet observance, just outside the circle of activity. She kept her face assiduously impassive and never let on what she made of us, those who were supposedly her betters. I expected her appraisal was not flattering.

Her presence in the George house was never fully explained. Oddly enough, it was only even lightly gossiped about. She seemed untouchable even to the busiest of busybody ladies as she sat, over in some corner or upright in a hard chair, as likely to be watching the gathering as staring out the window or turning the pages of a book, fingers running over the illustrations there as if trying to read them by feel, the expression on her face one of the lightest engagement with any external stimulation. There was always a shadow of annoyance and preoccupation about her, as if the mere presence of others was a provocation that interrupted some internal contemplations which she found much more interesting and engaging than our company. When she lifted her head and looked at her surroundings, her eyes were lit with scrutiny, as if she was seeking what might be out of place, what might need attending to. Those few times she looked at me, her stare was disturbingly frank and unrelenting, as if she was sizing up a piece of cloth before cutting into it, determining whether it was cheap muslin suited only for the kitchen or fine silk, fit mostly for hanging in the closet. She was full of assessment and yet without judgment. Lear said it best: "So young and so untender" was she.

When she was spoken of, whispered about, rare as this was, a variety of theories as to who she was were rumored and suggested.

It was most regularly posited, with a confident flip of the hand, that she was some poor relation. Mr. George, hardheaded as he was about business, was thought to have a soft spot for certain sorts of those in need. Some explained, with the undue confidence of pure supposition, that she was brought on as a favor to someone to be a governess to the George girls, and although she was no longer required now that the George girls were grown and off to England, loyalty and lack of opportunity and suitable situations on the island dictated the Georges keep her on. Of course, this made no sense given how much older his daughters were than she. Others arched an eyebrow knowingly and said that Mr. George had grown fond of her, laying great emphasis and thereby salacious overtones to the word *fond*. Once in a great while, someone who attended their parties in spite of harboring some grudge against the Georges hissed that she was the product of one of his liaisons.

As for her part, she offered absolutely no account of herself. She didn't even offer us the smallest scrap to go on by suggesting or implying anything. No, in fact, she offered only the minimum of what was required by polite society: a small curtsy, a nod, a twist of a smile that was almost more a grimace, followed by a quick retreat. She wore dresses as plain as possible. No adornments, frills, laces. Everything was carefully arranged, but more in the manner of a woman organizing her pantry than her person. Her features were regular—perhaps her gray eyes were a bit too close together, her nose and lips a bit thin and angular—but there was nothing that drew attention in either a positive or negative way. She showed not a single concern for her own attractiveness. She was always clean and tidy, but in a pragmatic, workmanlike way. No powders or rouge, hardly a curl to her pinned-up hair. However, there was one decidedly attractive aspect to her: her skin. This she could not hide completely. Her smooth wrist had to emerge from a sleeve, her neck gleamed from above a high collar, her cheek caught the soft light of the afternoon sunshine. Her skin, where it showed, required no adornment, but presented itself like a delicacy waiting to be tasted, something soft and warm that had been cooked gently at low temperatures in plenty of fresh butter.

I remember when I first had the unexpected pleasure of touching her. One evening, when everyone was called to dinner from the drawing room, I busied myself with an energetic attempt to plump and replace a pillow I had intentionally dislodged with the intent of lingering in the room, knowing as I did that she was always, determinedly, the very last to leave. As she passed near me, flustered perhaps by my ministrations to the sofa, she stumbled slightly over a corner of the rug that had been turned back. I stepped forward to catch her arm—which she quickly, albeit politely, snatched back—but as I did so, I detected a splattering of light freckles across her nose and cheeks. A bit of grated vanilla in the pudding. It was something any other woman would have tried to conceal. But not her. It was not just that she was young, a teenager still, which the freshness of her skin made clear. It was that she was so much not any other woman.

Most of the women that I met at parties and polo fields were of a certain type and breeding. Their discourse was as light as a soufflé, their interests and energies directed toward husband finding and social climbing. I was an easy target for these women. Back then, as a man in my early thirties, I was in the full bloom of my looks and charms and masculine powers—women flirted openly with me. I also had, it must be admitted, the additional sympathy of having been alone for a year after losing a woman I deeply loved and what would have been my first son in a single, horribly bloody night of hell. My sadness over that loss was real and deep.

My first wife was a shy beauty, an innocent, unformed, unhardened thing of twenty, who had not been long on the island when we fell in love and married. She came to visit relations. She stayed for me. Our courtship was brief and our marriage not much longer. We had an extended honeymoon in British Guyana, where I am afraid she caught some sort of illness that ruined her pregnancy and took her life. I never even met her parents, as they did not make it over from England for our civil ceremony. They were not wealthy, her father a country barrister, but they did give her a comfortable dowry, which I invested in the further development of my steam engine and the pursuit of patents. To me she was a fresh flower, its face upturned toward the sun, suddenly cut down and pressed into the mud by an unseasonable storm.

I am aware that this tragedy, as real as it was to me, also made me even more appealing to women who both felt sorry for me and admired my raw emotions, being surrounded as they were by much harder men, men who whipped horses and field hands with equal ruthlessness. The truth is, I could have had my pick of many a woman. Plenty of them wealthy, as well. I flirted, I toyed, I played with them all. Yet my attentions always were distracted by Rachel. Still, it is strange to me, given these circumstances, given the options open to me, given my desires to have a wife and a family, that I did not make a more concerted, thoughtful choice. That I did not consider carefully who and what I wanted my life partner to be. I wonder, more often than I care to think, how it came about that, in fact, I really made no choice at all. It is not just that I fell for this confounding, totally inappropriate young woman named Rachel; it is more as if I actually fell into her.

RACHEL

When did Henry's stories become not just something I overheard him telling someone else, but something told directly to me? Did he scoot his chair over toward mine, or did his voice draw me out of my hiding places? This much I know: he would start talking and, little by little, other guests would drift away from him, out onto the lawn or to cluster around other conversations. Then he would look up from his cigar or drink, as if wondering where his audience had gone, and find only me.

My small presence seemed not to bother him, to be enough for him. It seemed to please him, in fact. I was a good listener because, unlike the others, I was actually interested in what he had to say. I was a good listener because I wanted to know more. I began to ask a question or two. I guess, without really meaning to, I encouraged him. He began to seek out my company, and I began to be more interested in joining the parties.

I suppose I wanted him, wanted at least something about him. I suppose he was the first thing I'd ever really wanted. Maybe I just wanted the attention I got by giving him mine. Maybe the thing I wanted was less him and more of the promise his many tales held out to me. It was the promise of a different sort of life, the promise of being a part of the world beyond what the Georges, what the island, what my ignominious birth and low standing had so far held out to me.

HENRY

Some days I wonder why I stay in this blasted place. As I make my creaky stroll down the dusty road into Royalton—a walk which used to take me twenty minutes going, as it is downhill, and thirty minutes coming home up the hill, and now takes me almost twice as long—I tend to make a rather negative accounting. The heat is intolerable. It is freakishly fecund. It seems there is always a new critter that bites or annoys or spreads disease. The city, once a sleepy little town on a peaceful and protected bay, is filling with a cacophony of carriages, automobiles, feral dogs, and people coming down from their shacks in the blue-green hills looking for nonexistent work. No one has money to pay for my services, and those who do go to the other dentists in town. Everyone gossips. The locals whisper about each other over the market stalls, amid the flies and dust, and it is condemned as salacious rumors. The wealthy do it in drawing rooms, over cigars and brandy, and call it wit instead. The result is the same. A few snippy words and a reputation can be ruined, a family shunned. This entire island, which used to shimmer before me like an oversized emerald in a sapphire sea, has begun to feel hostile to me.

I had thought I might return to England. I had some good years there when I was studying. There, I felt understood, as if I was among my own. But then again, be honest with yourself, old man, your modest background was an impediment. I had no name and no standing, no rich relations, just some merchant uncles. Those who are born in England and then leave to make their way or find riches in a distant colony are given a grudging respect; those who try doing the same in the reverse direction are not. Self-made is apparently understood only as a one-way street. Another of those strange, unwritten, yet deeply ingrained rules of class and society. If I had been able to make a place for myself there, I might have stayed. I might have married a truly English lass. Instead, I moved on and eventually, like a long-lost homing pigeon, back to here. London was so many shades of gray; this place so many shades of green. Both are oversaturated with moisture, but the one is cold and clammy and the other, this place, hot and sticky. My doctor says the former will kill me, and the latter will keep me well. I know no one there. I know many people here.

Or do I? My brothers and sisters have almost all moved on to other islands, other countries. Or died. We were a close family as children, we visited each other in our youths, but as we grew up and settled into our own lives, started to make our own families, we did not stay in touch. Once our parents were both dead, we lost our center as a family. We had no hearth to gather around at holidays. We had no one person who drew us to her, as our mother did.

I have lived in many other places. I spent time in British Guyana, but that country lags even further behind us in its development. I found nothing profitable to do. I went to Panama after hearing about the supposedly vast opportunities as they contemplated their great canal. It was said there was work for any and every one. But the engineers, if you can even call them that, had little use for my advice, my steam engine designs seemingly meant nothing to them, and the laborers had little use for my dentistry. Yes, there was tons of work, if you were good at digging ditches. The best time in my life, I suppose, was my few years in the United States, working on developing engines for automobiles. Now those absurd and ugly tin lizzies have taken over the country. I maintain that steam is still the future for engines. Internal combustion engines, those noisy, clanking things, will never become the standard. In any case, I loved the broad plains in the center of the country where it seemed you could stare for eternity and see nothing but grass dotted with buffalo. Then there was the contrast of the congestion of New York City. I enjoyed the robust attitude of the Americans, for whom class and birth is so secondary to sweat and smarts. I acquired a rather large pot of money in the States, having few expenses and only myself to take care of, and I wanted to spend some of it working on my steam engine and fly machine. These two machines have proved as intractable, as unwilling to accommodate my wishes, to help me fulfill my dreams, as Rachel has.

I suppose I could go back to the United States. The one place where I have had some clear financial success. But so many years have gone by. Truthfully, I am now without sufficient means or connections. Of course, I am without means and connections here, but it matters much less, because here, many of us are without money, and we are all beholden to one another for something, whether we like to admit it or not.

And there is Vea. What would become of Vea if I left? Even more to the point, what would become of me without her? Vea was a friend to Rachel when they both lived in the George house. She helped when Rachel came to live with me. Vea visited us often, bringing us something delicious from the Georges' kitchen when she could. And now that both of the Georges are gone, she still cares for me. Out of nostalgia mostly, no doubt, as I can offer little in the way of payment. But I do believe she is fond of me. Her soft footfalls in the kitchen as she shuffles around in her slippers are a great comfort to me. Her gentle singsong as she works in the garden lifts my spirits. Her warm, strong hand on my shoulder is the only thing some days that sustains me. She has a small shack of her own somewhere, I gather, but she stays here often, comfortable with me and in this house. I would set her up in some sort of business if I could. A small shop, perhaps. A food stall in the main square. She would enjoy work that also afforded her company. Better company than am I, no doubt. But I have barely enough to keep myself in mangoes for whatever years I have left. I imagine, I hope, Mr. George settled some sum upon her, as I cannot. Oh, bother. Truthfully, all this might be overcome. A fresh start in the great city of New York might be welcome, even at my age. But if I am honest, the only reason I would go would be to see those who I am not sure would welcome me.

This island, this modest kidney bean in the midst of the Caribbean, must have seemed to my father much like America did to me: a fresh country, full of possibilities, unimpeded by many of the more ridiculous notions of class and tradition, even though it was a British colony. It was flanked by larger islands, but was nonetheless a jewel in the empire's crown, producing a substantive percentage of the world's sugar and desperately in need of workers, managers, and guidance. The world here was open to him; in England, a teenager from modest parentage would undoubtedly have been severely circumscribed in opportunities. Here, he could raise himself up by his own industry alone. He could become a banker on the basis of his own good skills and steady temperament. This strange small island gave my father everything he loved and then took it all away with its malarial pestilences and fevers.

What a love my parents had! The merest glance between them contained great oceans of affection and understanding. I was the eldest, and it seemed the birth of each of the ten children who followed me served only to increase their love for each other, their sympathies for each other. Mother adored and cared diligently for each of her children, but the largest serving of her love was always reserved for him. His face lit up hers like no other. As my mother aged, her swarthy complexion darkened and her body shriveled into itself, but still there was always that brightness that illuminated the deep coffee color of her eyes, that seemed to illuminate the creases in her skin. In his later years, Father's eyes grew weak, so she read to him in the evenings. They sat in their well-cared-for, immaculately clean drawing room in two deeply cushioned and elegantly upholstered chairs, a pot of tea on the tray. They never took even a sip of anything stronger. Mother would select a book from the shelves lining the walls, which were thick with volumes—reference books, histories natural and human, novels, poetry, and plays. The last two were their favorites, perhaps due mostly to long familiarity, and more often than not, Mother allowed the book to slip from her hands, and in the flickering twilight of the few dripping candles and the pulsating embers in the fireplace, they recited passages back and forth to one another from memory. It was a well-practiced call-and-response routine, repeated over many years, decades even, and their voices rose and fell with emotion, pleasure, and companionship until the fire burned itself out and they shuffled off to bed, arms interlinked as they made their way through the darkening house.

I miss the old man for his advice, good cheer, and cordial counsel. He encouraged my travels and my tinkering. He told me to chase dreams but to have a trade, to try everything once, but most things no more than once, that it was good to have enough, but not too much, as a little hunger keeps you on your toes. Even if I had money to give you, he'd say, I wouldn't. The only way a man has to learn who he is, is by making his own way in the world. He certainly made his, starting from the bottom as a bank clerk, ending on top as the head of a thriving financial enterprise. I named my eldest son, James, in his honor.

Mother had the mystery of the gypsy in her, the skepticism of the Semite, the warmth of the Mediterranean. Cordelia Henriques.

She was a woman of few words, but one who made each one count. She often said that English did not have the words she needed to express her deepest feelings. She was not unduly demonstrative, but the smallest touch from her carried great weight, gravity, feeling. Her palm placed on your shoulder conveyed remonstrance one day, approval the next, and appreciation the following. I do not know how she managed this subtlety and precision, but she did. She helped my father in his office, ran the school once he started it, taught languages there. With her upright carriage, pitch-black hair, tea-with-milk-colored skin, black eyes, and laconic ways she presented a figure that tended to pause conversations midstream. My father loved and admired this quality in her, this ability to make a quiet stir, to rock people back on their heels a bit. He spent his days in the most conservative of company and professions—banking, insurance. He relied on her to tweak the nose of convention just enough to keep people guessing, but not so much that they would throw him out of the club he worked so hard to be able to join. We were all in Mother's thrall, in fact, not just Father, but me and my brothers and sisters as well. I see that now, looking back. We all struggled with the opposing desires to know her mysteries and the equal craving for them to stay safe within her keeping. We all wondered if our father had found her depths, or if she kept whole chunks of herself apart. We suspected the latter. So sad that he died so young, not yet sixty, and then she followed less than a year later. She died, no doubt, from a broken heart. The center of her world suddenly gone. Apparently my heart is none too vigorous anymore either, but whereas hers was used up and worn out with the pounding of a deeply reciprocated passion, mine is desiccated for lack of the same.

As I now know, a woman like my mother, who retains much to herself, keeps her man interested and intrigued. A woman's mystery is her power. It is what draws a man to her. In my case, it has also pushed me away, made me mad with exasperation. Rachel was my mystery. I suspect I saw that same inscrutability in her I had seen in my own mother and assumed it hinted toward depths of character I craved to uncover. And yet, Rachel was not what I anticipated. The more I probed, the more she hid. The more I looked, the less I saw. I tried, again and again, to lift what I perceived as her heavy curtains of self-protection. I thought those dark drapes in which she cloaked herself could be lifted to reveal something soft and luscious within her. Did I do her wrong in this? Was this my own vanity acting out, imagining her to be some sort of magic lamp that needed only a gentle rub from my hand and mine alone to release the beautiful genie that would fulfill all my deepest wishes? Did I rub her raw in my endless efforts to find something within her that I hoped for rather than saw? Did I love her? Or did I only love what I thought she might become under my gentle tutelage? Was I disappointed and resentful? Condescending and cruel, as she accused me of being on more than one occasion?

Perhaps. I am trying to be honest. Yes, at least some of the time I was not the man I wanted to be and in fact the man she accused me of being.

She was, after all was said and done, just a woman. A woman perhaps damaged, certainly burdened with the layers of deceit others had built up around her. A woman abused, no doubt, by those who should have, could have, protected her. I am guilty of some of the same insults. I pushed where I should have encouraged. I was petulant where I should have been patient. I took what I should have waited to be given. I wanted, oh-so-desperately wanted, her to be something she was not.

But even if I was those things, did all those things, my punishment seems unjust. To take herself and my three youngest sons, Edmund, Percival, and Thomas, and my dear, sweet, freckled, ginger-haired Margaret, so far away from me, and when they were so young, not yet teenagers. Even my eldest, the one closest to my mind and my heart, James, went after her eventually, himself just fifteen—or was it sixteen?—so sure of himself, so determined, an adult before his time. I am left behind, an old man, all alone, lost, forgotten. It seems too much. It is as if she is punishing everyone who has ever done her wrong through her punishment of me.

MARGARET

THE FEELING OF DISLOCATION IS STRANGEST AROUND THE HOLIDAYS. I see something shiny in a window and think how much one of my brothers might like that. And then I realize that they are all gone, all died too young. I remind myself that I should write holiday cards and then I ask myself, "To whom?" I find myself dating a check and only thereby remember that the day is, in fact, my own birthday, and I, unlike the others, have somehow made it into my fifties. I check off Thanksgiving—just another day for me—and then Christmas, the same. January 1 is such a relief as I look forward at the almost ten months ahead of me without a reminder that I am a woman leaving middle age, single, childless, without either parent or any of my four siblings left alive.

My father died before I was thirty. James was notified by Henry's housekeeper, and then he wrote to our mother, who in turn told us. I had not seen him, had hardly heard from him since leaving the island at just around ten years old, so I felt distant from the man and remote from the loss. I had lost him, I suppose, the minute I set foot on that boat for New York. My younger brothers died in their forties; only James made it to fifty. Mother died right on his heels. These last losses came hard and fast. I seem to have mourned them not as individuals but as a group. I mourned the feeling of being suddenly thrust outside the concept of family as much as I mourned the individuals themselves.

However, I am not sad about my solitude. But being alone is my preferred state.

The rub comes from the expectations and assumptions of others, the steady and innocent querying over lunch trays about my "plans" for the holidays, the hints dropped about an attractive older brother, newly single, in the teachers' break room, the bombardment from every shop window that we, every one of us alive, should be doing something, buying something, cooking something almost constantly for the last few months of the year. I have yet to figure out some sort of gracious response, some light riposte that stops my inquisitor from intruding on my solitariness without leaving marks or wounds on either of us.

Maybe it was all those years in cramped apartments caring for my younger brothers that made me this way. All those hours cleaning up the small daily messes whose magnitude was increased by the close proximity. All those years of trying to carve out a small niche of privacy from the rank male presence. Don't get me wrong. I love—or is it now, more properly, "loved"?—my brothers. Eddie, Percy, and Tom. So much alike—not James, of course, being separate from us in so many ways—but the other three, so much alike and so much together, it was as if they were three parts of the same boy instead of three separate beings. Oh, their buoyant energy. Their disinterest in domesticity. Their carefree knack for making any space their own. Their endless and rambunctious teasing. Their raw physicality. I loved it all, especially in contrast to my own requirement for order and elbow room. For great expanses of unplanned, uncommitted time. For great expanses of unplanned, uncommitted space for my mind to wander.

For all their robust good health, they each died young. In this, even James followed suit. His heart failed him. Eddie fell prey to drink and dissolution. Percy, the smallest, the weakest, wasted away from a multitude of ailments. Tom was attacked in the street—robbed, badly beaten when he resisted and fought back—and died a few days later. He was tough as a kid and a young man. Even though, or perhaps because he was the youngest, he always protected his brothers and won his fights with the neighborhood boys. Perhaps when he was attacked this last time he forgot that he was no longer a young man.

I have two sisters-in-law, but we have never been close. Eddie and Percy were bachelors. James's and Tom's wives are both shrewish women. Energetic, ambitious, controlling. They both bossed my brothers around—to no apparent effect with James, but Tom's wife hardened him. Perhaps our own mother's bottomless reserve and self-containment led my brothers to look for more strapping, voluble female types. I imagine they didn't bargain for the strident nature that sometimes goes along with that type.

I have a few nieces and a nephew. Tom had two girls, James a boy and a girl. I have seen them little, but heard my brothers speak of them much. Disappointment littered their calls and letters to me. Even in my limited dealings, I could see why. These children are self-absorbed and superficial, angry and dissolute, spoiled by parents who had to do without so much in their own childhoods and in striving to keep their children from the difficulties they experienced gave them a completely new set of issues. These children—well, adults now, no longer children—look for problems where there are none and expect to be forgiven every mistake they make, even as they have little empathy for others and their mistakes. They demand money from their parents and not only rail against them and their alleged unfairness when it isn't produced, but criticize their parents' frugal ways. They take and ask for more. They scrutinize and criticize their parents' hardworking, prudent lifestyles even as they seek personal benefit from that same lifestyle. They are full of excuses for why they can't keep a job or won't work: delicate natures, artistic sensibilities, unfair bosses, a need to see the world, to "find" themselves.

I spent some time with James's daughter, Anne, when she came to New York. They had sent her to art school, where she studied fashion design. A dramatic-looking girl, with dark hair and strong features—a less delicate Audrey Hepburn—she had done some modeling, bit-part acting, all those starlet-wannabe things that pretty girls did back then in the forties and fifties, trading on their looks if they had them. Then she won a design contest and got her start with some blouse manufacturer here in the city. I invited her to tea, to dinner, to go to a play. She stood me up more than once, calling well after the fact to apologize with the excuse of a date with an up-and-coming movie star, a party that ran late, an impromptu trip to Europe with some man she had just met. When we finally did get together, she chattered about the people she was meeting and spending time with, artists, actors, directors, models. She made it all sound very important, as if there were weight and heft to what they were doing, even though what she described sounded lighter than air, a puffed-up confection. She asked a few polite questions about myself, but didn't listen to my answers. It was clear there was nothing I could show her about New York. It was clear she thought I was old, boring, dull.

I suppose, in a way, I was. An old soul, my mother always called me. Serious in nature. Pensive. Not that I minded. I found being around people like Anne exhausting. She was one of those who is always looking for some new stimulation, always vaguely dissatisfied, always aware of the impression they were making or trying to make. As if they were perpetually in front of a camera. As if they had an on, but no off switch. Poor girl. She had some early success in fashion, but then a precipitous decline into drink and dissolution. Last I heard, she was living as a homeless person, camping in her car or at the beach, terrorizing her mother from time to time by showing up at her house dirty and manic. Thankfully James died well before his daughter's deepest descent.

I suppose my brothers shared their disappointments in their children with me because they couldn't with their own wives. They probably felt I didn't mind listening, or would at least do so without advice, having had no children of my own. Forgetting perhaps that my days are filled with children. Other people's children. I suppose they never considered that as a teacher and librarian, maybe I had my fill of difficult children. No matter. I listened sympathetically, wrote back praising their endurance, kept my own counsel. What little I had. Which was very little.

In any case, I heard less and less from them as the years wore on. Especially from James. I always expected he would live to a ripe old age. When we did talk, he carried on about his health. About all his schemes to preserve it. The carefully controlled diet. The vitamins and supplements. The weight lifting and calisthenics. His letters were full of unsolicited advice on what I could or should be doing. Of course, he never directly asked how I was doing, what I was feeling. He took me for granted in his own distant way. I was always just a sister to him, never a woman in my own right.

These two boxes that his wife sent me are all that I have left of him now. It is not much to account for a life, two compact cardboard boxes stacked with pieces of paper that his widow had neither the time nor inclination to look through, much less care about, but fortunately, in a moment of inspiration, thought I might. I do have the interest, but I also have the fears. I am not sure what I am frightened of, but whatever it is has kept me from going through them myself. For many months now. I have moved them from place to place. I have tried hiding them in a closet. I have tried leaving them out. Still, I resist. When they first arrived, I skimmed the top few layers just as a means to get some sense of what was there. I found mostly articles on fad food regimens, advertisements for potions making great claims to longevity, extensive records on blood pressure, pulse rates, weight, and some other numbers of mysterious meanings. I could sense, somehow, heavier, weightier, more potentially dangerous things swimming, like a shark in opaque waters, at the bottoms of the boxes. This is what kept me from diving deeper.

There are several photos of James near the top layer. They each show him at various ages in a similar pose: wearing nothing but a bathing suit bottom and slippers, his chest smooth and hairless, his stomach flat and hard, his pectoral muscles well defined, his feet turned out, and his arms well contoured with muscles flexed overhead. The stance was a bit of unintentional, or maybe self-conscious, buffoonery, but still, one cannot help but be impressed by the consistency of his physical condition, even as he aged. It didn't save him, though. We all, in our own ways, run from the fate of our births. But they always catch up with us. Bad hearts run in our family.

HENRY

It seems that James has gone and stepped in it now. I don't know why he felt it necessary to grill the poor woman about her background. Of course, I did the same, but I was her husband, not her son. Not a son who has been separated from her for, what is it, two, three years? Then he appears at her home and starts demanding information and explanations. I was not there, of course, but I know my own son. I know how stubborn he can be in the pursuit of something once he decides he wants it. Apparently he wanted some answers from her. And now from me.

August 14, 1914

My dear son James...

How do I begin? How do I explain? I am racked with guilt that I gave my son a mother like his and yet, this very same woman, who has caused me such misery, is the one who gave me James, who remains my greatest joy. It is a confounding irony.

Your letter of the 20th just arrived. I am sorry to learn that you have not received the two letters I sent you. I have not yet been able to get an opportunity to send on your box. Everything in shipping is upset by the war and quite a number of clerks have been discharged. There is bound to be much suffering.

Oh, get on with it, man! Stop beating around the bush. The meat of his letter was not about shipping or boxes filled with incidentals. This is a young man who has had quite a shake-up, a complete rearrangement in his understanding of his own mother. He is seeking facts, which he thinks are his due, and he is hoping to achieve understanding through me. Something I am not sure I can give him, having so little of it myself. But I will try. I will try because I believe it is necessary for a son to think the best of the woman who bore him. How else will he ever be able to move forward as a man into romantic relations with women of his own choosing if he has a poor start with the first feminine presence of his life?

Oh, to go the other direction is easy. To have a wonderful mother robs you of suspicion and makes you see those higher qualities in almost any woman. You make excuses for all sorts of things in the women you come to know as a man if your mother is a kind, gentle, nurturing, wise sort, as was mine. This was the core, I believe, of my mistake. I have too open a nature, am too trusting, too willing to see the good in others. I would go so far as to say that I find the good in others even when it is not merely hidden, but actually nonexistent.

A daughter needs less from her mother, I think, having a more natural and innate understanding of, and sympathy for, the nuances of feminine emotions. A daughter also knows how to be cautious around the dark and treacherous caverns of the female soul. A daughter will love her mother, despise her mother, and love her yet again. A daughter, as I hope Maggie will do and has done, can become her own woman, no matter what her mother was. She has little choice in the matter, after all.

But a son—a son must make something of his mother if he is to make something of himself.

I must be forthright with him. He is not a boy any longer, but a man of eighteen years. He is on his way in the world. He will soon find out that many, many people harbor darkness in their past. I just wish his first experience of this knowledge had not been with his own mother.

I am sorry you have learnt all the evil things about your mother and her people…

If he only knew how sorry I am that I did not learn them sooner myself. But again, if I had, I would not have had James. I love the other children deeply, but James is more than a son—he is of like mind and temperament. He shares my interests and sensibilities. We have a relationship that goes beyond filial bonds.

Of course, we must be kind and remember that Rachel's beginnings were not her fault. She had no choice in whom her parents were, what she was born into, in the fate she was handed. Her parents tried to do well by her in their own perverse way, I suppose. They tried to create separation between themselves and her, and while it might have felt like abandonment, it seems to me they found a means to introduce her to polite society in a way that would leave no taint of her origins. Whispers and gossip, while evil, are normal, no matter what your birth—her parents found a way to give her a chance, at least. The strangeness, though, is that she, perverse woman that she was, accepted but made little of that chance. She seemed to care equally little about what she came from and what she was given. She took what came—including me, I suppose—with the same dose of equanimity. It is as if she came into the world with her character fully formed and whatever came next, good or bad, had almost no effect on who she was and how she conducted herself.

In the final analysis, we must say that the world dealt her a harsh hand. And that most of the fresh cards she pulled did little to improve that hand. I suppose we can't blame her too much for in her own way refusing to play.

And what of myself? If I turn the glass toward my own visage and closely regard what I find there, can I say I was a man more sinned against than sinning? Well, I was far from perfect, of course. Our relationship began in a rather ignoble fashion. But I was born of honest, hardworking people who believed in family and in bettering themselves and that is what I tried to do myself. I was vulnerable, I suppose, when I met her. I missed my first wife. I missed the child that never was. I was still heartsore and lost. And yet, also a bit full of myself. Emotionally defensive no doubt, but the myriad attentions I was receiving from such a wide variety of women made me bold. Stupid, perhaps. Certainly a bit blind.

Carry on, old man. Let go of your backward glances and get to the letter at hand.

It was a mistake to have anything to do with that class of people, but the…

The what? Blast, how do I characterize the degree, the magnitude, the varieties of my misunderstandings of her?

…the mischief…

Well, that's a word for it, isn't it?

…the mischief having been done…

Yes, once it was done, what did I do? How do I hold up when I turn my own cold eye to my own grizzled reflection in the mirror?

…I endeavored to do the best I could for my children…

Well, that I did! No one could ever accuse me of a paucity of love for them. No one could ever accuse me of excesses to my own person while they did without. What I had, I shared. Sometimes there was more than other times, but we all shared equally in whatever riches—or poverty—I may have brought into my family. And let us remember, shall we, that there are many kinds of poverty! My children always had a richness of education. Well, yes, not always of the formal-schooling sort, but through richness of experience, exposure to books and ideas and nature herself. I take great delight in the world around me, I see it as the very best sort of classroom, and this enthusiasm I shared with my children. I tried to enlist her in these pursuits, I tried to engage her in my interests, I tried to improve her. But she was stubborn and disinterested. She was not generous in her understanding of me. She was not completely unkind, either, to be fair. She was simply removed somehow from it all. Even as a young woman. At first and for so long, I thought it was perpetual innocence, a kind of naïveté I thought charming. Something she would grow out of. Of course, I also thought her much older than she was. So I saw her as simultaneously wise beyond her years and refreshingly without guile. She was, it turns out, neither. She was simply free of need or want, and yet in her remove, terrifically cold and cruel. At least to a man like me, who is so needful of warmth and sympathy.

...I endeavored to do the best I could for my children and to elevate their mother from her disgusting surroundings and connections, and keep you all with as clean souls as I could.

But it was not to be. Yes, sadly.

...but it was not to be.

No, it was not to be. So much was not to be.

However, and this is an important point, we must remember that we are made not of just one parent, but have generations on both sides to look to for inspiration and example. There is little on her side, but more than enough to make up for it on my side. That should sustain him.

Remember that at least on your father's side, your grandfather and grandmother were loved and respected by all who knew them. Keep that before you and let us hope that your sister may not follow in the footsteps of her maternal line.

All right. Enough of all that. I don't need or want to belabor the point. He needs to move on into his future and forget his mother's past. He is in a new country where she is unknown and the dark history that surrounds her is irrelevant. Let us stay focused on him and myself and what we have done and can do together in the future. There is still so much to be done. Even with this blasted distance. A situation I am sure is only temporary.

I had hoped to send your box on with a young man heading to the States, but he just rushed in to say good-bye. Business is jogging along. I have been laid up with a sore foot so could not walk for a day or two but am now very much better.

What more can I say?

Tell your brother I hope to hear a better account of his behavior and to write me a letter. The children I am afraid are hopeless. I do not think they have been brought up to any idea other than to despise their father. Give them my love and with love and best wishes for yourself and hoping that you may be able to kick that bunch into shape as that they may have some decency.

Well, sadly, this is the truth. I fear for them, now that they no longer have my improving influence to offset their mother's rough manners and limited resources. James is my only hope. I hate to foist more responsibility on him, but what choice do I have from this great remove? What else can I say?

Thanks for the clipping on starvation. I have seen that proposition before and there is something in it.

Of course, I have not the discipline to cleanse myself through fasting, no matter how propitious it might be for my health. I have tried from time to time. There was that fortnight that Vea was away and I subsisted on a light diet of mostly just fruit. I lost a full stone, but my insides were a mess for weeks following. I was very glad to have Vea back and in the kitchen from time to time. I regained the weight, but it was worth it. After all, who among us mortals would have the steel to decline any of Vea's cooking? I wish she was here more often, but I have little to pay her with other than free dentistry for her extended family and sharing the meals she makes and letting her take whatever extra is in the garden or hens' nests to use for herself or to sell in the market. She is kind to me because she is loyal to me. She understands my situation, knowing Rachel as well as she did. Perhaps she feels sorry for me. No matter—she keeps her pity to herself, and I am glad for her company.

Write to me whether you get letters from me or not because in the wartime mails are uncertain. I am very lonely here, but it is better for you to be there. All hope of happiness with the rest of the family seems dead. I long and hope for the time when we can be together again.

By the way, I had two offers of $12 for your boat, but like all things here, they did not come off.

With love from your affectionate father,

Henry

Of course I had heard all sorts of stories about the two of them, the preacher and his maid, the scandal that surrounded them. I had just never connected any of it with Rachel. Why should I have? There was nothing that drew a line from her to them. As is usually the case with these kinds of affairs, there is no way to know the full truth of the matter. Here is what seems to be irrefutable: two girls who attended the preacher's school ended up pregnant. The doctor who examined them found evidence also of rather severe beatings, flesh raised up all along the backs of their shoulders and thighs. These discoveries were not in and of themselves unusual, of course. Especially among the poor natives. But for some reason, suspicion began to fall upon the pastor himself. He was a dour, serious man. Maybe that was what caused the raised eyebrows and hissed whisperings to begin with. And then he left the island. Suddenly and with his housekeeper. That is the only incontrovertible fact in this muddied matter. Strange enough for a missionary to leave the community of which he is a part, the school he built, the church he created. But this man went even further. He left with no warning to his parishioners, his students, the families that relied on him. Or his superiors. With no immediate replacement in hand. And no explanation offered. This made the rumors seem suddenly like truth. With him not here to defend himself, there was no way to quash the talk. As to the housekeeper who fled with him? Colored, of course. That only added flame to the fire.

It is clear is that the two young girls in question were damaged and almost cross-eyed in their backwardness and skittishness. That there was abuse is not in question; the only thing unknown is from whose hand it came. This was a missionary school—missionaries were left alone to do as they saw fit because, frankly, no one cared much for the locals' education. Most thought it a bad idea, in fact, to equip them with the skills of reading and writing and arithmetic. We had enough labor troubles as it was. Plantation owners were desperate to find workers content to stay in the fields. Education made this effort even more difficult. They were being forced to bring in labor from India and other places. Which only made the locals even more belligerent.

The question no one bothered to ask was if these girls were backward and damaged to begin with, or if they became this way because of their upbringing or environment. No one bothered to wonder whether the damage came from within rather than without. Or if it did, in fact, come from some external force, if this force was someone other than the minister. The girls might have been abused at the hand of a relation on one of their visits home—they have strange rites, rituals, initiations, these people. Some do, anyway. It might have happened along the road as they walked—the shrubbery is so thick in places, one could hide an elephant just a few feet from the road. These things happen all the time. But people must have their stories to whisper to one another behind a skillfully raised fan as they stroll the croquet pitch, to titter over when watching the polo match.

I, of course, have reason to consider the matter much more carefully. I also have reason to try and find some less salacious reason for his escape. This man, after all, as I learned far too late and to my endless chagrin, turned out to be my never-known father-in-law. And even more appalling, the grandfather of my children.

So he might have fled the island because he did something unspeakable.

He might have fled because he was tempted to do something unspeakable.

He might have fled simply to escape the rumor and innuendo that he had done something unspeakable.

After all, the gossip is brutal in a place like this, where we are so isolated and so little new comes our way that we worry and fret and pick at what we have until we create wounds where none existed and then work to keep the sores of our own making open and oozing.

Personally, I do not believe he was guilty. I am a man of science and I have considered all aspects of the case. No other girls were harmed. Many came to his defense. The two girls were cousins or related in some twisted way and part of a family that lived way up in the hills and was known primarily for living in filth and trading in obeah. Allegedly, one could buy almost any kind of curse from them for little more than a few pennies or a crock of stew. Or, plausibly, a few moments in a rough room with a young and unresisting girl.

People say that if he was not guilty, he would not have needed to leave the island in that way. Well, people leave this place all sorts of ways for all sorts of reasons and no explanations. Look at Rachel. Far less than that sent Rachel fleeing this place. Also suddenly. Also with no explanation. And in her case, with children in tow and a husband and son left behind.

After all is said and done, what was Rachel guilty of? Not much more than being badly born. Poorly married. Rottenly temperamented.

19 December 1914

My dear son,

I am extremely sorry to hear you are not taking a trip this way and I shall not be able to see you again soon. At present I am ill and laid up, however I trust it will not be serious. I manage to hobble around with a stick. Business is very dull and the Island is under Martial Law. The Great War has come and all the Germans are prisoners of war. What vessels have not been captured are hiding in neutral ports, all their clerks discharged and no ship is allowed to carry wireless telegraph, except of course the men-of-war ships. The Suffolk recently came in, stripped for action, loaded in coal, and went out on the war path. However, the government allows very little news to be published so that probably you in New York will learn more about this Great War than we who live in a British Colony. As soon as I am well enough to go out I shall try to send you I hope $10. I shall also send on your box as soon as I can find a safe means of transport and when I can get out for I am laid up at present. Be of good cheer and give my love to the children. I shall write them all another time. By the way, what is your mother doing? Is she as bitter against me as she was?

Your affectionate father,

Henry

The word I used in my last letter to James was *mischief.* I suppose that is one way to put it. Not a very good way, but it is difficult to speak of these things out loud at all, much less to one's own son. Even if he was an adult, which he is not yet. Well, wait. Yes, he is. He is, in fact, an adult under the law and about the same age his mother was when he came into this world. Still a teenager. Just barely, but still. I didn't know she was so young. But still. I should have. Yes, of course, I should have known.

The mischief began, as mischief often does, innocently enough. I had thought of Rachel in my quiet moments, certainly. The image of her face, the memory of how she carried herself when she left a room stayed with me after every occasion of visiting the George house and rose before me regularly when I had my hands in someone's mouth and should have been focused on their teeth. I had considered her as a potential wife. But I was cautious. I had other options, I thought. I suspected I was not really ready for a new wife. Even though I was feeling the increase of years and the increase in my desire for a family. There were barriers. I knew I was much older than she. I thought, at the time, by a dozen or so years—it turned out by several more than that, even. She was of unknown parentage. For all I knew and much I suspected, she could have been Mr. George's daughter, which made things tricky. I knew he was fond of me, but I suspected he didn't take me seriously. Certainly not as a suitor to a daughter of his, even an illegitimate one.

These were thoughts that often buzzed around my head. Especially on a day like that one, a day when I was at my office and there were no patients on the ledger or in the waiting room. The day was heating up, and for company I had only a humming fan and a bothersome fly or two. I had cleaned all my equipment, wiped down my chair, arranged my tools in orderly rows. There was nothing else that needed to be done. I rocked back and forth in my oak chair, making a small sort of music with the steady creaking I created. I seemed unable to put myself to any good use. My mind was wandering the deep silence of the room trying to find some place to land its swirling thoughts, which were slowly turning my mood sour. I began contemplating a project I had been noodling on for some time. I pulled out a pencil and made a few notes. I was puttering with the development of a piece of labor-saving machinery that I thought could be utilized in the cane fields. The price of sugar was plummeting. The locals were giving up fieldwork to tend their own meager lots. The importing of laborers from India was proving expensive. The problems of wrangling more money from the same piece of land were being discussed in every smoky club and stuffy drawing room. I had ideas for mechanization. As usual, I lacked the funds to make a prototype that I could use to apply for a patent to protect my invention, and so my plans were firmly stuck in the two dimensions of lines on paper and in the haze of my own imagination.

I hesitated to speak of my inventions in any degree of specificity to anyone. I had unique theories that I did not want to expose to the possibility of theft. Yet I increasingly found myself considering the possibility of enlisting an investor to help me see one or the other to completion. I had money set aside from my years working in the United States, but I was raiding that store more than I had intended to, as dentistry was proving less remunerative than I had hoped, mostly because my patient stream was far less consistent than I had anticipated. I would not share theories related to the fly machine or the steam engine to anyone—other than eventually James—as these inventions had far too much potential not only for riches, but for changing the future of industry. However, the cane-cutting and -processing machinery I had in mind, well, that would address some immediate needs. There were options for business partnerships right at hand, potentially all around me, individuals who stood much to gain and could readily see the benefits, both in time saved and yields increased, two effects that would improve their bottom lines.

I had floated a trial balloon or two to Mr. George, querying him about his own field processes and positing the idea that there might be a smart way to improve them. I tried to engage him one evening at a soiree when we had been fortunately seated next to each other and were enjoying the fine bouillon of our host. In response to my efforts to direct the conversation to my ideas for mechanization, he merely slapped me on the shoulder and changed the topic, pointing out that we didn't want to bore the ladies or upset our digestion.

Of course, he was right. So I demurred and turned the conversation back toward softer topics. But I wanted to bring it up to him again, in a more private setting. I was sure he'd see the sense in my ideas and front me some cash, given how solid was the prospect of high returns. I also had some ideas about exporting the locally made, highly colored cloth. Or perhaps panama hats. If he might put up some capital, I could call in some favors with some merchants I knew in the US. I still had friends there. Back then, anyway.

It was the heat of the afternoon when I set out toward the George house, the sun's rays long and brutal. I approached his property, unlatched the gate with the rather intimidating, wrought-iron coat of arms set in the center, and, after beating the street dust from my clothing with my hat, strolled up the drive. All was oddly deserted and quiet, creating a strange pall that seemed to envelop the house and grounds. I assumed this was because everyone was resting, waiting out the hours of high sun, but truthfully, his home was increasingly quiet these days, no matter the hour. His wife, who was rumored to be very tough on the help even in the best of times, was becoming more and more irascible and demanding as her moods swung and her health declined. Even in public, she seemed, with alarming frequency, to be on the edge of hysteria, cheering a bit madly on the sidelines during a polo match, laughing somewhat loudly when taking tea at the hotel, walking the streets with her head uncovered in the heat.

I think Mr. George was trying to keep his wife at home more. Sadly, it appeared her increased presence was not having an improving effect on the place. The house and grounds were starting to take on a frankly mangy tinge—not the barns or fields, of course, as Mr. George ruled those domains as if on a military campaign—but everything in the domestic realm had an air of disregard and being left too much on its own. Beating back the jungle and the rot in this place required a diligent hand, in fact, many diligent hands; yet I had heard that Mrs. George found her staff increasingly irritating and infuriating and was regularly kicking people off the property. Or they left when they could stand her moods no longer. New help was not forthcoming. She was never a good house manager, was Mrs. George. Vea had always done most everything. Steady and stable she was, with her otherworldly equanimity that allowed her to simply shed the hostilities like rain off a windowpane. She was the only one who stayed on. Well, along with that scuffling, fawning, lazy-eyed Sarah. Something kept her there, too. Probably simple awareness that no one else would have her. Apparently, the only one Mrs. George tolerated when she was ill was Rachel. In public, she was dismissive to the point of rude to Rachel. She never met her eyes. Referred to her in the third person when she was in the room. Had taken to calling her "that girl" instead of by name. But Mr. George confided in me once, on one of those rarest of occasions when one too many bourbons at the club had softened his mood and turned him chummy, that Mrs. George relied on her almost obsessively in private. To the point of being paranoiac when Rachel had been out of her sight for too long.

In any case, on this most fateful day, none of them were in evidence. I wandered cautiously to the front door, which was ajar. I stood in the hall for a bit, stamped my feet, cleared my throat, but no one was forthcoming. I peered around the doorways in both directions, but all was still. Vea must have gone into town. Sarah was probably asleep somewhere. I went back out of doors. For some reason, I was reluctant to return from whence I had come. It was not just that I wished to not be thwarted again in my quest to have a constructive business conversation, but the day was even more beastly hot and humid than was usual for this latitude. I did not relish turning back to the road. Nor back to my empty office. I wandered the yard for a bit, hoping to be noticed. I looked toward the stables, strolled to the side yard, peered around the back toward the kitchen hoping to catch the eye of someone removing slops, but again, nothing. The thought that I would have to go back as empty-handed and full headed as when I arrived began to take hold. I twisted my hat in my hand. I was not looking forward to adding a new layer of road dust to that which had already accumulated on my sweaty countenance. Then I came up with the cheery idea to just find a quiet spot of shade and sit for a while. Someone might turn up, but even if they didn't, waiting out the heat seemed a good idea. I recalled spying a small kitchen garden off the back of the house. I thought there might be a bench there. The refreshment of water, even.

When I turned the corner of the house, the garden was indeed there, looking lovely, peaceful, inviting. It was set in a protected piece of the property, bordered by the back of a large barn and hemmed in by trees along one side to provide shelter to the more tender crops. Surrounded by a fence covered with some kind of twining vine, intended to keep marauding pigs and other animals out, it was a kind of practical and private sanctuary filled with tidy beds of lush vegetables that were trimmed with simple dirt paths. I believe I sighed at the sight of it, such a respite it seemed to offer from the dulling temperatures and the frustration of my quest. I entered through a small gate and stood still for a moment, my eyes adjusting to the shadowy light in front of me. I saw a bench at the far end of a path, set under the trees. The sunlight caught a metal cup set on the handle of a water pump just next to the seat. Of course, such a heavenly sight on a day like that beckoned to me. It was just ten or twelve strides away—steps that would change my life forever.

I don't know how it is that I did not see her at first. A trick of the variations in the afternoon sunshine. Or, more likely, a trick of the mind, already focused as mine was on the idea that the area was deserted. But there she was, sitting on the bench that was my goal, with the light and shadow playing over her pale dress, her mahogany-colored hair, her freckled skin, so that she seemed to be a part of the wall of greenery that moved behind her in the ever-so-slight breeze. I didn't even realize who it was at first, as her usually careful appearance was in an unexpected state of dishabille, with her hair only loosely pinned and many damp strands falling about her flushed face, her bodice opened, the laces hanging down beside her bosom, and her skirts hiked up, revealing pale, smooth legs defined with feminine musculature. It was Rachel. And it was Rachel as I had never seen her before. Even more startling than her disordered clothing was her expression, the deeply private look it carried in its unawareness of my presence. Her face was normally closed in on itself, inward looking, a box that held the promise of mysteries, but remained latched and locked. Yet, here, in this setting, on this afternoon, I found her countenance unguarded, open, taking in the sun and the occasional bursts of warm air. Her eyes were bright, glittering objects, a smile did a little dance around her lips. Something was giving her delight. I had always found her compelling, even though she was without the conventional forms of beauty. And yet, on this day, in this state, she was lovely. So lovely.

I confess the rest is a bit of a blur. Oh, my memory is certainly punctuated with moments of clarity, like bright spots of sunshine coming through dense greenery. I remember her eyes as I approached, not yet registering that it was me, not yet surprised, just clear and inscrutable, like brook water. I remember the feel of her uncovered legs on my hands, soft, yet not, like a warm pudding. I remember that no words passed our lips, which were suddenly pressed against each other's, hers giving way to mine, as if a ripe piece of fruit were dissolving in my mouth. And how can I forget the discovery, when my fingers ran up the inside of her thighs, that she had no knickers on. If there was any hope of stopping me before that moment, there was certainly none after.

I am also quite clear on this point: she did not resist me. It seemed, in fact, as if she had been waiting for me. As if she had been hoping for me. I know this sounds ridiculous. I am not insensitive to the fact that this may be my own ego speaking. Be truthful: it is just as likely, nay, more likely, that this is the backward-looking explanation that seeks to absolve me of my own guilt for acting without thinking, for taking without asking permission. Of course she did not reject me. She was young, uneducated, with neither means nor relations. I was older, established, a close friend of the household. What choice did she have? Shock alone could have dulled her into compliance. I should have acted better. I should have had more self-control. Christ, she was seventeen years old and I a thirty-three-year-old man! I didn't know she was that young, dammit. She had the poise and self-possession of a woman in her twenties, a woman who had seen much of the way the world operates already.

How ridiculous this all sounds now. How much there was that I didn't know.

But still. But still.

Be truthful with yourself, man. This is one of the few compensations of finally reaching grizzled old age—a willingness, perhaps even a necessity, to be honest about the mistakes and miscalculations of our youth. I saw flirtation where there was perhaps only surprise. I saw desire where there was perhaps only deference. I saw seduction where there was only frankness. I saw maturity where there was simple lack of experience. I saw depth where there were only still waters. It is the curse of many a man.

I don't recall how we separated. I don't even recall how we faced each other after the fact. I recall her soft, low moans in my ear. I recall how those sounds of hers, which I experienced as the expressions of a woman's pleasure, began to mix and mingle with another sound, that of a child waking from a nap, the small noises of its lonely mewling as it reenters the conscious world. Yes, this is what drew her from me without the requirement of conversation or even postcoital eye contact. There was a baby that had lately made itself known around the George residence. Here it was, nearby, in a bassinet tucked in the shade, waking up from a nap, its discomfited cries drifting up to us.

So this was what had put delight on her face. She had been regarding the child in her care. This small creature had been the most recent subject of much overheated gossip. Everyone assumed it the offspring of some affair of Mr. George's. We indulged many a man his affairs; it was so common as to be unremarkable, but Mr. George's were forgiven even further, given the apparent physical illnesses of his wife. Not to mention her growing mental instability. The speculation was that Rachel had been sent off to help care for the sickly mother and baby for a while, and when the mother finally succumbed to some fever, Rachel was brought back to raise the little girl at the George house. It was posited that this particular indignity was also what sent Mrs. George running to her bedroom with her latest ailment, as well as the reason there had been few entertainments about the household for some time. The Georges had, in fact, ceased social events altogether recently. I, like everyone, thought the baby was Rachel's charge. I thought Rachel was the nanny, nursemaid, and governess, and the girl was Mr. George's child. I had at least part of the equation correct.

RACHEL

The first time I asked Vea to curse my womb was after Mr. George came to me. No one knew that she had obeah powers. If they did, it would have caused troubles for her. First from too many people asking for curses, and second from them blaming her when her curses came to pass. But I knew. I knew because I asked her to help me. At first, I asked her to find someone else to curse my womb. Then, when I saw the look on her face, I realized she could do it. She would do it. Because she loved me and wouldn't risk me having someone else do it. Her curse worked, but it worked in its own way. Which was not at all the way I thought it would.

She knew Mr. George had come. I don't know how, but I know that anything at all that happened in that house was known to her. In her bones, as well as in her mind. That first time he came, I fought him. I clawed and bit and kicked at him. Then he pinned my arms with his hands and my legs with his knees and told me to be quiet. It was like my mother's voice all over again. Be quiet. Don't make a fuss. I folded up like an animal retreating into a small hole it has dug for itself in the dark, damp earth. He said that he couldn't help himself. I gave up because I knew that the longer I fought, the longer it would take for the inevitable to be over. Afterward, he said he was sorry. And that he loved me. Love. That was just something for him to tell himself, to make himself feel better. I said nothing to him with my voice; what I had to say to him was written by the bruises I left on his body and scratches on his face, marks I heard him trying to explain away to the stable hand the next day—said a piece of harness had gotten tangled when a horse reared and fought being bridled.

I suppose I was that horse.

The next time he came, he cried and asked forgiveness. He said it was because his wife was so ill. He said he loved me this time, too. If this was love, it was a twisted and ugly form of it. Uglier even than my mother giving me away out of love. I knew I was nothing special to him. At least for this kind of act. I knew I wasn't the only one he visited. I tried to be thankful that at least he came to me in the dark, in my bed—the others he took where he found them, the stable, the kitchen, the fields. The third time he was quiet. Then it was over. Never said he loved me again. Never said much of anything to me after that.

Vea was right. Vea was always right. She didn't express an opinion on much, but when she did, you might as well take it as the truth. She told me it would not last. I don't know how she knew that either, but she did. It was the morning after his first visit. I came into the kitchen, fixing a pin that had slipped loose from my hair. I caught her looking at me a few times as I tied my apron and got started on making the bread dough. When I was wiping the flour from my hands, she took my chin in her thick, powerful fingers and turned my face to hers. I had a hard time meeting her eyes.

"He won't keep at it," she said.

I tried to turn my face away, but she held on.

"Once or twice more, maybe," she said. "He's a good man, but he is hurting and that's why he does this."

Now my eyes locked with hers. I felt anger flush my face.

"I am not excusing him," she said. "There is no excuse for what he does. But it will be easier for you to bear if you can feel the pain of his that he puts into it."

Hot tears rolled down my cheeks then, and I whispered my wish to her.

"Curse me," I said. "Make it so no babies come."

Children, from what I had seen, were too often the fruit of men's evil to women. And too often, instead of hating the men like they should, the women hated the children instead.

Vea shook her head.

"No," she said. "You do not know what you are asking for, child. Magic has a way of doing what you want, but not in the way you expect."

"Please," I begged, as my tears dropped off my chin and her fingertips.

"No," she said again. Then she let my chin go and muttered, "Not yet."

I held on to that "Not yet," and when my monthlies stopped, I asked Vea again.

"Please," I said. "Curse my womb."

She said nothing this time. But a few days later, she handed me a mug with something thick and foul smelling in it. She nodded at me, and I gulped it down. It burned hot and prickly inside of me. The baby grew anyway. As she predicted, it would take many decades for the potion to take effect. In the meantime, I got sent away again, but this time to a convent up in the hills. This was a different sort of being sent away than my coming to the George house. Because this time I loved where I was sent to. There were few people, just the cloistered nuns, who asked no questions and left me to my own devices, thinking a pregnant woman was not fit for work. I wandered the long, quiet hallways, sat in the neatly tended vegetable garden, found quiet corners where I mended and sewed clothes—they discovered I was good with a needle and thread and this work was deemed sufficiently nontasking for what they considered my delicate state. Everything in that place had a role to play. There was nothing extra or frivolous—only simple, functional things. My months there were the best of my life. I loved how my own personal quiet blended with the quiet all around me until I felt cradled by nothing but peace. I watched my belly grow and felt the baby start to kick and started to think that maybe this child would be a good thing. A good thing that came from a bad thing.

Then the baby came—pale and howling with red wisps of hair and a pronounced scowl—and they tried to take her from me. So I had to fight all over again. I didn't hurt the nuns like I did Mr. George, but I made my intentions clear. I never let them near her. I set my teeth, put stones in my voice and steel in my eyes and said that if they took her I would kill myself. I might have done it too, I don't know, but I did know that this was a sin they would not abide and so they would leave me alone. Which they did, eventually. Being stubborn is considered a bad trait, but I have always been able to use it to my advantage. I was not going to let them take from me the one thing, the only thing that was my own. I was not going to let them take from me the one thing, the first thing I had truly, blindly loved.

They kept me on for another few months. I kept sewing for them. When they had a pile of fresh habits, the mending basket was empty, the baby had nursed long enough that we could put her on a bottle, and my breasts had gone back to small and my stomach back to flat, I returned to the George household. Now the story he could tell was that the baby came from a relative who had died, and I was coming back from where I had supposedly been staying with this ill and distant family member to take care of this baby who supposedly belonged to this nonexistent family member.

Seems to me that the important thing about a lie is not the content, but the way it is told, the spirit of it. That's what makes people believe it.

I don't think anyone spent much time trying to figure out the real truth behind all the lies that Mr. George and his friends told each other about who was born to whom and who was doing what to whom. But that didn't seem to matter. What mattered was pretending together, keeping the story alive together, like they were all in a play together. All the real stuff, all the things that had consequences, in the form of babies and broken hearts and spilled blood, happened offstage. For people like Mr. G, people with a certain amount of education, a certain amount of money, people with something to lose, for them, the play was the thing. For the rest of us? Well, we had nothing to lose and just as little to gain, so we lived in a world of slaughtered livestock, hot kitchens, dirty barns, and bellies that swelled up no matter how hard we fought back, no matter how many nights we spent wishing otherwise, no matter how much of Vea's bitter brew we might drink.

In the end, I won. I won because I got the baby. I called her Margaret after a girl at the convent who had been nice to me; she held my hand and wiped my brow with a cool cloth when Margaret was on her way. Called her a blessing. Said she wished for siblings but her parents were dead, and wished for children but had married Jesus instead of a flesh-and-blood man. I imagined marrying Jesus—I hadn't found flesh-and-blood men to be all that appealing. I imagined staying there in that cool, quiet, peaceful place, but it was too late for me. Not because I thought they wouldn't have taken me, but because I would have had to give up Margaret, and after all was said and done, she was all I had. Besides, she made me smile, made me happy, two things I was unused to and found I liked. I guess the word for it is *love*, but I hear that word used so often as an excuse for so many things I am careful about using it myself. When I looked at her, it seemed I had a reason now for being in the world. It wasn't much of a reason, it wasn't a good reason, what with the way she came into this world, but she needed me, that much I knew, and I wasn't about to give her away. Being given away was something I did have experience of. I knew giving her myself wasn't giving her much, but it was all I had and I gave it willingly.

Mr. George did dote on that girl. Called her Maggie. Maggie, Maggie, Maggie, he made a song up about it. If anyone really had wondered who the girl's father was, all they might have done was look at his face when he sneaked into the kitchen and pressed sweets into her fat fingers and into her warm, wet lips. I was the only one who ever saw that, though. It wasn't often, but it was enough, I thought. More than I got. Some kind of love from both parents. That had to mean something. It had to add up to something.

The next time I asked Vea to curse my womb was after Henry found me. It was a thick, hot afternoon and I was sitting in the yard, trying to find a breeze. I loved that moss-mottled bench where I could remain hidden in that small corner of shade near the kitchen garden. Here I could pull up my skirts, loosen my hair, kick off my knickers, watch the hummingbirds dip and weave among the flowers, without anyone finding me. I had my blouse unbuttoned—I still had a little milk, and I sneaked Margaret to my breast from time to time. She had been feeding, emptied me out, and was now asleep in a bassinet tucked in the deeper shade nearby. In that spot, I could rest. I could be still. These things may not seem like much, but in a life of constant occupation, in a life where one is beholden to others who care for you out of obligation rather than love, it is a rare luxury.

I did not hear him approach. I was peacefully adrift on my own empty sea. Some scuffing of a foot in the dirt made me lift and turn my head, and there he was, standing in a patch of sunshine. I remained hidden in the shade. He looked a bit lost, like a young man washed up on unfamiliar land. I was so used to seeing him in complete possession of himself that I smiled a bit at how vulnerable he appeared. I suppose I should have moved more quickly to push down my skirts, button up my blouse. I am afraid he took my stillness for an invitation. As if I'd put myself right there, in that way, for him. Men's egos. It's fine when they get themselves in trouble, but so often they take others with them.

Henry was a man with a ready supply of charms and admirers. I had watched many women who tried to snub him—he was not wealthy and had a reputation as a bit of a dreamer—succumb to his sly humor and gentle flirtations instead. Within moments, they'd be giggling behind their hands at something he said. To me, he was always polite, always respectful, but he seemed to restrain himself, keep me at arm's length, as if I was a niece or some such. He did not see me as a candidate for anything, I thought. I felt I had no attractions for him, having neither looks nor connections, neither money nor standing, neither grace nor skills beyond what was necessary to keeping a house. And yet, I cannot pretend to have been surprised or unwilling to find him at my side, his lips on mine, his hands on my uncovered legs. I had liked that he didn't see me as a candidate for anything and in spite of this, had always been kind and attentive. I liked that he never bothered to flirt with me. Instead, he'd simply spoken to me. Spoken with me. His words over all those times prior to that day had softened me, made me ready for him in a way I had not expected. His touches were tender and affectionate. I had so little experience with affection of any kind that when it came, I succumbed to it. When passion took over, his ministrations were skillful. Something else I had no experience of. My body yielded, and my mind followed right behind. I felt like I was sinking into some large, muddy body of water. There was so much relief in leaving my earthly concerns behind.

If I had thought about what might follow, what was probable to follow, I might have stopped it before it started. It would have taken only the slightest resistance to break the spell of that heavy afternoon. But then again, I might not have. Because after all, what other options were open to me, a woman burdened with nothing but gossip where a family should have been? I also didn't stop him because I thought he was a better, more authentic man than other men I had met. Because the other women often said he was handsome, and while I wasn't sure what value there was in being handsome, I did enjoy the way his mustache twitched when he talked and the way his eyes disappeared behind deep creases when he laughed. I didn't fight him off because I'd already been damaged. Because he held my face in his hands and kissed my mouth first. Because he was gentle.

But then I needed a curse from Vea again. She said I had to stop nursing so it wouldn't harm the baby. So I stopped and she gave me the bitter muck once again. And once again, it did not work. Here's the thing: Vea loved babies. She was just starting to show with a baby of her own, a baby whose father she would not name, but I had my suspicions, so maybe she gave me something with no potency just to keep me quiet. In any case, after that, I gave up on curses.

HENRY

My mind turns of its own accord back to that day, the day I discovered her betrayal to me. It is like my thoughts keep finding themselves pulled into an unwelcome eddy and have not the strength to swim themselves back into the main part of the stream. It is a problem of age. And lack of sufficient occupation, as the days here are longer and emptier all the time. So many people have moved away, not counting just my own wife and children. If you can call what they did moving. Fleeing is more like it. For the others—maybe for her as well—they want something more. The markets have changed and everyone is quitting this once promised land for the new one in the United States where jobs are plentiful and the economy is booming. People are shuttering their empty stores, closing up their moth-eaten homes, and jumping on any damn banana boat they can find. The war was good to them and bad for us. There is little money here for anything but essentials. This is a disaster for me, as people are letting their teeth fall out for lack of even the few coins I would charge to yank out the rotting, offensive things. When they do come in, they are as likely to pay for their dentures with a pot of fish stew as with hard currency.

Rachel has abandoned me to my fate here. When I think of what she did, the precipitous course of action she took, there is one thing above all others that makes the gorge rise and my heart sink: I thought everything was just fine. I was, dare I say, happy. Of course, she infuriated me, but only from time to time. Of course, there were struggles, but this would be the case in any relationship. In my estimation, we had settled in to a comfortable enough routine. We needed more money, but doesn't one always? We had our immediate needs covered by income from my practice. I had good prospects with my forthcoming patents. I educated the children in the afternoons and evenings by reading to them—Shakespeare was a favorite for all of us—by capturing plants and bugs and observing them under my microscopes, by working sums and fractions utilizing discarded teeth. The children greeted the lessons I put before them with enthusiasm.

We were companionable enough, she and I. We had only one course of regular conflict. She wanted to send the children to what she called "real" school. She even went so far as to suggest the mission school, which surprised me, given her very personal experience with missionaries. I thought the paucity of her own meager education at her father's mission school was evidence enough of its insufficiency. The unsavory reputations of her parents we did not discuss. I was sensitive to how painful those memories might be to her and saw no reason to rub salt in wounds that might still be only lightly scabbed over. Perhaps even still raw. But even more important, I reminded her, was that my own education was far superior to anything any simpering churchman could offer. Besides, there they would be with half-breeds, mulattoes, and local children. I would not have them picking up bad habits. Rachel had picked up enough of them herself from her too-infrequent hours in a classroom and far-too-frequent hours with the kitchen help. I had tried repeatedly correcting her mangled grammar and had begged her to forswear speaking the local patois in front of the children. I had little success with her on these counts and did not want to have to take up the effort with my own children as well.

I reminded her that my parents had started and run a well-respected school. As I told her many times, my father, who came to this island from England at only fourteen years old, his younger brother in tow, began his life here with nothing but a few shillings between the two of them. He worked his way up through simple dogged hard work in banking and insurance and became part of polite society without the benefit of a so-called "real" education—he was educated by his own life and his own efforts. He was able to marry a wife from a class well above the line of small merchants he was born into. She was a Spaniard and a Jew, which some held against her, but she was kind, refined, and brilliant. She helped him set up the school, managed it efficiently, and taught languages there, even Hebrew. I expounded on this story many times to Rachel, maybe too many, but eventually she gave up on her repeated requests to send the children out of the home for education. She had held out that the reason I didn't want them to go to school was because I begrudged the fees, that I spent money on what she more than once and very unkindly referred to as "scrap," when those funds should more rightly have gone to some under-educated bureaucrat or sheltered spinster schoolteacher. This was not the case. Not the case at all. Yes, the necessary funds were not readily available, but if any one of my patents had come through, I could have sent them all to the finest universities in Europe! I was merely prioritizing my efforts.

Then she left, and I lost all my energy for pursuing my inventions. Oh yes, I dabble, but it is as if I have let my sail go soft in the wind.

That day...back to that day. It is as if I am searching the same spot over and over again for something I have lost, wondering over and over again why it does not materialize. James and I had gone out to the club for an afternoon of sailing. Perhaps we watched a polo match. Yes, I remember that I was intent on returning home and he suggested this one other event. We squabbled a wee bit on this point, and then I relented. He so rarely asked for anything. There may have been a girl he was hoping to see. It is difficult to recall, truthfully, as my memories are always clouded with breathtaking hurt. I do remember the strange sensation of returning to an eerily quiet house. I do recollect standing on the veranda, the doors flung open, and staring into an emptied house. I was aware of James at my side, my emotional mirror, both of us speechless, unable to comprehend or explain to one another what our eyes were seeing, the yawning void where there should have been children running to greet us, the absence of noise when we should have been hearing the sounds of a meal being made ready in the kitchen.

Of course, my first thoughts were of robbery. But what was there to steal in that house? Our holdings were simple, of necessity. And anything of value to me was worthless to anyone else: my books were no good to the illiterate locals; my pieces of equipment frightened them, as they thought they were used primarily for some advanced form of white-man obeah. And besides, these items were still in place. What was missing was the furniture. Each room expanded before us, open and empty, like a mouth without teeth. All the everyday items used for all those quotidian tasks of eating and resting and sleeping were gone. I turned away in horror from the sight in front of me and noticed for the first time the ruts a laden cart had made in the soft soil of our yard. I panicked for a moment, wondering if she and the children had come to harm. But the scene in front of me had no signs of a scuffle, nothing was broken, nothing amiss. Everything was simply gone. James and I sidled silently through the echoing rooms like we were ghosts returning to haunt the place instead of two men returning home, expecting the warm embrace of family.

Oh yes, she'd left behind a few things so we'd not be totally inconvenienced—a few plates, a bit of cutlery, the kitchen table, two narrow beds, a pair of chairs. Otherwise, the house was literally and figuratively swept clean. Of herself she left nothing but her unmistakable citrusy scent on our sheets and a short note announcing her departure, with the other children, to New York. She reiterated that she wanted them to attend school. She heard it was free in the United States. She wrote that she didn't want to separate me from James. It occurred to me then that we might have passed not far from each other on the docks. I imagined her scuttling the children in front of her like a busy hen, shooing them up the gangplank of some rough steamer as James and I tied up that small sailboat he had scrimped and saved for. There was nothing further in her note. No kind word for either me or James. No apology. No explanation for the secrecy. Of course, none was needed. If she had tried to be open, the plan would have fizzled like a drop of water in the dry dust of a hot day. I would not have gone. I would not have allowed her to go. We would have had a great row. Our relationship might have soured beyond saving. What I cannot accept is that it was already soured enough to cause her to leave.

I can still conjure a slightly fuzzy image of her note in my mind. The sheet so small to hold such big revelations, her handwriting so careful and childlike for such a grand gesture, her grammar so simple and plain for such a vast treachery. I wish I had the memento still. Of course if I did, I would just worry over it, pick at it as if it were some small piece of shrapnel from a long-ago war trying to find its way out of my body. But it would be something. Something to make the event, which seems like the stuff of a bad dream, real. It would be something of her. At the time, I didn't know that I would ever want such a thing. At the time, I was so angry, so blind with my outrage, that without thinking, I twisted the note in my hands, and in the heat of my emotions, the sweat of my palms ruined the writing. Then I tore it to shreds. Little did I know, it was the last I was to hear from her.

Before she left, I had been happy. I was quite sure of my happiness. Well, I was at least happy enough, that much I know. But upon what was my happiness based? If it was derived from some basic misunderstanding of her, of what was between us, of what she was capable of, was it happiness at all? Dammit, she took so much from me. She took my children, and I don't know how or if I can regain them. She took the things that brought joy to my face and hope to my days. Can an old man hold on to the memories of the happiness he once had, or must I give those up to her as well? Does my current rather depressed and gloomy state of mind negate all the happiness I once had? Does that residual happiness still exist somewhere, anywhere? If I die in sadness and solitude, does this taint what joys and successes I may have had in my earlier years, as if my current life is a skim of mold on the fresh bread of my earlier years?

Oh, these are unprofitable thoughts. Bad for my head, my heart, my soul. I must put myself toward some occupation. Write a letter. Go putter on your machine. Read a book, man. Yes, and be reminded that my hand shakes when I hold a pen, my joints ache when I bend over my worktable, and the print swims in front of my dimming eyes.

I miss my children. It is that simple. That profound. I miss seeing them skittering about in the yard, chasing butterflies, bringing me a skinned knee or bruised elbow to kiss, a lizard or bug to inspect. The boys especially. James is my true son, so like me, so sympathetic to my soul. Edmund was the classic middle child, a smiling, easygoing smoother-over of things. Percival had more of his mother's temperament, brooding, a bit dark. Thomas was a scrappy young man, as one is when he is always trying to keep up with his elder siblings. They came so fast, they were all so close together in age, they are like many parts to a single child. I can barely conjure their faces anymore, I am sad to say. As the years have gone by and they are no longer here to make new memories with me, I am enraged and confounded that their individuality is blurring. In my mind, I see only a cluster of children playing, their highly pitched voices drifting along on the afternoon breeze, distracting me from my tasks, beckoning me to come see what they have discovered, to referee a dispute, answer a question, enlarge upon a topic.

I saw a group of little ones the other day in town. They were standing outside the general store where I used to bring my brood, comparing their penny candies, sharing and competing at the same time, as children do, waiting for their mother, no doubt, to complete her purchases inside. There was a brief moment of confusion and dislocation when I thought, crazily, they somehow they might be mine. My heart banged unsteadily in my chest with joy and then for a long time after that with melancholy. There was a bench in front of the store and I sat there, trying to catch my breath. And catch some of their chatter. I searched their faces for something, anything familiar. Too long, perhaps, as they began to throw suspicious glances my way. Then a tussle broke out between the two boys and the girl tried to intervene and only got her hair pulled and her ribbons mussed for her trouble. Oh, that reminded me of my Maggie. Maggie, the elder sister, always the elder sister. She was like a sheepdog, fussing over the boys, trying to corral their disordered energy. I see her with a sibling only the slightest bit smaller than herself propped on a hip as she wipes a dirty face with the edge of her dress. I see her bent over like a miniature matron, lacing a shoe with her small fingers. I hear her voice, comical in its high-pitched effort to be commanding, calling them off some argument or in for a meal.

The mother to these other strange and wonderful and very real children tumbling around in front of me came rushing out of the store at the sound of the minifracas and hustled them away. I sat for a bit, I was so shaken and unsteady. Then my cooler thoughts kicked in and I reminded myself that my children would be much older by now than those I had seen. I might not even recognize my own children if I passed them on the street, they would be so changed and grown into young people completely unknown to me. That sobering thought settled me down quite a bit. Settled me down into sadness.

Of course, it would be different if the child in question had been James. I know him not just by looks and familiarity, but by the sympathy within our souls. James carried himself apart, always wise and sober. He did not engage as much in the other boys' games and silliness, aligning himself at an early age with me and my jobs, my tasks, aligning himself always with work. He took something from us both in this regard. I focused my energies with the work of the mind, Rachel with the work of the physical world. I was interested in the intellectual, she the domestic. I wanted to solve problems; she wanted to create order. James wanted all of these things, was all of these things. I loved all my children, but it was different with James. I loved the company of his mind. His personality sometimes veered almost too close to his mother's, but he had, where she did not, at least a sense of humor. He had, where she did not, a native curiosity. And he, where she did not, seemed to enjoy my company.

I remember that I would try to snatch a kiss and she would turn away. The children are clear evidence that she was not always cold to me, but as the years accumulated between us, her affection for me seemed to wear away. Whatever energy she once had for me went to chores. She tasked herself with cleaning, rearranging, fixing things that would have been left well enough alone. Always scrubbing something, washing something, tidying something, her face averted from mine when I tried to engage her in conversation or affection, occupied, always occupied with something else.

Our house was compact. She had help with the heavier chores from Vea, but she was relentless in her efforts, as if through dogged attention she could burnish our meager holdings to some higher level of shine. Strangely, she rarely turned similar attention to her own children, who ran around, much more often than I thought appropriate, with dirty noses, torn shirts, black eyes, bare feet. She let them live like feral animals. Yet she upset our entire domestic applecart on the pretense of wanting to educate them? The contradictions in that woman continue to confound me these many years.

According to letters from James, she is little changed. And she did little to improve her life by abandoning us. Or more accurately, I suppose, abandoning me. Of course, he tries to protect me from the news. He says little, evades my direct questions, but it seems the children's education is, in fact, highly erratic, a by-product of her moving so frequently to keep ahead of landlords and back-due rent. She takes in sewing, but there is less and less of that—everyone wants store-bought and ready-made. The boys attend school for some time and then forgo the classroom for the opportunity to make a few cents selling newspapers, running errands, stocking shelves. Or, I imagine, simply playing jacks in some alleyway. I would send her money—I have little enough, but I would help as I am able, if only she would ask. Blast, if only I knew even how to reach her. But no. She has not written to me once. I have no address for her. I will not ask James. I will not make him an intermediary, ask him to share the contact information she has given to him but not me. She is lost to me, stranded somewhere on that other, faraway island. She is too full of pride. As is often the case with one who came from so little. Who has so much to answer for.

3 May 1915

My dear son,

Your letter dated the 16th duly received and made me very happy.

We do get the war news down there twice every day, but of course we can only estimate the state of the two contending armies and judge the truth by such results, for when the British and French reports tell of a great victory, next day a German report is exactly the opposite. Anyhow we have to come out on top, but it may take some years to do so and in the meantime the whole world may be drawn into the trouble.

I may have my fly-machine ready before the end of the war perhaps. I got one engine, best part of another, two boilers, three burners, 20 lbs of aluminum, some steel tubes, one chassis and a lot of junk delivered for 8 £. I have the body frame of the fly machine built of bamboo, wings and tail not yet sprouted—outlay in cash to date 10/8. The boilers are 16" x 12" high of steel with 300 brass tubes each in good condition. One engine is cleaned up by me and in good condition, the other can be put in order with some little trouble and expense, however I only want one and I have it. Engine 2 cylinders, 2½" diameter, 3½" stroke, double concentrics link motion reversing gear. If my system works out it should develop from 5 to 60 HP. Weight when all fitted up will be 75 lbs…

Of course, never mention my principles on steam to anyone and hope that it will work out all right. If it does, we will soon get together again.

Business is very dull. Last month scarcely paid expenses. I am living almost entirely on oranges and grapefruit. Sometimes bananas and pears and only go to the restaurant twice a week for a good dinner. I have not weighed myself, but have taken up 4 holes in my belt.

I am sorry you and your brother do not get on. Treat him kindly and he will get over it in time I hope. Of course there can never be any order or regularity in your mother's house, that is certainly bad training and the children are brought up with very bad habits. It used to drive me nearly mad and I cannot blame you for wishing to live away from it. I am glad you are settled in a place until you can get a job with a dental office.

I am expecting Jipijapa hats and shall send some on as soon as I get them; perhaps we may be able to work up quite a respectable business in that line.

I enclose $1 for the other children. They no doubt care not a snap for me, however remember me to them.

With love and affection from your father,

Henry

I wanted to marry her right away. It was not the pregnancy. I didn't even know she was pregnant. I couldn't have, the first time I asked her to join me in matrimony. We separated from one another that fateful afternoon, somehow. We reordered our clothing in some degree of discomfort and perhaps confusion. She collected the child and the cradle and went indoors. I waited on the bench in the shade for quite some time. I thought she would settle the moppet and come back. I thought we could have a conversation about what had transpired and what would happen next. Already I was formulating my proposal. After all, I had considered and reconsidered asking her for some time already. But the minutes stretched away before me, and the house and yard remained still. The door she had used to enter the house remained closed. I began to fret and pace around the garden beds, working myself into a bit of a lather. I thought about entering the house. I talked to myself. I considered the options. What if I ran into Mr. or Mrs. George? What account would I, could I, give of myself? Maybe the child would not settle. Maybe she was called off on some other duty. Maybe she did not want to see me right now. Or at all. I finally settled on the explanation that she must naturally be embarrassed by what had transpired and that I should move on so she did not have to face me right away. I thought I would give her some time. I told myself it was only a matter of time.

I then tried to seek her out several times over the ensuing weeks: I walked by the house pretending to be on a stroll; I made an excuse to come chat with Mr. George, to ask his advice on a made-up financial matter for myself; I glimpsed her in town and quickened my step to catch up with her. In every instance, she met my eye with a brief nod and then she dodged me. I finally sent her a note asking for a private meeting; she did not reply. I sent her a note asking for a meeting in a public location, a stroll along the wharf, a faux bumping into each other in town; again, she did not reply. Weeks stretched into months. I wrote her again offering both an apology for what had happened and a proposal of marriage. I assured her that I was not merely being gallant, that I had admired her for quite some time, had considered asking her for quite some time, was able and willing to be a good husband and father. I admitted that my house was not as grand as the Georges', but pointed out that she would be mistress of it rather than beholden to it. Again, she frustrated me by not replying.

I was flummoxed. I wanted just a small note, anything, even just something to put me off. All it took was a pen and a scrap of paper, a moment at her writing desk. If she had such a thing in her room. After all, I reminded myself, who did she have to write to? I resolved to try again, in person. I returned to the George house at the same time of day as our assignation. I was at my wits' end. I needed an answer of some sort. I was desperate for resolution, a yea or nay, an explanation. I was desperate to know whether I was admired or shunned. This time I was in luck. She was in the garden tending plants. And we were once again alone. She looked up as I came in the gate and this time held my eye. She set down her trowel, straightened her back and legs, brushed her hands off on her apron. She turned and took a few steps away from me and my heart sank. I thought at first she was fleeing. But then she looked over her shoulder, inviting me to follow. She moved toward that embarrassing bench. She sat, arranged her skirts so there was room for me beside her. I sat primly, upright, and as far away from her as possible without letting myself tumble into the dirt. I fear I started badly.

"Why have you ignored my letters?" I said.

I had not intended to begin with an accusatory tone.

"I have not ignored them," she said. A pause. "I have simply not replied to them."

I sighed. This was the first time I was to see a quality in her that eventually came to wear on me: she was tiresomely exacting, and always about the wrong things.

"Yes, well then, why have you not replied to them? Common courtesy might dictate that you tell me something of your feelings for me." I paused, and then added with perhaps too much of a dramatic flourish, "Or lack thereof."

She busied herself with brushing some soil off her skirt.

"I am not as comfortable with sharing things of that sort in writing," she said. "I am not confident in expressing myself in the written word."

We were quiet for a few moments. I was unsure what to say. Perhaps she was, too. We were waiting on each other. Finally, I could wait no longer.

"Rachel," I said, entreaty entering my voice as I turned to face her. I reached out to take her hand, but she was just beyond my grasp. My hand fell back to my side as I addressed her profile. I swallowed hard and carried on. "Rachel. Marry me. It is my most fervent wish that we be joined in the law and under God."

She said nothing.

I persevered. "I have long admired you," I said. "Surely you felt this from me. I find you lovely and competent. I am in need and desirous of a wife. None of these foolish fancy ladies are for me. But you, with you, we could make a life together."

She stared out into the middle distance. I was out of words for the moment. I was anticipating rejection. I was hoping for acceptance. In what I would eventually learn was a distinct quirk in her character, Rachel found a means to give me neither.

"There is no need for us to marry," she said in a voice so low I had to lean forward to hear her.

"What do you mean?"

"I mean there is no need for us to marry."

She set about rearranging her skirts.

"But I have no objection to coming to live with you," she said plainly and shockingly. "As mistress of your house, as you put it," she added. And then, "And as mother of your children."

Confounding woman.

"But why not marry? If we are to have children, we must marry," I insisted.

"No," she said. "There is no need for it. Plenty of people have children together and don't marry." Then she added, "I have no wish to be married. Not to you. Not to anyone."

I was completely flummoxed at her absurd proposal. Unusual for me, I was also at a loss for words. We sat in silence for some moments. She regarded a fluttering butterfly, and I regarded her.

"Yes, people do that," I said slowly, careful with my words. "Island people do that. That does not make it right. Or desirable. What if we were to have children? You would have children together without the benefit of marriage?"

She was quiet a long time. I fear I had raised my voice a bit. I felt my face had flushed. Finally, she turned to me, stared at me, her grayish-brown eyes flitting over my face. I felt exposed, as if she was discovering and assessing every flaw, counting each gray hair and wrinkle.

Finally she said, her voice firm with portent, "Henry, we *are* going to have a child together."

I leaped to my feet, so strong was my shock and consternation. She remained unruffled. I stood there stupidly for a moment and then sat back down. I found myself thrilled by the idea. I so wanted a child, a family. I so wanted to be surrounded by the busy noise of children. I had grown up with many younger siblings, all of us in the warm embrace of a happy marriage. The ache of this so far unrealized dream now fought in my body with the potential joy of its coming to pass.

"Rachel, this is great news! We will marry as soon as possible. I will go speak with Mr. George right away. He will be sad to lose you, but he will be happy to see you well wed."

"Henry," she said, her voice a single, sober stone pulling my enthusiasms back to the earth. "I will come to live with you. I will mother our children. I will tend to you as a wife would. But I have no desire to marry."

I did not know then that this was a conversation we were to have many times over the coming years. At that moment, I thought I would give her time and in a few weeks or months she would come around. I thought I could prevail upon Mr. George to talk sense into her. I thought that the worst case would be that after the baby was born we would have a proper wedding. I latched onto her words about filling my life with herself and our child. All I asked is that she make the move soon. I wanted to start our joined life as quickly as possible. Before she began to show. She nodded. Then she had yet another surprise for me.

"Henry, there is one more thing," she said.

"Yes, darling," I said, taking her hand properly now, caressing it within my own. "What is it? What can I do for you?"

"You must welcome Maggie as your own."

Maggie. Maggie. I drew a blank. I wondered whom she was referring to. Then I remembered. The baby. Her charge.

"Well, yes, of course," I said, warming instantly to the idea of having an immediate and rapidly growing family. It seemed natural to me that she wanted the little crumpet to come, that she had grown attached to it. It was somewhat parentless, like herself. I honestly loved the idea. "Are you sure Mr. George won't mind?" I asked.

"He will not mind," she said, with a resolution I would only come to understand much later. "I am quite sure of it."

So it was done. We became as one on that day, in that rather unorthodox way. In my mind, we were married right then and there, on that bench, with Mother Nature as our only witness.

I did, a few days later, seek out and discuss matters with Mr. George. He asked no questions and said the decision was hers to make. She was a free woman. He was only there to help her.

"Yes, but she won't actually marry me," I pointed out, rather painfully. "She says she will only come to live with me as a wife in deed, not in name."

He shrugged. Truly. That was all. I was rather surprised at his cavalier attitude.

"Don't you think you can make her see reason?"

He looked at me long and steady then, with a frank and assessing stare not dissimilar to Rachel's.

"Rachel," he said slowly, determinedly, "has more reason than any person I have ever met."

I sighed.

"I will care for her and Margaret at long as she chooses to stay, we will part as friends if she leaves, but I will not interfere to influence her judgment either way," he added.

Apparently, there was neither incentive nor pressure that could be brought to bear on the case. She was steadfast in her position. I wanted her, I wanted the child who would become James and who was starting to stretch her petticoat and threatening deeper embarrassment to me. I even by now desperately wanted the adorable child Margaret. So I accepted her terms. A day was arranged for her to switch households. I hired a cart and trundled over to the Georges' yard. She and Margaret were waiting in the front hall, one small, pitiful, hand-me-down suitcase between them.

"Where are the rest of your things?" I asked.

"This is all," she said.

I detected the hint of irritation in her voice. I had hoped this liberation from the George household would be a cause for some happiness on her part. I regretted the shame or embarrassment I may have caused her by the impertinence of my question.

I still did not realize that she was incapable of shame or embarrassment.

There was no one who came to send her off, to say good-bye. I suppose all that had been effected already. Mrs. George was undoubtedly in bed, Mr. George off in the fields or working over his dwindling sugar-cane sums—I had told him to switch to bananas and mangoes, but he didn't listen to me. We climbed aboard the awkwardly empty cart and started toward my small house in the foothills. We rode along in silence. Her face was turned away from mine—she seemed stubbornly fascinated by the unchanging wall of greenery on the side of the road—but Margaret gazed at me unceasingly, as if I were a strange animal at the zoo. Her frank stare gave me my first chance to really look at her. A pretty and serious baby, with strawberry-blonde curls and eyes the color of morning mists. Those eyes were already reaching into my heart, so deep was my longing to be a father. I smiled and winked at her; her expression remained impassive. I reached for Rachel's hand, but it sat there, inert, in my own, so I let it go.

I wondered then the thing that I would wonder often in the ensuing years: What sort of strange creatures had I compelled to come live with me? At that time, they seemed glorious in their mystery; later, they would seem simply exasperating. Their quiet, the depth of it, their comfort with it, their clear preference for it, made me nervous. I was both given to and accustomed to lively conversation when in the presence of others, but I bit my tongue, let them both have their own thoughts, uninterrupted by my inquiries or small talk. I imagined they both, even little Maggie, wondered what they were embarking on and had their own worries about the coming changes. I wondered if Rachel doubted her abilities to run her own home. I wondered if she was considering her good luck in acquiring me. Ha, my vanity was still intact back then.

We arrived at the house. It was modest, but with a nice veranda. The previous owners had painted it a bright set of colors, island style, which I found festive and so retained. Besides, the repainting would have cost a sizable sum, which I did not have at the time, having recently invested in lawyers' fees to pursue some important patents. Mr. George had lent me Vea for a day, and she had scrubbed every surface so the entire place glistened. She had also arranged the cabinets, stocked the larder, aired the rugs, washed the linens, and even set out flowers in various locations. I was thrilled and grateful. I took in the smell and sparkle, so glorious to an unwilling bachelor like me, and indulged a fantasy that this was just the start of what Rachel would maintain as regular habit.

Rachel stepped down from the cart carrying Margaret and then wandered the rooms like a cat unused to being indoors, peering cautiously around the few corners and doorways. She took Margaret to her small room and unpacked her few garments, hanging them on pegs and placing them in the bureau. She propped her homemade doll against the pillow on her narrow bed while the child held unsteadily to a chair leg. She left the two of us regarding each other while she stepped into the kitchen, where she conferred with Vea, speaking to her in the native patois, which I never could understand. Margaret and I stared at each other some more. I suppose neither of us knew quite what to do with ourselves. She suddenly lost her balance and sat down hard. I expected tears, a wail that would give me an excuse to come to her aid, but got only a dim look of surprise that left me even more unsure of myself.

We had a quiet and simple dinner—Vea had left us a few delicious and ready-made meals for our ersatz honeymoon. Rachel put Margaret to bed and we wandered the house and property together. There was not much, but I pointed out the corner of the yard that got sun most of the day and told her I had thought to put in a garden there. She nodded and said she would start on it in the morning. I absentmindedly noted how overgrown the vines around the veranda were. She assessed them and said it would take no more than an hour or two to give them some shape. We sat on the swing and as we rocked I shifted my weight a few times. She said she would make some cushions. My intent was not to give her chores, but her intent seemed to be to find them. I wanted to speak to her as a husband and wife; she seemed locked into a self-view that relegated her to a role as a house manager. I thought she needed time to soften her harder edges, for her to relax into a gentler form of herself. I looked forward to watching the process. How optimistic I was.

Eventually she stood and said she would go check on Margaret. When she did not return to me, I waited, thinking I would let her go into the bedroom first, give her some time to collect herself, to change. I relit the stub of a cigar. I enjoyed the evening air. I smiled at my sudden and complete transformation into a domestic union. I let myself feel happy. Eventually I went indoors. I peered into the bedroom, where the door was ajar and a candle flickered. She was sitting in a chair by the window, still fully dressed.

"Is everything all right?" I asked.

She looked up at me and her face was inscrutable. I thought I would learn to read its nuances. I was wrong. But at that time, I still tried.

"Yes," she said eventually, her voice a mere breath. "Yes. Margaret settled down nicely."

"I meant with you," I said, stepping further into the room.

She seemed vaguely alarmed and certainly confused by the question. Later, as I came to know her better and reflected back on this first and subsequent nights together, I wondered if anyone had ever asked her about her own feelings. She seemed so unaccustomed to attentions of almost any kind, she practically flinched under even a gaze gently directed her way.

"Yes, yes," she said, nervously. Then a pause and she said, her voice taking on an oddly formal tone, "Thank you for your kindnesses to us."

She spoke as if I was an uncle rather than a lover. In that moment, my heart broke for her, for all the normal affections she had missed. I stepped to her, raised her up from her chair, and clasped her to my chest. She remained rigid, but I thought I felt her soften a bit in my arms. I held her away from me for a moment. She stood still and stiff, her eyes downcast. I repeated my embrace. When I held her away from me again, I stroked her cheek.

"Rachel, you are my wife. Marriage or not, you are my wife, my heart, the mother of my children. I hope to never be anything other than kind to you for the rest of our lives."

Her cheek twitched.

Thinking she was frightened, I continued, "Do not worry. We will not be intimate again until after the baby."

Then she shocked me with a kiss. She seemed to lift herself from the ground and came at me with such vigor, I was forced to take a step backward and clutch her arms just to keep my balance. Her kiss was hard. As if she was hunting for something hidden. I searched for passion in it. I found determination instead. Then she was all over me at once, pushing back my coat, unbuttoning my shirt and pants, and we slowly collapsed together onto the bed. I was taken aback by her aggression, her passion, especially given her delicate state of growing pregnancy. I was, however, I will admit, also very pleased. I thought this spoke well of what was to come. Indeed, our relations were robust, and her pleasures real and deep. As were mine. Afterward, we lay there together, side by side, our breathing slowing and becoming synchronized, my heart filling with happiness and hope. I told her I loved her. She remained quiet. I wondered if she heard me. I knew my voice was quite distinct, that it carried weight. My mood darkened suddenly, and I let an insecure question slip from my lips.

"Rachel," I asked. "Do you love me?"

She was quiet for so long, I began to wonder if she had fallen asleep.

Then she said this: "Is it necessary?"

I inhaled sharply. What a freakish inquiry! I hardly knew what to make of it, how to respond. What a thing to say on what was the equivalent of our first night together as man and woman, if not husband and wife! Her words repeated themselves over and over in my mind, each time with a jabbing sensation. My astonishment at her question opened up into a dark, cavernous empty space. Finally, she took pity on me, showed she had at least some small capacity for tenderness. She even used my name.

"Henry," she said. "I am sorry. I know I am not what you hope me to be. I *will* try. I can promise you that. I will try my very best to love you. To do right by you as a woman. And a mother."

This was her promise. If I am fair, it was a promise she worked hard to fulfill in her own unorthodox and unexpected ways. She did try. I have to give her that. She tried her very best. In turn, I tried to have her very best be good enough for me. In this effort, I fear I failed.

RACHEL

I REMEMBER THE FIRST TIME HENRY ASKED ME TO BECOME HIS WIFE.

"I would like to marry you," he said. "I have no riches to offer, but I have been rich before and I may be again."

I think he was nervous, as he did not pause for me to respond, but kept talking, moving the conversation quickly away from this issue at hand and instead to one of his contraptions, some kind of an engine, that he was sure would result in a huge fortune. He went on for some time, but it seemed the more he talked the less I understood. I at least tried to follow the line of his talk as it veered between patent offices and propulsion, mathematical formulations and compound materials. I had seen him do this before with other people. I had seen them nod politely, then roll their eyes when he wasn't looking. I always wanted to smack those other sniggering fools.

"What have you done?" I wanted to say to those men. "What do you even try to do?"

Those men, content to live off of their fat inheritances, playing polo and drinking wine, batting a tennis ball around and eating delicacies imported across the high seas as if those things were as important as life and death itself. Even those men who had farms satisfied themselves primarily with striding through the cane, conferring with their head man once or twice a week, and beating a field hand with their whip once in a while, showing off their own suspect authority. They hired others to do everything from bringing in the crop to counting their money.

But I didn't say any of this to Henry. What I said to Henry was, "You don't need to marry me."

That stopped the flow of his talk.

"My dear girl," he said. "Of course I do!" Then he took my chin in his fingers and tipped my head back. "I need to because I want to," he added.

"I can take care of the baby," I said.

He looked at me, searching my face for something.

"I won't tell anyone," I added.

He shook his head, not understanding.

"That you are…" I paused. "Who the father is. I won't tell."

Not telling was something, after all, that I was very good at. He turned from me then. Stood up and walked away, actually. I thought he would keep going. I was both afraid and relieved. The feelings swelled and rumbled in me like potatoes boiling over in a pot, the relief solid, heavy, sinking; the fear frothy, liquid, overflowing. But he came back.

"You have been too much in the company of the locals," he said.

Now it was I who searched his face, not understanding.

"That behavior is fine for the local women," he continued, looking down at me, his face more serious than I had ever seen. "It is understandable when the men are less than responsible," he said. "If I had only those sorts of men to choose from, I would stay independent myself. It makes sense for those women. But it is no good for you. It is no good for the child, for my child."

I remembered then that he had been married before. That he lost his wife and baby at the same time. When he should have been bouncing a baby boy on his knee, he was instead dressing in black, mourning both his losses. He wouldn't want to lose another child. I understood that. But I didn't understand why his tone had changed so much. Now he talked to me like he was teaching me something, like my father used to talk to his students. He kept on, and in his keeping on, he began to lose me. He did not notice, of course, because I did not let on.

It is true what he said about the local women. Vea told me more than once, "No reason to keep a man just because you have a child." She always said, "The child is a blessing, the man a burden." But I also learned from watching the white women. Before they married, they were free and easy with each other, chattering and giggling together like birds on a wire. Once married, they stopped laughing so much, started always looking at their husbands before they said or did even so much as pick up a fork. The other thing I learned from the local women was how to keep my true feelings from showing on my face. Which I did as I listened to him with half my attention, the other half preparing responses and explanations that I knew I would never share with him. But I had to give them voice in my own head.

He carried on.

"It is not just for the child within you that I want to marry you," he said. "I have long admired you, I have long found you captivating in a way I am not quite able to explain or even, honestly, to understand. I don't pretend that you have the same feelings for me. I understand that I am much older—I see how much gray is already in my beard! I know I am not a dashing young officer like those who you undoubtedly see in town and I daresay sometimes here at the Georges' house, even. Those days are behind me now. But I do feel sure that these same qualities of steadiness and maturity and experience will become valuable to you over time, especially as you see what a mess those dandies tend to make of themselves. And often enough of the women who have the weakness of spirit to fall for them. I know you are fond of me; I know you care for me. I am confident this will blossom quickly into a love that will be sustaining to us both. And to our children, if we are fortunate to be blessed with more. If you feel unable to commit yourself just now because you are unsure of your own feelings, then consider committing yourself for the child and trust that your feelings will catch up."

I was quiet for a bit after he said all this.

Then I said, "I am quite sure of my feelings."

But what I thought was this: it is not that I am unsure of my own feelings; I simply have little use for them. The truth was that I spent no time considering my feelings. That was a luxury for others, an indulgence my own life had not afforded me.

What I said next was this: "You are a very good man, Henry."

What I thought was this: there was little to object to in Henry. There was less to object to in him than any man I had ever met. There were quite a few things to recommend him. I could imagine myself listening to his voice for a very long time. My objection had to do with marriage, not with the man.

"Then there is no impediment!" he declared. "I will go and speak with Mr. George directly."

I put my hand on his arm to stay him. I said, "I will go with you, Henry, to live. But not to marry. I will give our child his or her father. But I have no need of a husband."

This is also exactly what I thought.

He stared at me and his face darkened. "Have you no shame, woman?" he said. "To live with a man without the benefit of marriage?"

I shook my head.

"No, Henry, I have no shame," I said.

This was true. It was also, I knew, one of the best and only benefits of being outside of so-called polite society. I had no use for shame and shame had no use for me.

HENRY

I CONTINUED TO ASK HER TO MARRY ME. ACTUALLY, A MORE ACCURATE description might be that I continued to ask her why she would *not* marry me.

"No need for it," she would say.

"We are going to have a child," I would say. Then, eventually, "We have a child," and even later, "We have children."

"Plenty people have children and don't marry," she would say, her diction lapsing into island talk, kitchen talk.

"Not," I would say, fighting with myself, trying not to say that word that she detested so much, especially when it came from me, but saying it anyway. "Not if they want to be *respectable*. Respectable people do not live together, raise a family together without the benefit of marriage. Without the sanctity of either God or state."

Respectable. She hated the concept, thought it weak charade. She thought there was some sort of strength in flouting convention. Or maybe she just had no use for, no interest in convention. Whenever I brought up the subject of marriage—or, really, any societal norm or ritual—she gave me that look. Just her eyes moved toward me. They were that unsettling shade of dark in-betweenness, like a deep pond, stark against the whites, a powerful contrast to her light, thick lashes, which she refused to adorn, and which therefore offered no distraction, no break from the intensity of her gaze.

Her hair was usually loosely, hurriedly, simply arranged, barely softening the angularity of her features. Features I once considered somehow strong and noble, but which I came to judge as simply hard. It was impossible for me to ascertain her internal thoughts, even after years together, but it was always clear to me that she was thinking. It was not judgment that I found in her countenance; no, that would be too obvious, too easy and expected. It was that damned assessment she had in her look. When we had conversations like this, she was looking at me and readjusting her sense of who I was and what place in her world I could or would inhabit. I had seen her do this with others and had been proud of her discerning way with people. I liked it much less when she did it with me.

I was reminded, again, every time we had this talk, every time she directed that peculiar expression toward me, that she had no need of me. This was not just a stance on her part, I came to understand. She truly would have been, would be, fine without me. She would find her way. As she eventually did. This, among other things, was what was so maddening. In spite of pregnancy or children, in spite of her complete lack of prospects, means, family, she would be all right. She had no need of anyone.

Finally, after leveling her stare at me, she would repeat the word, but in her mouth, it turned into something despicable.

"Respectable," she would say, her voice quiet and filled with distaste, as if the word itself was a dirty thing. "A little late for that."

I fancy she was referring not just to what had transpired between us, but her life entire.

"And we live in the wrong place for a thing like that," she would add, low and muttering.

Again, we would find ourselves at a familiar and intractable impasse. It was not just that I wanted her hand; it was that I wanted her to want something from me. I had learned to not expect her need. But her desire—for something, anything—that's what I wanted. I thought, at one time, early on, that I had her craving. What had happened in that yard, that afternoon, what some might have characterized as ugly and rude, was to me spontaneous and beautiful. To me it seemed that we crashed together in the manner of rapidly moving and still water. I wanted to believe that my desire brought us together, that her desire allowed it to happen, that hers was equal to mine. That perhaps her yearning for me had been even more evident to herself than mine for her was to me. I was older, yes, but that would have been, should have been considered an asset to a girl like her. I was considered handsome, I daresay a bit dashing. I had my charms. I was known to be a genial, witty dining companion. I was a tinkerer, a dabbler, an inventor, yes, and also a professional man, a medical man, a dentist. My parents had been well known, well liked, respected, admired. By marriage to me, she would become all of these things as well. It was what any woman of my class, and certainly any of hers, was brought up to cherish.

It never occurred to me back then that she might not want, might not care a jot about these things, or any of the other things that polite society leads one to believe are meaningful. Important. These are, after all, the things that hold society together with the glue of simple understanding and shared values. Confounding woman. In all our years together, I never was able to determine exactly what it might be that she did care about. All I managed to do, I fear, was accumulate a long list of things she cared about not at all. I also managed, I fear, to put myself near the top of that list.

She did, I will say, maintain a robust appetite for relations with me. This surprised me, but was not at all unwelcome. I certainly had a robust appetite for relations myself. Having been without a wife for some years, during which I was not inclined toward prostitutes or mistresses, the sudden presence of a woman in my bed every night was a delight to me. If I am brutally honest with myself, I have to say that she seemed to require more than actually enjoy these activities with me. She tackled them with the same dogged gusto with which she would attack a dirty floor. We both felt better afterward, but I am not sure we felt any closer. I continued to try affection with her. She submitted to these softer ministrations and demonstrations with a degree of uncomprehending, reluctant caution, as a feral dog might accept a pat on the head. I learned to keep my hands from her anywhere other than the bedroom if I did not want a caress to be rewarded with a flinch. Deep pleasure and spontaneous delight of the kind that came so naturally to me seemed completely foreign and unnecessary to her. I wonder, often, if having been born into such ignominy, having been separated so early from her parents and raised without the busy bustle of a real family life, made her incapable of not only giving, but also receiving more gentle sentiments of love.

I should clarify, as I am trying to be fair to her: she was always tender and affectionate with the children. Not perhaps with the full energy or raw emotion of a more natural mother, but she had a quiet command with them. They drew smiles out of her. She never raised her voice—or needed to. She tended to their requirements without recriminations or complaints, and gave them steady if not overly demonstrative attentions. They repaid her workmanlike parenting with adoration and obedience. Well, James not so much as the others. He always was diffident and dodgy around her. Especially later. But he loved her. They all did. I loved her, too. The children always seemed confident in her love for them. This is where we differed. She cared for me much in the same way as she did the children. I learned to do without the emotional succor or adoration I so wished for from her. I learned to accept what she offered and try to appreciate what I had without constantly tabulating perceived slights. But sometimes I slipped. I whined. I railed. I accused her of coldness. She usually accepted my insults as if I were simply a donkey braying in the yard. No point in asking it to stop, just wait it out and the noise will soon be over.

I do remember one time in particular when I hazarded that emotionally loaded question once again. It was a Sunday afternoon. I know this because it was this day of the week, this time of day, when sometimes a bit of melancholy came over me. It was a time when I found myself taking the measure of my life. I would rock on the porch and consider the week in front of me. If I knew my appointment book was empty, if I was waiting once again on a lawyer or the patent office to determine the fate of my future profits, I might find myself casting about for something positive to look forward to, something to brighten my mood. Usually one or another of the children would bound into view and take my mind off my troubles. But this day they were not in evidence. The afternoon light was low, the shadows around me crept in. Then Rachel appeared, glass in hand. She was generous with small, thoughtful kindnesses that way, bringing me a drink of water with lemon. Or if I had had a good month, something stronger. I motioned for her to sit with me. I knew inactivity made her nervous. But this time she indulged me. We were quiet for a few moments. And then, without thinking, the words slid from my lips.

"Rachel," I said. "Do you love me?"

She drew her breath in, sharp with unpleasant surprise.

I should have stopped, not spoiled the peace that had descended between us, but for some stupid reason, I plowed ahead and added, a bit pitifully, I admit, "Have you *ever* loved me?"

She turned away from me then, looking out to the side yard, leaving me only the contour of her cheek to contemplate, along with her hands moving, as they always were, fixing, fussing, arranging, cleaning, busy this time twisting a dish towel she had brought out with her instead of leaving it behind in the kitchen where it belonged. I had regained enough composure by then to keep my mouth shut, thankfully. She took her time answering.

"I have done the best I could, Henry," she finally answered.

The towel was finally properly folded and settled at her side; that activity had been replaced with her rubbing her hands against one another as if they were raw and painful to her. Which they might have been, given how hard she worked them, how much they were in hot water, hard soaps, garden dirt.

She swallowed visibly and added, "You have had everything from me that I was able to give."

Then she got up, let one of those aching hands rest on my shoulder for a moment, and went back to her chores. I was left, again, empty hearted. I know she told me nothing other than the simple truth. It's just that I wanted that truth to be something other than what it was.

RACHEL

He asked me if I loved him. I liked him well enough. I wasn't sure where the line between like and love was. I didn't know how to turn one into the other. I wasn't sure what difference it made. After all, the people who had used the *love* word with me? Well, their actions told a very different story. I had little experience of men, even less of desire. I had few if any feelings of need or want. This might be a character trait I learned, but I suspect I was born with it. Regardless, wanting seemed to be a big part of what people expected from love, and it was something that did not come naturally to me.

What did I feel about Henry? I liked the sound of his voice drifting into the kitchen, especially when he was playing with Margaret or James or any of the others. His voice rose and swelled and then dropped back to a growl as he teased and taught them. The tones were rich and varied, a masculine singsong that softened me somehow. I liked the smell of cigar smoke on his mustache and beard when he rubbed them against my cheek and neck when I was standing at a counter in the kitchen or sewing on the veranda. I liked the feel of his warmth and bulk, his chest hair pressed against my back at night. I liked feeling that he wanted to know me. Even though I didn't know how to talk about myself, what to tell him. I didn't feel the past was worth discussing and the present he could see for himself.

I enjoyed our relations. I liked feeling him reach for me in the night. He was always gentle. A big man who was soft in his ways. The only other men with whom I had any acquaintance, my father and Mr. George, were slight, fair, balding; hardly men at all, in the physical sense. Small men, hard in their ways. In the darkness, in our bedroom, Henry took care of me. It was important to him. To be good at love. And he was. Of course, the results were as much for his self-satisfaction as for my pleasure, but nevertheless, a pleasure it was. It gave us something to go on. For a while, anyway. And it resulted in children, which gave us something else to go on. For a time.

HENRY

FINALLY, AFTER ALMOST SIX YEARS OF LIVING IN OUR IN-BETWEEN state, when I had given up completely and the idea of formalizing our union had gone stagnant in my soul, she confounded me yet again with the announcement that she would, in fact, marry me after all. I don't know what caused her change of heart, but, I admit, I was happy about it. I suppose I hoped it was indeed a change of heart, the start of something fresh and soft in her.

"I am ready," was what she said to me.

I recall the words exactly because I responded, "Ready for what?" Thinking she meant an excursion of some sort, or ready for our next meal.

"I am ready to marry you."

I was thunderstruck. I sputtered. There was no introduction, no warm-up, no discussion. We were standing in the kitchen. I had merely stepped in to inquire after the hour when supper would be ready. After this statement, she turned her head away from me, scuffed her foot a bit.

"You want to marry? Me? Now? Why? Why now?" I asked stupidly, so uncomprehending of her remarks that joy at the fulfillment of my greatest wish was not even possible.

"I think it is time," she said simply, her voice just above a whisper.

"You think it's time? Why?" I asked. "Why so suddenly now?"

"Do you no longer want to be married?" she asked.

I thought I detected the shadow of hurt cross her face.

"No! I mean, yes! Yes, I want to marry you, for God's sake. I meant, why now? Why after these years do you suddenly consent to legitimize our domestic arrangement?"

She busied herself with something in a bowl that apparently required a vigorous mixing at just that moment. When she did answer, well, it was still no answer.

"I don't have a reason," she said. "It just seems like we should. I feel ready now where I did not before."

I stared at her. She must have known I needed something better than that for a reason.

"I would like to," she finally said. "I would like to be your wife."

She smiled as these words crossed her lips. Light from some invisible, internal source suffused her face. This look of hers dispelled all doubt and confusion in me and replaced it with delight. I threw my arms around her and picked her up off the ground. She didn't even resist me as I spun her in a circle, but softened within the hearty round of my embrace.

"I will go to the church tomorrow and set a date," I shouted as I set her on the ground and kissed her soft cheek.

But even in this happy moment she had to be difficult.

"No church," she said. "Please, no church."

Well, even that bit of stubbornness was not going to take the edge off my happiness. A civil union was fine with me. In the end, she was probably right about this point. What church would want to sanctify our unholy union? But no matter. We were to be married, finally. She was to make an honest man of me. It was not romantic to go to city hall. But it was romantic to be finally married. It mattered to me. It also mattered, perhaps even more, that she had finally given me this one thing that I wanted so dearly.

The marriage made me happy. I felt content and peaceful in a whole new way. Yes, other than a slender gold ring on her hand and a slightly larger one on mine, there were no obvious outward changes. But I daresay it made her happy, too. Happy enough to have the result of Tom within the following year. Once the marriage point of contention was no longer between us, well, we settled into a companionable, comfortable routine. I was regularly frustrated by her decidedly hands-off management of the children, but I kept those concerns to myself. Mostly. They were happy children, freer than most, and when they looked up at me with their broad smiles, I tried to look past the grime that was lodged in their dimples and the twigs that were entangled in their hair.

The only worry was money. Of course. I tried to shield her from our thin resources as much as possible and was mostly successful. I had just enough coming in from dentistry to keep us in flour and fish. She kept a large garden that supplied a steady stream of vegetables. The jungle itself offered fruit. But I was beginning to feel cornered. I had put almost all the money I had made in my years working in the United States into my efforts to gain patents—lawyer's bills, application fees, the supplies I needed to create working prototypes. Which often enough failed to work adequately. Over time, dentistry was proving less and less remunerative. Others were coming to the island and creating competition with their new equipment and theories of dental health. My patents were not forthcoming. The fly machine remained firmly grounded in my mind and on paper only.

I came up with a scheme. I honestly thought I was creating a mechanism whereby both my family and Mr. George would benefit. I honestly thought he would want to help, and had not offered simply for fear of hurting my pride. The girl, after all, was his daughter. I assumed, in any case, that she was. He was clearly not overly attached, as he had not asked to keep her when Rachel left, but men like him thought little of their illegitimate offspring; I was happy to have Rachel bring the child with her to my home, as she clearly *was* attached. She and I had raised Margaret as our own. She called me "Father" and Rachel "Mother," and we never corrected her or led her to believe we were anything but father and mother in blood, as well as name and deed. I had never asked for a penny from Mr. George. I felt sure he would want to do right by the girl, and I was equally sure he had the means to do so.

I had not been back to the George house since the day I picked up Rachel. We were busy with our rapidly growing family. I saw him from time to time in town, at the club or hotel, both of which I frequented less and less for reasons of other commitments, as well as cash. He was always polite in his greetings, but in truth, I detected a profound chill had grown over our relationship as soon as Rachel went away with me. I did not attribute it solely to my taking her from his home, as I had ascertained through some discreet inquiries that this same chill had extended over the George household entire. His wife had died and he had less help around. He never entertained anymore. I heard he might be unwell. It occurred to me that he might be considering his legacy and making plans for the disposition of his estate, as any man of his standing, wealth, and age would be.

I wrote him in advance, asking for a meeting. I did not say what I had in mind, but he wrote back with a date and time at which he said I was free to call upon him. Maybe he suspected. I arrived at the agreed-upon hour and found him even more brusque than usual as he ushered me into the drawing room. I asked after his daughters in England, both of whom had married well. There were now grandchildren, he mentioned. Said one son-in-law was worthless and the other dull, but fortunately both were quite rich. I asked after the plantation. He shrugged. Some years are better than others, he said, but the problems with labor, weather, and markets never vary. His demeanor never warmed and his conversational efforts were minimal. There were several awkward silences. He was too polite—or perhaps disinterested—to ask directly what this visit was all about. I was unsure of how to get to the matter.

Finally, he cracked open a door for me when he asked after Rachel and the other children. This gave me the chance to steer the conversation toward Margaret. I told him what a good girl she was growing into. He stared off. I said that she had a great love of books and took exceptional care of her brothers. Nothing seemed to pique his interest. I mentioned her intellect, thinking this might make him proud. Her exceptional handling of sums. This gave me the opportunity to segue into the expense of school fees. Clothes. The steep increases in the price of food. It was all a bit clumsy, and I fear I beat around the bush. Then he turned suddenly to me and his eyes, which had seemed cloudy with age, were now dark and full of storm.

"Are you asking me for money, man?"

His voice was expelled from between his teeth. He drummed his fingers against the arm of his chair and then threw back what remained of his drink before his eyes once again locked onto mine.

"Well…" Frankly, I stumbled. I had not expected him to be so blunt and was taken aback by the raw force of his question. Of course I was doing just what he suggested, but I had hoped our transactions could be handled with greater delicacy.

"I suppose," he said, his voice now lowered, almost contrite, "she told you that the child is mine? This is why you are here, floundering like a fish on a dock, filling my ear with little tales of the girl's wondrous nature? Her delightful personality? As if she were some sort of a doll?"

"Rachel has done no such thing," I answered honestly. "Rachel rarely speaks of you."

This was also true. I had tried to get her to tell me of Margaret's provenance, but she always answered with a variation of, "What difference does it make? She is ours now."

"Yes," he said, his voice bitter. "I suppose Rachel thinks little of me. Rightly so, no doubt. Such a sensible, astute girl she always was." He paused for a bit, deep in thought, then returned to the main part of the stream. "But you assumed," he said, "that Margaret could only be my daughter?" He was staring steadily at me.

"Well, yes, I suppose I did." His unrelenting gaze made me squirm.

"And who," he asked, his lips curling into a tight, dark smirk. "Who do you assume is the mother?"

This rather frightening, snarling change of tone animated what was the first real expression to inform his face since I had arrived.

"I did not bother much to think about that," I replied, again honestly. "I supposed it mattered not much to me. Someone's maid, perhaps. A girl you visited when traveling on business. As you know, these things are common enough." I swallowed. "Especially for a man like you. With your wife so ill and all." I rushed onward. "I assumed only that Rachel had grown attached to the child, as would have been natural to a young girl caring for a baby. I was content to have her come along with Rachel. I thought it would ease her transition to my household. And I am so very fond of children. I suppose having so many younger siblings might do that to you," I added.

He, thankfully, took his eyes from my face and directed them out the window.

"Unless it turned you against children altogether," he mused.

I decided to ignore the pique of this last comment and sit quietly for a moment or two to give him space to consider what I hoped would be a generous contribution to our household. The silence stretched out for an uncomfortable distance and I began casting about for a way to once again take up the thread.

"I thought," I said, pausing, as I was painfully aware that I was treading into delicate territory, but territory that might make him more amenable to my cause. "Well, I wondered actually. I mean it crossed my mind in any case, that Rachel and Margaret might be, well, perhaps, they were sisters." I stood there stupidly and waited for a reaction from Mr. George. As I got none, I carried on. "Or half sisters. It's just that they look so similar. Their attachment is so deep and so natural."

He looked at me blankly for some time. It was as if shock had removed all emotion from his countenance. And then he broke out into a sudden and completely unexpected snorting sound that it took me a moment to recognize as laughter. I was quite taken aback. His guffaws increased in volume and intensity. This was not a man naturally given to humor. I was a bit alarmed when he threw his head back and then doubled over in great heaving roars.

"Oh yes," he finally sputtered out. "That is rich. That makes perfect sense. Of course you'd see it like that. I can't believe I never thought of it that way myself. Perfectly natural. It must be what everyone on this godforsaken island thinks."

Then he stood, went to the cupboard, and poured me a large snifter of a rather exceptional brandy. Which I had no idea how much I would need. He also lit two cigars, and as we puffed and sipped, he told me, frankly, honestly, every bit of Rachel's life story and Margaret's life story, leaving out nothing of the darker and more sordid bits. This is where I learned of Rachel's parentage, of her abandonment, of their flight. This is where I learned that Rachel and Margaret were not sisters, or even half sisters, but mother and daughter. And Mr. George himself, yes, horrifying as it was to consider, he was the father. He gave himself full credit for the care he gave Rachel, and full damnation for his abuse. He quite beat himself up over the whole thing, heaping a range of epithets on his own head and filling his glass more than once as he did. His face began to flame and his eyes water.

I sat dumbfounded and badly shaken. I did not blame Rachel for not sharing all this information—what woman would want to revisit the deeds he described? She must have been terrified this baggage would turn me against her. Perhaps even worse, against poor, innocent Maggie.

He said that this whole sordid tale was why he did not intervene when she decided to come and live with me.

"I thought it a capital idea," he thundered, his reedy body shaking with the force of his emotion. "Get that fine, fine girl away from here, from me, from the memories of what I had done to her, from my evil defilement."

I hardly knew what to do with this new information. It was so horrible and yet, sadly, so common. It explained so much, and yet was a complete shock. It tied up every loose end I had been wondering about this woman, who was now in every way my true wife, but also left me wondering if I'd ever really know her at all.

I never told Rachel all that I knew—what decent man would want to shame his wife so? I also didn't want to tell her about the rather generous check he gave me that day.

As he tore it out of his register, George said, "Rachel is ten times more decent and one hundred times more deserving of this than my own daughters are. I wish I could give it to her directly, but you are her husband, and so it must go through you. See that you spend it on her and the children, man, and not on those stupid gimcracks of yours."

I also didn't discuss any of what had transpired between him and me because I didn't want to tell Rachel about the other checks he saw fit to send my way from time to time.

7 July 1917

My dear son,

I understand why you have pressed your mother for details of her past, because of course, it is your past too. But please do not tell Margaret what you have discovered of her parentage. I have been the only father she has ever known and she is the only daughter I have ever had. I have loved her since she was a tiny, ginger-headed girl, toddling around the yard, chasing lizards and hummingbirds. The memory of her sweet smile and marmalade curls has sustained me many a time.

Her true father was not a bad man, and was from the same or, if I am truthful, perhaps better class than I—she has no cause to worry about her heritage from that side. But I am the one who loved her, who fed her from my own plate, who kissed her skinned knees and bug bites, who pulled her brothers from her when you played too rough, who willingly played her pony, crawling on my hands and knees as she pretended to whip me with a switch from the garden. It was me she ran to when she tripped down the front steps of the veranda, it is me she curled up next to in the hammock on still, hot summer days, it is me she cried out for when a nightmare woke her in the night.

Her relations with her mother have always been stiff. I fear her mother saw too much of the girl's true father in her. Maggie's creation having been a severe wound, perhaps the woman held it against her. Gentleness and sympathy did not come naturally to your mother, as you know. Let Maggie alone. Do not disturb her love for me, her innocence of her birth. She has had enough trouble in her life—let her remain ignorant of the trouble that caused her to come into the world. She is the one good thing that came from that trouble. Let it stay that way.

I remain your affectionate father,

Henry

He asked once to see her. He surprised me by coming into my office; he had never darkened my door before. It was late afternoon. Like many of these afternoons, I was free of patients. I fear he caught me drowsing. I had barely risen from my chair, shaken off the clouds of dreams, before he got right to the point; he didn't even give me a chance to offer him tea. Sadly, I had nothing stronger.

"I've just been to the bank," he said, producing a register and plopping it on my cluttered desk, unceremoniously shoving my inkwell and a few sets of dentures aside. "Had a good sale. Finally."

"Thank you," I said. "It's not necessary, you know. I—"

"Oh please," he blurted out. "I am well aware of just how necessary it is, man."

He had me there.

He scribbled furiously, ripped the check out of his book, and folded it so I could not see the number he had put there. There had been great variation in the amounts he had given me, but every one was helpful. Increasingly, necessary. The checks usually arrived via messenger, a silent, somber man he kept in his employ as a clerk in his office. They arrived without any note or explanation. Not that any was required. Now he held his arm out toward me, check in hand, and I reached out to accept it. It was not forthcoming; he maintained one small corner of it between his thumb and forefinger.

"Listen," he said, staring at the check. Then he looked up at me. His eyes were yellowed and rheumy. I hadn't noticed until then that he looked unwell. Quite unwell.

"Yes," I said, not letting go, yet meeting his gaze, expecting he wanted to ask me for something. "What can I do for you? How can I thank you?"

I was terrified of what he might say next.

"I want to see her," he said.

I was a little unclear whom he meant. I furrowed my brow in question.

"Not Rachel," he said, gruffly. "It's Margaret. I want to see her. I want to see the girl."

"Of course," I said cautiously. I was panicking at the idea of arranging something behind Rachel's back. "What did you have in mind?"

As if reading my thoughts, he said, his voice brusque and dismissive, "Oh, don't worry. It's nothing dramatic as all that." He released the check, finally, into my fingers. "I just want to lay eyes on her. I just want to see what kind of a girl she's turned out to be. It can be—it should be—from a distance. I have no desire to upset the girl. Or Rachel."

"I have to think the best way to arrange a meeting," I said.

"Just tell me sometime when Rachel is likely to be out," he said, closing his register, picking up his hat. "I don't want a 'meeting,' as you call it. I don't want to confuse her. I just want to get an image of the girl I can keep in my mind."

Relief welled over me. This kind of an arrangement was not hard to fix—Rachel had a regular marketing day. I often stayed at home those mornings. Worked on the fly machine or wrote letters and kept one eye on the children. Sometimes this was when we had our lessons. Having him stop by unbeknownst to Rachel was actually not of great concern to me. What began to worry me was how the children would present themselves, how the house might look when he came to the door. He had never seen just how modest our domestic situation was. And recently, it had become increasingly unpredictable.

Rachel was a hard worker, I give her that. But more and more she would go into dark spells when she did little around the house. Dishes and dirt piled up. Beds went unchanged, laundry stayed on the line for days, the garden filled with weeds. She would sit and stare off into the melancholy middle distance while the children ran in the yard barefoot, bringing home snakes and bugs, their faces smeared with grime, snot coming from their noses, bruises from a brotherly brawl sprouting on their faces. All this she ignored. She would stay stranded, brooding in her dark fog, for hours. More often, days. Sometimes it lasted a week or more.

At first I railed at her. I could not stand to see my home life so topsy-turvy. She remained impassive, ignoring me. I told her the children were being left to run wild, like animals. She shrugged and said they were animals. I begged her to come in off the veranda, to fix her hair, to pull herself together. She looked up at me, her eyes vast pools of dark water, and said one word: "Why." It was not a question so much as an observation on the state of the world. There was no getting through to her. The children and I learned to simply wait her out, scraping by on leftovers, fresh fruit, and sandwiches. Once or twice, in desperation, I called Vea in from Mr. George's to help. She tiptoed around Rachel, paying her absolutely no mind, picked things up, tidied our surroundings, put a cup of tea into Rachel's hand and a bowl of stew at her side, and left, without creating the slightest ripple in my wife's still surface.

Then suddenly, with as little warning as we had at their descent, the dark clouds would lift, and we would find Rachel on her knees, skirt hiked up, splashing soapy water around as she furiously scrubbed the floor, or out in the garden, yanking weeds and hacking at overgrown greenery like a maniac. The children would, one by one, be plunked in the bathwater, the detritus removed from their clothing and bodies with a vigorous soaping, and they would emerge some minutes later fresh and pink like newly plucked chickens. Order would be restored and maintained. Until her next spell.

Fortunately, when the day came for Mr. George's visit, we were in the midst of a tidy period. I told the children they could play on the veranda, but not to go beyond our small front yard. I told them if they obeyed, I would suspend lessons for the day. I went indoors and busied myself with drafting letters to my lawyers. I kept one ear pricked for what seemed like hours, but there was no knock on the door. Eventually Rachel came home with her gleanings from the market. The children jumped and pawed at her like puppies looking for a teat. I thought he had lost either courage or interest. I was, frankly, relieved. I didn't relish Margaret being confused by his presence. I was even more dreading having her say something to her mother about "a visitor," and having to fabricate some sort of an explanation that was plausible. We never had visitors or guests. Anymore. I sighed with a deep relief and helped Rachel unpack her groceries.

Then, at dinner, little Margaret shattered my calm with the announcement that she'd seen a man that afternoon.

"He stepped out of the greenery," she said.

Rachel looked up, her eyebrows closed in on each other, and asked, "Who did, Maggie?"

"A man," the child replied, the picture of innocence.

Rachel's face grew more serious with concern, as she asked, "What sort of a man, Margaret?"

It seemed to me she was trying to control her voice. I feigned passing interest, opening my eyes and lifting my brows as if to offset Rachel's expression.

"He had reddish hair and was very pale. Very tall and scrawny, too. Kind of old," Margaret said. "He smiled at me, and I was going to speak to him. I thought I should ask him in for a lemonade. He seemed very hot. I turned around because Tom was yelling at me about being too far out in the yard. Daddy told us to stay close to the house this afternoon. To stay in the front yard only. If we were good, he said, we didn't have to have any lessons."

"I had some letters to write," I protested.

Rachel stopped my explanations with a mere shift of her eyes. She let this minor deceit on my part pass as she pursued the larger mystery Margaret presented.

"Then what happened, Maggie?" she said. "What happened to the man that you saw?"

"What man?" Maggie said.

"The one you were telling us about," Rachel persisted. "The one with the red hair who came out of the trees."

"Oh, him!" the girl said. "When I looked again, he was gone."

She put a forkful of food into her mouth. It was rather a large bite. I gave her a stern look and she chewed quickly.

"It was like he'd never been there to begin with," she continued.

"Maggie, don't speak with your mouth full," I said.

Rachel looked at me and then at her daughter rather intently. Margaret went back to sawing away at a piece of meat on her plate, frowning at my reprimand. I held my breath, a satisfied smile plastered on my face. Apparently he had meant exactly what he had said: he just wanted to see her. Nothing more, nothing less. I hoped this was the end of it. Rachel said nothing and went back to her own plate. I exhaled relief.

Then into the silence that settled around us entered Rachel's voice: "It was probably just a duppy, honey," she said. "Nothing to worry about. This place is full of ghosts."

She ruffled Margaret's curls in an uncharacteristic show of playful affection. *Isn't that just like her,* I thought. *Here she goes and puts the idea of a ghost into a child's head and then tells her it's nothing to worry about.*

We had some years of relative peace. There was little to argue about. There was little money, of course, but that in itself tended to forestall dissension because we had to spend on food and necessities and then there was no more. But there was one aspect to our lives that continued to rankle me. It was the business with the children. It was how offhanded she was about their management. She let the children run, to my estimation, far too wild. Other than dinner, there were no set mealtimes. There were no set boundaries for their play and they roamed the roads and jungle equally. I called it negligence. She called it letting them be children. To me, she seemed devoid of what should be a mother's expected caution about her children. She showed little concern about their injuries and scrapes, about what they might encounter in dangers from man or beast. She let them wear rough clothes, which she called "comfortable," "practical." Margaret even wore her brothers' clothes sometimes, favoring especially their pants, insisting skirts were uncomfortable. Rachel not only allowed this, but agreed with her. She told me she wished she could wear pants herself. The children dug in the dirt and played with half-wild dogs. She delighted, in her quiet way, in their scrappiness. It was perhaps the one of the few things she delighted in.

I spoke to her about this highly irregular approach to child-rearing many times. To no effect. Oh, she might try for a few days to straighten things out, to clean them up. But she was clearly only humoring me. There was no question about that. Because after only a day or two or three, she once again let the children have free rein.

So I hatched a scheme. Yes, it was dubious. No, I should not have done. Of course, there were other options open to me. It was born out of frustration. Exasperation. She was so obdurate to my entreaties. Like many a bad plan, this one seemed, the more I considered it, brilliant. Effective. Foolproof. It turned out to be none of those. I never meant to scare her so. Well, I wanted to give her a scare. But just a small one. Just a cautionary jolt to wake her up a bit. I never anticipated how deeply shaken she would be. I was stupid. I thought it was something we'd be able to laugh about once it was all over. Maybe we would have. If she had not discovered my hand in it all.

Had things gone according to plan, she would not have been so terrified. At least I don't think she would have been. I simply didn't know how else to get through to her. My words fell on deaf ears, so I resorted to action. She called it a kidnapping. Well, it wasn't truly a kidnapping, it was just made to seem like one. I singled out Tom because he was the most adventurous of the bunch, the toughest, and most adaptable. He was also the youngest. Which I thought might give an extra kick to my message about the dangers of her negligent parenting style. The men I hired were supposed to stay with him. Times were getting tough, there were many idle men about, so it did not cost much to enlist some help. They were supposed to take him someplace not easy to find, stay with him for a day, an overnight, and then return him. Make it seem that he had simply followed them like a stray, and that they hadn't known what to do with him. That it took them a bit to figure out where he belonged.

Well, Tom's spirit of adventure was more than I anticipated. He outright challenged the men. Bragged about his knowledge of the jungle and his abilities to be self-sustaining in the wilderness. Where he came up with this stuff I do not know. He was only eight. No, I guess he was just seven. In any case, they thought his bravado so funny, they decided to teach him a lesson themselves. They rowed him across some mountain lake, showed him a cave, and then challenged him to spend the night there. They told him he'd be all alone, with just a burlap sack and a box of matches for protection. They promised me that, in fact, they stayed nearby, though out of Tom's sight. Yes, he was very young, but plenty of children that age are already working and making their way in the world. No harm was done to Tom; no harm came to him. As I say, this extra challenge was not the plan. As I say, he was tough and adaptable. And again, I say, no harm came to him.

Well, yes, they did extort more money out of me. But that was harm to me, not him. I am still not sure how she discovered that part. Maybe she just assumed, given the sordid nature of the entire debacle.

The adventure itself she discovered from Tom. After, of course, a night of panic, which she spent pacing the house and yard, running up and down the road, calling his name so loud and for so long that she went hoarse. I tried to calm her. I played along, calling for him myself. She cried in my arms and then tore away from me to hunt for him some more. As the morning light came over the trees on the far hillside, I hazarded a gentle remonstrance that I now hoped she'd see that keeping the children on shorter apron strings might be a good idea. She glared at me with such darkness of feeling it chilled my heart and shut my mouth. She pulled away from me and refused every entreaty to see the reason in my complaint.

Fortunately, Tom appeared soon after. He skipped into the yard, dirty and hungry, which was nothing unusual, and none the worse for wear. Then he blurted out the entire story as Rachel knelt at his feet, gripping his arms with such strength, I thought she'd bruise them. He was so excited, he'd had so much fun, he told her every detail. Including how the men came to the house and shared a glass of brandy with me before taking him away, while I waved good-bye. Straight from the mouth of babes, as the saying goes. Sigh. He had been sworn to secrecy. He had been told that his having this adventure was completely dependent on his keeping it a secret. Another miscalculation on my part. He was a bit of a braggart and wanted all his siblings to be jealous. Which they were. As he babbled on, completely insensitive to my hand motions directing him to stop and my efforts to redirect his tale, the other children became breathless with excitement. All of them completely missed my role in orchestrating the adventure and wanted nothing so much as their own turn being rowed across a lake and spending the night in a cave.

Rachel stood stone still, her eyes widening, her face hardening. She, of course, did not miss my part in the charade. She also did not express the worry I had hoped for. No, I would characterize her emotions as sheer horror at what had happened. Once the cat was, at it were, out of the proverbial bag, I tried to make light of the entire escapade. I pointed out how much fun Tom had had. I said it was a maturing experience. I described a range of native traditions, especially in America and Africa, that required boys to go on expeditions like these. I reminded her that my own father and uncle had been not much older when they set out, not across a pond in familiar territory, but across a great wide sea to another country, unaccompanied.

I soon realized that I was arguing at cross-purposes to my original intent and reminded her again that this was the kind of thing that could have happened spontaneously and with a much worse outcome if she did not keep closer watch over her own children. I said that I hoped she had learned an important lesson from my rather expensive piece of commissioned theater.

Rachel said nothing to me. She just watched me talk. I became nervous. Her eyes became dark clouds. Then she asked me a single question.

"Are you really concerned about the children's safety, Henry, or are you worried about what the neighbors will think of you?"

The way she said my name was terrible. The emphasis she laid on that one word was chilling. I tried again, but the more I tried to explain, the more I realized the folly of my scheme. Not just the folly of it, but the cruelty of it. The raw dangerousness of it. My heart pounded. My eyes filled with tears. I was suddenly terrifically frightened, as if the hoax had been played on me instead of by me. It turned out all right for Tom, but it might not have. It did not turn out all right for Rachel. It hardened her to me. Her parenting style did not change. She simply took herself further, if that was even possible, from me. She seemed frightened of me. Especially around the children. I would catch her watching me as I played with them, her eyes huge as she peered around a corner or peeked out from behind a curtain. She refused affection, comfort, or sexual relations. I don't think it was the sex she had enough of; I think it was that she wanted no more children. Maybe, it must be said, she'd just had enough of me.

RACHEL

I TRIED TO MAKE OUR MARRIAGE, OUR FAMILY, WORK. I TRIED TO find a way to give Henry enough of what he needed as a man and to give the children most of what they required, some of what they wanted, and also plenty of what I hoped was good for them. I tried to make our little house in the hills a home. For some years, we eked out a tentative balance. We had good days and bad days, and on balance, I honestly felt the sum was more than a mere addition of the parts.

Sadly, it seemed Henry could not make the same accounting. He tried, too, I suppose, but always found me wanting in warmth, insufficient in maternal feeling, inadequate in social graces, too unconcerned with the proper forms of things. It seemed more and more that when I looked in his eyes, I saw only disappointment reflected back at me.

He was not the only one in need of small acts of kindness and consideration; however, unlike me, he was capable of asking for these things outright and became bruised when they were not forthcoming.

Still.

Apparently, I underestimated the extent of his hurts. The distance he would go to even some internal score he was, unknown to me, keeping. I could manage everything that did and didn't transpire between us. I was capable of making do with whatever he was willing to give me, good, bad or indifferent. But when he used our child as a pawn in the battle he was waging with me, it was too much. It was just too much. If only he had not decided to use his love for them as a cudgel against me, things might have turned out differently.

HENRY

James and I entered into a new routine when Rachel and the others left us alone. Simple breakfast of tea and bread. Mornings with patients. Simple lunch of a sandwich. Afternoons doing calculations and plans, letter writing and research. Evening dinner at the hotel. Some days we took his boat out. I encouraged him to socialize more, but he seemed to have no stomach for it.

Then he got it into his head that he had to go to college. He told me there was no way he could properly further our plans if he did not get a solid education. Which he felt impossible on the island. As much as his sentiment rankled me, because it echoed his mother's voice, how could I stand in the way, no matter how painful it was to me, no matter how much I wanted him to stay? Of course I think college a noble enterprise, there is no doubt, but certainly it was not necessary. If he was going to go to college, my choice would have been England, not the United States. For our purposes, an apprenticeship would have been enough for him. He could have learned a trade and then worked with me on my—on our—inventions.

But no, college was what he wanted, what he had his heart set upon. Which necessitated finishing high school. Which necessitated his leaving me. He didn't want to go to Britain, he wanted America; he wanted to get his education not in the old way, but in this new country, in this fresher system. I encouraged him, of course. I was, have always been, deeply proud of him. Truly. He set out for new lands and adventures just as his father and grandfather had before him. With his heritage, how could I expect it to be otherwise? Let it not be said that I was ever a barrier to his pursuit of his own dreams. But my hope was always that he would return, education in hand, to me, to our projects here.

This never happened. A fact that pains me more and more deeply than Rachael's decamping.

I blame that damn dentist. If James had just stayed in New York City. Even if he had to keep selling papers and such. But no, he found employment with some dentist in what he called "upstate." I guess it was booming with so-called engineers and laborers involved in expanding their canal. Stupid politicians spending ridiculous sums to direct men who had no idea what they were doing to abuse immigrants desperate for work to cut stones from cliffs and widen their ditch full of stagnant water so barges belching smoke could move goods through rough country.

In any case, James found this dentist, this place upstate. Perhaps a newspaper ad? Somehow James made his way to a town called Utica, lived in some sort of a boarding house for young, unmarried men, attended high school at night, and apprenticed to a dentist. I worried for him, but also admired his gumption, I must say. So like a Ford, he is! In any case, this dentist took an interest in him and had him to his home regularly for dinners and soirees. Such as they might be. James suggested to me that this dentist was quite successful. Whatever that might mean in a place like that. He said the dentist and his wife were the center of the city's social life. It was at this dentist's home that he met some men with fancy surveying equipment and elaborate drawings. It was from these men that he got the idea to go, not to Harvard, which I had suggested, but to the Massachusetts Institute of Technology. It was also from these men that he got the idea to study engineering, because of course, they were self-styled engineers.

In his telling, it all seemed so exciting. He loved Boston. I was not surprised, as it is the American city closest in temperament and heritage to England, after all. I had been there once or twice myself during my years in the States. He shared with me the processes and practicums he was learning. I followed along for his first year or two, told him of my own experiences with the challenges of applying ideas from a lab to real-world models. But he shared less and less with me. Apparently, that blasted college began to fill his head with ideas that led him to question all the principles that I had spent a lifetime working on.

I warned him to be cautious of mere book learning! What can those professors of his know, stuck up in their classrooms with their chalk-dusted jackets? What have they tried with their bare hands, as I have? What have they done besides talk, talk, talk, squeaking their theories across a blackboard, with a sea of rapt, jejune, and unquestioning faces turned toward them? Even James, who I thought had enough experience to be more critical, was apparently rapt with attention and awe for their complex theorems and myriad mathematical equations! These men put the ideas in his head that turned him away from me and my ideas, that made him want to stay in America, to work in "industry," as he called it, to design aircraft for other men to get rich off of, instead of designing them for ourselves. Oh, America! You are such a flirtatious country, full of promises for what might be—you have charmed so many young men, including myself, of course. But why is James wasting his talents making other men's dreams real? Why is he not pursuing his own dreams, his own designs, our dreams, our fly machines?

But do I tell him these things? No, I will not be that kind of father. He is young, I remind myself. He needs to try out his own ideas, explore his own life. As I did, I tell myself over and over again. I will not be bitter and strident with him. I will not pit myself against his new experiences. Many a father has taken that tack and ended up only turning their sons against them. Irrevocably. He will find out for himself. He will learn. Let him go out in the world. Let him try all his newfound knowledge. He will see. He will see. And then he will come back to me.

22 January 1918

My dear son,

I am sorry you are not feeling as bright as you would like. Cheer up and hope for the better times. Believe that everything that happens happens for the best. You are young and have much before you. I am going down the hill. I shall be 62 and everything looks blue. Have not had any patients the last two months so have plenty of time to work on the Fly machine. Progress has been slow, still I see no insurmountable difficulties even if I break my neck when I go to try it.

For the last 20 years everything seems to have been a failure. And here I am at 62 in this hole with no one who cares a snap whether I live or die. It is truly hard at my time of life. We have been having quite severe shocks of earthquakes and very heavy rains for a week at a stretch. I have had no word from that patent office. It is like the carburetor that they held up for 6 years until my possibility of doing business was dead. Another failure when things looked so bright at first.

Yes, I am very blue. I have worked hard to have all end in failure. We must stick together to the end. You might see some business chance outside of dentistry. You do not seem able to do anything with Panama Hats. I had hoped you would have been able to do something in that line.

I got letters from your siblings. It makes me sad to think I can do nothing for them, and their mother I suppose drilling into them that I am such a bad father. Well I cannot help that so I must leave it to future and chance.

I have not heard from the British Admiralty about my proposition for submarine destruction—another failure. I am only sorry that I am too old to go to the front where I do not think I should fail to get killed. At least I would have done something for the British Empire.

Well, I will not write anymore in this blue vein.

With love and best wishes for your future,

Your affectionate father,

Henry

It is not as if I have not considered going after them. It is not as if I have done nothing but mope since they left. But. But what? Well, there was the cost of passage. I have been quite strapped for some time. I considered borrowing, but there was really no one for me to borrow the funds from. Once she was gone, I certainly could no longer approach Mr. George. I had a few friends left, but no one with any funds to spare. It is not as if I could shovel coal for my passage as James did. Then there was the problem of what I would do once I got there. How would an old man with outdated dentistry skills and nothing extra in his purse make his way in the new world of New York? There would be nothing profitable for me to do. If I went for just a visit, well, the cost of a round-trip ticket was beyond my means. And the trip itself! I have not been in robust health for some time. The heaving of a great ship upon the vast ocean would have been too much to bear. Not to mention the winters in New York! The horrific cold that seeped into your very bones. I had neither the wardrobe nor the heart for it. My doctor had warned me that cold weather could kill me. Of course, all this might have been overcome if one of my patents had come through. Then I could have set myself up, kitted myself out, arrived laden with gifts for the children, and the means to set us up again as a family. This is where I begin to squirm in my seat. Because what if, in spite of everything I had to overcome, I did in fact manage to get my creaky self to New York, and instead of being greeted by children rushing into my arms and the quiet smile of my estranged wife, I was instead looked upon as a stranger? Or even worse, what if she has put so much bile into their tender ears over these years about what a bad father I am that I was greeted with skepticism, derision, or malice? That I could not bear. The mere possibility of it froze my heart in my chest and made my feet like lead in the soft soil of this damned island.

3 April 1920

My dear son James,

I cannot say how glad I was to get your letter. I did not answer in detail your last letter because I did not want to bother you with a lot of new theory with regard to thermodynamics which would only interfere with your work and may retard your progress in examinations for the profession as it now stands. The American thinks he knows everything, is crystalized in that opinion and wants to rule the world.

My health seems pretty good at present. I am still bothered with that pain in the chest when I walk, but not so much as before. There seems to be a great deal of money in bees at the present high price of honey and I want to work up an apiary which I have begun on a small scale in the back yard.

I have no bitterness for the old woman. The marriage state as you have seen it is certainly not encouraging, at the same time your grandfather and grandmother as far as I remember lived a perfect life of happy marriage state. Now as to advice on the subject from me, I can only quote some fellow, I forget who, "If you do not marry you will live to regret it. If you do marry, you will live to regret it just the same."

Thanks for the bunch of Boston papers. I should rather have had a letter. Did you get the second scholarship and how about your new job? I should like to know something about the two boys. They never write me so in fact I do not know them.

With love,

Your affectionate father

Henry

I find these days that I wonder less and less about the why and more and more about the how. Given her temperament, her churlishness, her exasperating way of withholding all emotional succor from me, I am no longer surprised that she chose to leave. The pain of the fact that she did leave cuts at me less than it used to. It is, in fact, undoubtedly better for me that she left. I have more time for my inventions and I have less frustration at trying to manage her moods, less emotional aggravation now that she is gone. Which frees my mind to think longer and harder on the vexing mechanical and technical problems of my fly machine.

But I do wonder how she was able to do it. How she was able to find the money to buy passage for herself and the children. It would have added up to a not insignificant sum. Even if she did, as I suspect, subject herself and them to the indignities of steerage. Given her peevishness, I would not be surprised to hear that she made the boys shovel coal while she and Margaret chopped potatoes for their passage.

I should have suspected her plot. There were signs that she was scheming up some sort of independence. First it was the sewing. She was a talented, effective, and damn efficient seamstress, that woman. She could crank out a quality shirt or petticoat in no time. When I found her wrapping up shirts in a paper package and giving it to Vea, she explained that she was making a few shirts for Mr. George because he had lost his needlewoman. That I could tolerate. At first I thought it just a favor. An odd favor, perhaps, for a man who once abused her, but he also cared for her; I suppose that caring part dramatically outweighed and outnumbered the other part, and their relationship was undoubtedly a complex web of loyalties and ties that I did not pretend to fully understand.

When fabric continued to come into the house and shirts to go out, she said that he had single men working for him and they favored the quality of her workmanship. Then she admitted that he gave her some money for them, just for expenses and a bit for her time, and she only accepted the money to be polite. She said she had the time, that she wanted the occupation. She said that this money was good for the children. She didn't bother to specify why exactly. We had plenty to eat, after all. Well, we did seem to have more meat on our table at that time. What could I have done in any case? I was at my office pulling teeth all day. And even if I wasn't, I knew that her stubbornness ran in a far deeper vein than did mine.

Then there were the chickens. They appeared one day, squawking, in the yard. Fresh eggs every day, and when a layer got old, well, she could go into a pot of stew, Rachel explained. Also, yes, good for the children. She had paid for them with her own money, so what was I to do? It was clear there were more chickens laying more eggs than we could stomach, but I wrote that fact off to her lack of practical mindedness. I thought that an expression of womanish enthusiasm for the creatures, not cold calculation. Naive. I was always so naive about her and her capacities for deceit.

My suspicions were not even alerted when she enlarged the garden. It happened bit by bit. I was not much of one for digging in the dirt, so I rarely visited that part of our yard. What set me wondering was the day I noticed a certain degree of effort on her part as she was gathering baskets to take to the market. I lifted the cloth off one and saw it brimming full of vegetables, a veritable cornucopia.

"What is all this?" I asked, trying to keep the alarm out of my voice.

"We have so much extra," she said lightly. "I am bringing it to the church. I thought we could share with those less fortunate than ourselves."

I bought it. I even went so far as to praise her charity. It was unlike her, but instead of being suspicious, I was pleased. He who is without deceit rarely suspects it in others. Then I saw her accepting money from Vea. I held my tongue the first time but kept my eyes open. It happened again. And again. I confronted her.

"What is this all about? I demand to know."

"Payment for shirts," she said.

"That is absurd. You have not sewn any shirts for some time."

"I was owed for shirts sewn some time ago."

I stared at her, waiting her out.

"And the church had no need for the extra vegetables at this time…"

I closed my eyes and shook my head.

"…so Vea sold them in the market for me."

I was stunned silent.

"Along with the extra eggs."

She had no shame whatsoever.

"And a shirt or two. Now that George's men are well kitted with them."

Ah, now I had the picture of it. How unseemly. How sordid and low class. Trading for a few coins and rumpled bills. I knew she would find my class-consciousness distasteful. I had to find a different approach. I took a deep breath and modulated my voice.

"Why have you not asked me for pocket change if you need it?"

She gave me a look I could not read.

"Pocket change?" she finally said.

"Yes, spending money." What could possibly be unclear about my remark? "Is there something you need or want?" I asked her.

Again, that inscrutable look.

"It is not for me," she said, staring at me, her eyebrows beginning to furrow. "It is for the children. I am putting it aside for the children."

"I can provide for my own children," I said. The heat was rising in my voice.

"Well, Thomas needs shoes. As does James."

"Then they shall have them," I said.

"Yes, they shall," she said. "They are on order. And already paid for."

"Then you needn't keep selling."

"There will be more shoes needed. By the other children and as they grow. To say nothing of clothes and books and meat and milk."

"Have I ever not provided?"

She didn't answer for a moment.

"There is always more we could do for them," she finally said, her voice lowered. "And…"

"And what?"

"There are school fees. I would like to send them to school."

This was an old argument between us.

"I am perfectly capable of teaching them myself," I said. "As I have reminded you many times. Each and every time we have this discussion, in fact."

"Henry."

She had a way of saying my name that made the heat fly into my face. Just the one word, yet I heard it loaded with recrimination. She sighed and started over.

"You have your work. Your office. Your inventions. You are busy."

She was trying to smooth things over. I recognized the effort. All the more notable for its rarity. Yet I felt only patronized.

"I can teach them," I said. "I have more education than any teacher at any school on this damned island! The children can learn from me until they are ready to go to England. By that time my patents will be accepted, and we will have more than enough money for them to be as formally educated as they wish. I know what I am doing. My parents did have a school," I added.

She stared at me for a bit.

"Yes, well, so did mine," she finally said. "But they don't have one anymore. And neither do yours. And neither do we."

And then she was gone. Out the door, clucking to her hens, throwing them some kitchen scraps. The conversation was over.

Now, these many years later, I wonder now how much she was able to put by. Was it enough for passage for all of them? To say nothing of getting set up in a new city, renting lodging for a whole family, staying out of bitter poverty until she could find work there? A few extra cabbages, a handful of working men's shirts? But this did go on week after week. How much could she have cleared? How much did she set aside? Some days I torture myself wondering how she did it.

I must stop this nonsense, arrest these trains of thought. I must focus on the future, on what I may still have ahead of me. Assuming my health holds out. Assuming James returns to me. I suppose I have my few friends. I am still waved at on the street, although not much invited to tea. People do drop by the office, if not to have their teeth cared for, then to chat. But even that is less and less.

Were it not for Vea, I would have no one to talk to. As it is, I spend more and more of my hours here, out on the veranda. Filling my lungs with smoke, my head with ghosts.

I am tortured by the likelihood that my patents will never come to pass, my fly machine will never sprout wings, that nothing more of good may ever happen to me, that I will die here, unreconciled, a fistful of someone else's rotten teeth in my hand, buried by my maid, mourned by her and her alone.

"Absence from those we love is self from self—a deadly banishment."

I am all alone, a bitter weed in dry soil, waiting desperately for warm rain.

MR. GEORGE

RACHEL WAS THE VERY DEFINITION OF AN OLD SOUL. SHE HAD that look of otherworldly calm about her, as if she had not only already seen and understood everything one could of a life, but had assimilated and accepted it as well. She had a gaze that set you back on your heels a bit, especially coming from a young girl. A girl younger, no doubt, than we realized.

Her father brought her to me because he was afraid he was going to be driven from his church. It was more than that, really—he was afraid he'd be mobbed, burned out, hunted down. He was afraid he would not even be able to escape without harm. He wasn't sure where or if he'd be able to set himself up properly in a new place. He loved Rachel enough to want to protect her from that. He'd been able to distance himself from her by keeping her mostly hidden, but was afraid they'd discover her parentage, and then they'd harm her, too. He thought he might be able to send for her later. I'm not sure what happened to him. He disappeared and that was the last I heard from him. For all I know, they changed their minds, split up, died of fever. There is no way to know and there is no one to ask.

Beastly business with those two girls. I doubt he touched them. He just didn't seem to have it in him. Nor was he defensive. He just said he needed to leave. That if he didn't go, he'd lose his life in addition to his church and school, already almost emptied. Any uncle or farmer could have gotten those girls pregnant. And then beaten them for the very same thing. The girls themselves never blamed him, they never pointed at him. Some jealous or petty or just plain mean person started the rumor. It grew from there, fed and fanned by people with too much time and too little occupation.

He was living more openly than necessary with his housekeeper, that much was true. That was what left him open to suspicion. I don't blame him. She was lovely to look at and sweet in disposition. He was hard and cold. But not with her. He tried to get her to stay behind, but she would not let him go alone. Those two. They tried to hide their sweet looks and small touches but it was clear they were in love. Deeply so. Unusually so. The kind of love that makes you squirm a bit in discomfort and also envy. Just because I have never experienced love like that does not mean I don't recognize it when I see it in others.

So he brought me the girl, and I agreed to keep her, to raise her for a few years, give her some culture, let them get established in a new place—they had hardly two nickels to rub together and he refused all my offers of financial assistance. He said he would be in touch once they had a roof over their heads. He said he would send for her once he had a new school going. He had kept her so much behind closed doors that no one knew where she came from. Of course, unmarried housekeepers with children a few shades lighter than themselves were so common as to be unremarkable. There have been a few in my home, if I am honest. I agreed to take Rachel only because he came to me in desperation and at the last possible moment, literally in the dark of night, with the mother stoic in the cart and the ship waiting at the quay, but also because I was looking for a bit of freshness in the house. I didn't even realize that my own home had grown so cold around me and that I was desperate for some new energy, a new something, anything, until I saw her serious face with the spattering of freckles over her nose looking up at me. Those opaque, inscrutable eyes reflecting the lamplight as she unpeeled herself from the folds of her mother's wrap. The small hand that went to her mother's cheek as the woman whispered some parting words into the child's ear before she turned away and stepped out of the cart. Forever.

In her face, I saw the hope of something. I don't know what it was, but I knew I wanted her to stay.

People think me hard, I am aware of that, but that is simply the thick carapace that business on this island and my own unfortunate marriage has built up around me. My daughters, who I once doted upon, were gone to England, living with rich, childless aunts, getting educated. By which I mean being shown off to society matrons in the hunt for rich husbands. My wife and I were growing more distant. Cordial, formal, with a distinct if polite chilling of the passion we had once had.

I found this girl Rachel compelling. She was like no young person I had ever seen before. I suppose so many hours spent in only her own company turned her into the most self-contained person I had ever met. Still to this day she holds that status with me. She seemed to want and need nothing. Yet she always made herself useful. Without ever asking. This was her way, I suppose, of making herself at home. She saw what needed to be done and stepped right to it. Quietly. Without drawing attention to herself.

I tried to be fatherly to her. At first. But let's face it, I am not very fatherly. Nor, I should point out, was she very daughterly. We lived peacefully together as if we were distant cousins. She participated just enough in our lives to attract only scant and mostly unobjecting attention, but no more. We had some rather pleasant times, sharing a few words in the garden or barn. She had a fondness for animals, and they for her. She was especially useful at lambing and calving and other times of stress for the stock. She helped the house run more smoothly. Especially as my wife became more erratic. She easily earned my respect, my admiration, which few can say. I daresay she earned my love, as even fewer can claim.

My love. Such as it is. Such as it was.

I shouldn't have done it. I know I should not have done. Not a day goes by that I don't flog myself for it. It was wrong, shameful of me. The first time it was just rage. Not at her, no, not at her. At the damn plantation, the drop in sugar prices, the impossibility of getting workers to stay on the job, the riots when you tried to bring in laborers from outside the island, the damned raw difficulty of making the enterprise work. I wanted to lose myself in something. She was a far too easy, available escape. After all, how could she say no? She had nowhere else to go, no one to turn to. I pretended I did not have power over her and then abused my position anyway, pure and simple. The next time? I suppose some part of me wanted to find a crack in her, wanted to find a way through that impenetrable shell of self-containment. When that didn't work, I suppose it was just because I favored the feel of her flesh. But I did not abuse her for long. I did stop myself after just three times.

I am not the first man to find sex an escape from the stresses of business. I am not the first man to find the intimacy of relations with my wife more of a chore than a release. Women never understand this. For them, it is always about love. For them, the act is never without the burdens of emotion. It is not that men do not want sex enriched by feelings of love; we do. But we are also capable and frankly sometimes prefer the ease, the freedom and irresponsibility of the simple animal act. In this place, there is always a local girl easily accessible for these purposes. They even often enough seem to enjoy it. Sex with a white man for some of them is a badge of honor. But my wife's illness, bad humor, and abusive treatment sent most of the local girls away. Only Vea, with her bottomless well of patience and her steady, even temperament, could stand my wife, I am sorry to say. Her calm acceptance was a comfort to me on more than one occasion. It was what enabled me to stay away from Rachel.

This place has a way of corrupting soft things, and my wife was one of these soft things. In England she was a delicate beauty, nourished on fine foods and moist air. It was as if her skin had never been touched by anything other than soft breezes, and her ear had never heard a harsh word. She was even thrilled with the idea of coming to the island, elated for the adventure of it all, completely, childishly naive and innocent of how drastically different it would be. She did well for a while. She brought her sensibilities with her and arranged her dinner parties and soirees. But it was as if a fungus grew on her in this place, and little by little ate away at everything fine within her. She was not made of stern enough stuff for this climate, for this culture.

This happens to so many people when they can neither make this place into what they want nor accept it as it is. They wish it to be England, only warmer. I have never had that wish. I am not one to get all mopey and sentimental about that country. It is old and settled and spends far too much time and energy licking its wounds. There is little new there, only people bent on preserving what once was. I have made riches here and lost some, too. Perhaps I have been corrupted a bit as well. But face it, if I were in England, I would be corrupted in a different way. And it would have been the little Irish housemaids to soften my hard days instead of the local women here.

I am nowhere near as gentle, but certainly also not as rough as many a man. At times, I have been far too insistent in taking what I need, but I have never beaten my way into a woman. I have sent a few off to make a new life in a new place and thereby improved their lot substantially. Like I did for Rachel. Perhaps it was too little, too late, but it was what she asked for. I gave her what she desired. Given that I had never heard her ask for so much as a second helping or a single shilling, I know it was significant that she asked at all.

It was bad, in a way, to split the family. But it was also good to get her away from him. She never wanted to marry him in the first place. I had a hard time working out how she ever ended up pregnant from him, how they would have found the time or place. But I am well aware of the strange sorcery of her attractions. I should not be surprised that he was similarly drawn. Of course she was no help when I asked her what had happened. When I tried to solicit some need or regret in her. She would not betray anyone, myself included. She just bore what life—and men—gave her.

I doubt she would have married him at all were it not for me. While she was diffident and in her own otherworldly way fond of him, she showed little ardor for him. Maybe the eventual marriage was no good for her, but it was for the children. Children benefit from legitimacy. And he did love them. He was full of paternal passion for them. All of them. Margaret maybe even more so than the boys. He was closest to James, but that was a bond of the brain. Margaret lit up his heart; she put a smile on his face.

It was I who encouraged her to marry him. Pressed her, really. It was probably just another idle rumor, but when I heard from my lawyer—who of course knew all about Rachel and Margaret—that he had heard that there might be a wealthy relative, some nouveau riche merchant or something, back in England, and that Henry might someday come into real money, well, I felt obligated to tell her. I felt obligated to counsel her to marry him or else she would be left out of whatever might be coming. Of course she cared nothing for herself, but when I pointed out that the children could benefit, well, that changed her mind. We both agreed not to tell him. It would have just sent him on some wild goose chase to find some coins that he would turn into scrap and dreams.

I guess, as it turns out, there was no wealthy relative after all, but, as I say, the marriage was good for the children. Even after she took them away. They had a father, a real father. Flawed, yes. But never by a paucity of love for them.

She never really knew her own father, never had the experience of that kind of robust and forthright love from a father, so there is no way she could understand just how valuable a thing that is. He could not openly claim her as his own after she was born, and then he disappeared before she was even ten years of age, never to return. She had done without a father's love, and, in her way, did fine, so she didn't know what she was taking from her children. From him. Because if she had, she never would have been able to take them away at all.

MOTHER

I never intended to love him. My only intention was to serve him and, by serving him, serve God. Whom I already loved. Love for this man took me over. It crept into me and filled me, quiet and full of power, like sunlight reaching its bright arms into a dark house after a strong rain. I never knew I could love like I did. I never knew I could be loved like I was. I never saw any person have such feeling for another person like we did for each other. It is true that in finding love for this man, I lost my love for God. For this man, it is a bargain I would make again.

Our love was a house made of little bricks. A cup of tea brought to his study without being asked, just because he'd been holed up in there for so many hours. A book lifted from his chest and a shawl draped over his shoulders when he fell asleep in his chair. A bit of balm rubbed into his sunburned neck. I did these small services for him at first because I was his housekeeper and I wanted to keep my job. Then I did them because I wanted to, because he seemed lonely and apart from everyone, even the people who came to his church, even the girls who came to his school, and I wanted to reach through that solitude and give him some tiny bit of human contact.

I never meant for him to fall for me. Even after I felt love swelling in my chest so big I thought it might burst apart my blouse, I tried to keep it inside of me, I tried to let it out a side door by giving myself some chore, by scrubbing or waxing something extra hard. I knew he was not for me, a white man, an educated preacher and schoolmaster from England. And I knew I was not for him, an island girl, an illiterate housekeeper.

Apparently, love had other plans. One evening I entered his study, found him as I often did, asleep in his chair, his tea gone cold, his book slid to the floor, his mouth slack. His expression, as it often was in sleep and rarely in wakefulness, was soft. Like he was thinking about something lovely instead of the serious things he spoke about from the front of the church or class. I tiptoed to pick up his book. I held my breath as I reached for the tea tray. The feel of his hand on my arm was so unexpected, so startling, that I almost dropped the cup. I looked at his fingers against my skin, light against dark, and then let my eyes move up his arm, across his neck, into his face. The expression I saw there made me tremble. I set the cup down onto the tray. He did not remove his hand or his eyes from my person. We stood still like that for a few moments. We were waiting on each other. Then he drew me into his lap and enfolded me in his arms. Apparently, love was going to play by its own rules.

Those girls. They were bad girls. There was no good in them to begin with and then they got worse because the men in their family abused them and the women in their family let it happen. They were both like a piece of fruit with a bad pit that you then drop on the floor. You can cut away the bruise, but the rot has begun from the inside. The whole thing is ruined no matter how careful you are to pare away the ugly parts.

He never touched them. I know because I was there. Always, I was there. And, of course, I knew their families. All he tried to do was teach them. Make them less ignorant and foolish. He did not succeed. When their bellies started to swell, it was easy to blame him. They were mad because he could not make their brains learn a thing. He could not make anything stick in the empty space inside their heads. They thought since they could not get learning from him, they could get money from him instead. They thought those church ladies would pay them to be quiet. They gave those church ladies credit for having kindness toward him in them. Which they did not have. They gave those ladies credit for having spines. Which they did not have. They thought those church ladies loved their pastor. They didn't know that to those ladies, church was just something they could tell their friends they did. Something to fill a few hours on a Sunday when they had nothing else to do. First sign of a stink, those ladies covered their noses with their handkerchiefs and ran away. Didn't matter if they believed those stupid girls or not. Truth had nothing to do with it. My man, the look on his face when he watched those ladies who had listened to him Sunday after Sunday talk about charity and kindness, and "let he who is without sin throw the first stone," and that "judgment is for God to confer," not us, just turn their stiff backs and walk their finely dressed selves away and leave him to figure out what to do all by himself...it was a horrible thing to see those soft, gray eyes of his fill with so much sadness.

I knew those babies would come out full black coffee, not a bit of cream to dilute their blood or skin. But it didn't matter. It was too late, the blame already off and running, a rabid dog snarling and snapping at everything it comes across.

The God that I was taught to love would not have condemned us the way the people of that church would have if they knew about us. So we made sure they did not know. I wondered how the spirit of love could condemn the expression of love. Because God may not have looked badly upon us, but he allowed those church ladies to look badly upon us. He allowed everyone in that backward town to look poorly on us. A true God would not have said our love was not allowed, not as good as some other people's love. He would not have forced us to hide our baby, to keep our beautiful girl behind closed doors, to make us run away and leave her behind because we were scared to bring her out into the open. He would not have let what happened to those girls happen. He would not have let all these things stain a man as good as my man, a man who served God by serving those whom God had created and man had deserted.

This was a man who was kind, smart, and gentle. A man who took the weight of the whole wide world on his shoulders because his desire to make things better was so deep and so wide. He wanted to lift each and every person he met from the dust of ignorance. He wanted to make each person able to make a better life for himself. He thought that everything he did, everything he gave, was a gift that every person who received it would take and give away again, and in each passing, in every hand that touched that gift, it would grow and blossom and eventually take over every bad, ugly thing in this world with light. He believed that. Truly. My man never expected badness like what started with those girls could sour everything good he had ever tried to do.

"Rosa," he would say. "I did nothing wrong, so no wrong can come to us."

Innocent of evil he was. He believed he could make it all right. He fought to stay, to fix things. He defended those girls for their backward ways and unjust accusations. He said they were only misguided. He met their sin with compassion. But no one stood by him. Something inside of him folded up and in on itself then. Kept folding and folding itself into a little hard wad. When he saw that everyone turned away, no one would meet his eyes, not any of those folks who came to his church and dropped their small coins in his plate would step up, and not even those church people back in England offered to help him, he finally realized that evil can sometimes be bigger than good. That sometimes evil will win.

Only a handful of girls stepped forward to defend him. But they were too small, too young. Their defense only made the grown-ups around them suspect my man more. Those girls' voices, mixed with their tears, did not carry into anyone's ears, much less their hearts.

"This is a test from God, Rosa," he would tell me. "I will pass this test."

This was not a test from God. I do not believe that. Because if it was a test, he would have passed. That is how good was his heart, how big his love, how deep his service. God cannot love those the most that he tests the most. Because sometimes the test isn't just something on a piece of paper, it's something about life and death. And love and babies. If I am to give God credit for all that is good in this world, I also must credit him with all that is bad. His power cannot go in only one direction. This is why I came to believe there was no God.

"We will see, Rosa my dear, that this was all part of God's plan," he would say to me. "We cannot see from our short vantage point all that he has willed for us. But one day, when we are together in a new place, when we have our new school, and we have our own money, and are married with Rachel beside us again, we will look back and understand."

I never did tell him that I lost my faith. He had been so hurt already, I could not hurt him more. I could not tell him that as sure as I once was that he existed, I became more sure that God is absent. Church and all that stuff in the Bible is just something powerful white men made up to keep other people small and scared and unquestioning in their thinking. Now I know. There is only nature. She is cruel and she is blunt. But at least she does not make promises she has no intention or ability to keep.

I did not love my man more than I loved my child. I loved them both big, big and different, as is natural and good and right. He did not love me more than her. He loved us both with everything he had. And then some. Because when the love he once had for his church and his community and his God faltered in the face of their abandonment, all that love came to us. Once everyone abandoned us and we could be open, we filled every space we were in with our love. We placed our girl between us, and we wrapped our arms around each other, and we danced around the small rooms that the church people had given him to live in. We sang songs to each other, our foreheads tipped together and our lips moving just above her soft, sweet-smelling head. The hugeness of our love, suddenly set free, flew out the windows and seeped under the doors.

Here was our plan. We had only a little bit of money—he put so much of the small salary he made back into the school that I actually had more set aside than he did. We were going to get away, start over, make a life where we were not known and could become man and wife, and we would start a school of our own. He knew Mr. George because Mr. George had given some money to help build the school we were leaving. Mr. George was not one of those who thought locals and girls should not be educated. He wanted the school for the children of his field hands. My man promised me that Mr. George would take good care of Rachel until we could send for her ourselves.

We wanted to surround ourselves with children. This child of ours was so beautiful. So quiet. Such an easy girl to love. She made us want more. We did not need much. We would have our classes outside and write our sums with a stick in the dust, if it came to that. We would take a dressed chicken or a pound of cane for payment and be happy to have them. We would build a simple shack to live in. We would have our love to sustain us.

God failed us first. Then nature did.

The boat was small and there was no moon. This was the way we wanted it. So much easier to get away. There were only us, two bags between us, and the man we'd hired to take us to the other island. I had never been in a boat before. I had never been in water higher than my thighs before. It was a calm night. We sat side by side on the wooden seat and held hands and stared into the darkness all around us. We did not speak. It was like we were holding our breath, waiting to get to the other side of something. The man did not speak to us either. We gave him half the fare when we set out. Promised the other half when he got us safe to the other shore. I tied my bag to my waist with a rope to make sure it did not fly out of the boat. The bag had our money in it. That bag had our future in it.

The change crept up on me. My legs started to ache and I realized it was because I was holding myself stiff against the motion of the boat. An up-and-down slapping against the water motion. Once I felt it, I could think of nothing else. The motion was big and getting bigger. A few times it lifted me right off my seat and then dropped me back down again. We did not look at each other. We linked our arms through each other's and held on. I was too scared to know I was scared. I kept my eyes forward, pushing them into the black emptiness, trying to see something that was not there, that was nowhere to be found, willing land to appear where there was only water and waves. I felt myself in the boat, a part of the boat. I was pushing the bones of my buttocks down into the hard wooden seat beneath me. I felt the *thock thock thock* of the front of the boat slamming into the water over and over. There was a break in the rhythm. The boat rose up into a moment of absolute quiet. I took in a deep breath of cold night air. Then I was in that air, a part of that air. Then I was in the water. I felt my dress spreading out all around me. I swung my arms wildly through the sudden shock of the heavy, icy water. It filled my ears and my eyes and my nose and my mouth with its nasty, biting saltiness. My arms, my legs, my face found nothing but more water. I felt something pulling at me. I didn't know what direction it was trying to take me. Then I knew. My bag. The bag I had tied around my waist was filling with water. I tried to untie it. My fingers could not work the rope already swollen with water. My breath would not come. My eyes could not see. I swung my arms again. My hand found flesh. His flesh. His arm. Then his hand. Then his other arm came around me. Just like at home when we would hold each other and dance. With our girl squeezed in between us. Now there was nothing between us but water. We held each other tight. We went down, together.

MARGARET

I was married before. Like my birthday, I tend to forget this seemingly important detail of my life. I am, perhaps, too encased in my own solitude. I walk too much in the same paths, creating a few deep ruts instead of a delicate latticework of a life. It's not that I forget my husband exactly; it is more that I forget I was once a wife. It was so long ago. So much of my life is unchanged from that time—I still live in New York, I still work in a school, I still have few friends who seem to be as fond of their solitude as I am of mine, so we see each other rarely. My time with Marcus sometimes seems to be a book I read a long time ago and enjoyed enough to return to several times, enough so the story has stuck with me. Parts of it, anyway.

Marcus and I quite literally bumped into each other on the street. I used to have the bad habit of skimming a book while walking. Strange and improbable I know, but I was often reluctant to let go of a book, even if I had somewhere to go, even if I was just heading to the park to read on a bench with the pigeons. I often spent many hours of my weekends there at the public library. I was comforted by those two lions, the imposing set of broad stone steps. Sometimes there were shows and other light entertainments in the courtyard. But mostly I went there to read. Books took me places I could not go on my tiny salary. I coasted on the pages of other people's imaginations. I read the classics from the English authors: Dickens, the Brontës, Austen, and marveled at the profundity of class barriers. I read the American writers, Fitzgerald, Steinbeck, Twain, Wharton, even Hemingway, and marveled at the subtlety and yet persistence of our own class issues. In both instances, I sat amazed at the destructive ennui of the rich.

I also sought out travel narratives. Nonfiction of this sort was daunting to me; the raw reality of it all, the swashbuckling nature of the authors' various adventures took my breath away. Travel books, especially those written by women, were not easy to find, but I uncovered a few. *The Mulberry Tree* was my favorite, as I found Ms. James an entertaining and sardonic guide to the island I had left as a child. I tried to imagine experiencing the place as she did, but I was not a mature woman when I lived there, nor was I a writer, nor did I have means to explore. She might as well have been writing about Africa for all I recognized of the place and experiences she described.

I was especially fond of the Brontë sisters. *Jane Eyre*—I have read that book countless times. The image of Bertha haunted me. The woman from the island, so misunderstood, so misplaced that she went crazy. I never believed she was born crazy. I thought Rochester made her so. A man can do that to a woman. A mismatch like that marriage was can do that to a woman. More so than to a man, I think. Especially in that era, when women had so few options, when, if a door closed for her, the only opening left might be a high window.

For a big book like that, one I didn't like to be parted from, one I wanted to read many times, I sometimes bought a cheap paperback copy and broke it into parts and carried with me whatever section I was reading at the time. It may have been that book open in my hand when I met Marcus. It would, of course, seem too convenient, too literary, too much of a coincidence if it was that book, that particular story, that caused us to meet. But life is like that, sometimes. We only take note of the times that things unexpectedly overlap and collide—we have no way of knowing how many times we have been subjected to a close miss.

In any case, I am sure it was my fault that we bumped into each other. But he helped me pick up my broken book, my spilled purse, and offered to buy me a cup of coffee as apology. He was like that. Gracious. Ready to take responsibility for any injustice, even, or perhaps especially, those he had not caused. I was not accustomed to having someone be so solicitous of me, of my feelings, whether expressed or not. To my brothers I was just an annoying older sister, always interrupting their forward motion with my efforts to turn down a skewed collar or wet down a piece of stuck-up hair. To my mother I was her only assistant in the constant barrage of small domestic battles that made up so much of our daily life.

I don't remember what Marcus and I talked about, but I remember looking up and seeing it had gone dark outdoors. I remember being shocked that we—that I—had talked so much, for so long. It was very unlike me. I was usually the one who asked questions, because I was interested, yes, but also because it meant I could talk less. That was another skill Marcus had, drawing people out, gently, with just the right amount and degree of curiosity and interest to keep the words coming. He got you to let down your guard without even realizing you had been holding it up. This is what he did to me. And kept doing to me every time we got together for a walk or a meal. Our dates—they were full of words.

I got him to talk of himself, too. He had so many dreams. He was working in a lawyer's office, running errands, filing, making coffee, whatever was needed. He wanted to go to college, to law school. He wanted to make a difference, he kept saying. I pushed for details, but he wasn't sure yet exactly how or who or why. He just wanted to help people. That was what he said. With passion and conviction. And ambition. I admired the vigor of his goals, his confidence that he would make a difference. I suppose I had dreams back then, too. I was teaching in a little nursery school. I enjoyed the predictable structure of my days and the tidy order of my classroom. I looked forward to the noisy affection and eager faces of the children. But I wanted…well, just something *more*. More than my little walk-up one-room apartment with the nosy landlady and a hot plate. Oh, what a cliché it is to think of it now, and yet, don't so many of our younger years seem a cliché when we look back on them? I wanted to see things, to be enlarged somehow. My world seemed so small, my stimulations so minimal, just the callow children, the other teachers, all women like me, the blocks between my job and the four close walls of my room, an occasional show, an occasional outing with my colleagues. Our tiny salaries didn't allow for much, our fears, worries, and lack of imagination allowed for even less. I didn't know any women with ambitions back then, so I didn't know that I had any, wouldn't have known what to do with them if I'd recognized them. When I met Marcus, I felt as if I could ride on the back of his temerity, my arms wrapped tightly around his waist.

I also wanted to touch his skin. It was smooth and soft and colored with a hint of caramel. We held hands, his so much warmer in so many ways than mine. He had come from the island, too, but he came to New York with his parents as a teenager, older by several years than I was when I came. His parents had since died in one of the waves of consumption that had overtaken the city. I never asked, so never knew whether they were mulatto or black and white or some other combination. It mattered nothing to me. I didn't think much about his race; perhaps the fact that he could so easily pass for white made it easy for me to think race mattered not at all. We had almost no memories of the island to share, but he tried more than once to connect me to the culture he—we—had come from. The city was being flooded with immigrants from the West Indies. Sugar prices had crashed and the doors to the United States were open. Most of those coming had been educated, they were a professional class, and they remade in New York the churches, social clubs, and neighborhoods they had known at home. They were outsiders on my island of New York; I was an outsider in the island within an island they created. Marcus tried to help me bridge the gap between these worlds. But I remained an outsider. I was content to keep my distance and observe but not participate in the activities of those who came from the place I was born but could barely remember.

One day, at the end of a long, languid stroll around Central Park, he asked if I would go to city hall with him. I had no idea what he was referring to. I thought he was asking me to attend an event of some sort. I cocked my head and furrowed my brow in question. He pulled a slender silver ring from his pocket—really just some twists of wire a craftsperson must have made—and held it up in front of my face.

"Yes, yes, yes," I said, suddenly understanding and instantly thrilled with the idea of imminent marriage. It was as if my whole person wanted to repeat the word *yes* over and over, enough times to make the concept of our union real. I was elated. I had never been desired in the way that ring and his smiling face behind it seemed to tell me I was desired. We had not been dating long. More than six months, less than a year. Perhaps it was a bit of a whim. But we truly liked each other. We were, as corny as it sounds, in love. At least we thought ourselves to be. We craved one another. Many a marriage has been made on less.

It was only after we were married that I brought him to meet Mother. It is not as if I was avoiding her; I just didn't see her much. I checked up on her and made sure my brothers were checking in with her, too. I guess since I was so recently freed from the tight confines of her nest, I was not anxious to return. Truthfully, we were not close. There was no animosity, no rancor. I admired her hard work to keep us in shoes and stews. It's just that she was not a warm, maternal woman. She managed her children almost as if they were farm animals, feeding us, cleaning us, housing us as best she could. The effort of which, I suppose, under our cramped and penurious circumstances, wore down whatever softer feelings there might have been under her rough exterior. Then again, maybe she had none of those feelings to begin with. But even if she did have, where in those crowded rooms would there have been space for a caress or a tenderness? Where at that table jammed with dinner, ragtag bits of homework, the sewing projects that brought her meager income, would there have been room for a joke? It did not take any of us long to get out and set up our own housekeeping. Eddie and Percy never even finished high school, opting instead to get to work as soon as possible, first delivering newspapers and then laboring in the printing of the things. Tom just barely finished, getting by with his skills at painting and drawing more than reading and writing. He found work in the theaters, rigging at first, but eventually making sets.

In any case, while I saw no point in introducing her to a boyfriend, I certainly wanted her to meet my husband. So Marcus and I trudged up the dark, dingy steps of whatever apartment she was in at the time. He had bought a bouquet for the occasion, and the flowers were a strange bright splash against the faded wallpaper and dim hallways. She came to the door, hair piled atop her head as always, wearing a simple cotton dress, but it looked new. Her lips were a straight line, as usual, and they did not move when Marcus handed her the flowers. Her eyebrows did—they shot up as if he'd handed her a live fish instead of some beautiful blooms. She set them on the counter in the tiny kitchen. They spilled over the space, like an adult in a child's chair. Of course, she had no vase. She had nothing to fill with water to arrange them in. She had no mantelpiece to set them on. So they stayed on the counter, ungainly, an awkward, blaring presence at our little gathering.

She made tea and put some butter cookies she'd made on a plate. We sat around the well-worn table she had refused to give up even when my brothers and I offered to replace it as a Christmas gift. She gave us her congratulations and asked after my work and his. Then the conversation stalled. She was never one much given to chitchat, and even Marcus's usual charms chilled to a standstill under her cool demeanor. Then, from the depths of the silence that surrounded us, she interjected a complete non sequitur.

"What island are you from?" she asked Marcus.

I had not told her he was from any island, much less ours. He had no discernible accent, having worked hard to adopt a completely American vernacular. More often than not, he had been taken for Italian or Spanish. I have no idea what she saw, what she recognized in him. He was taken aback a bit by the directness of the question, but covered it with a laugh and answered honestly and at length. He told her about his parents, the store they had in the capital, how the bottoming out of sugar prices made their business dry up, as no one had much money to spend. How they came here and opened another small store that was doing well until they both grew sick with consumption when he was twenty-two. She nodded, listened closely, unblinking, as he spoke.

While he was good-natured in his response, her query made me bristle. I saw something racist in it. And his polite response irritated me as well. I saw something fawning in it. The conversation died after he finished speaking, I made our excuses, and we left. I swallowed against the bitterness that had risen in me and tried to forget the incident and my feelings about it. The three of us were almost never in the same room again. The few times we got together, my brothers were there too and their hearty camaraderie used up all the air in the room. As it was, Marcus and I kept to ourselves. He worked long hours and took classes. He had almost no free time and when he did, I was not about to share it with anyone else. Especially not my mother. In spite of my efforts to put aside her comments, I am afraid I nursed my suspicion that she didn't like Marcus because she suspected he was mulatto, that he had black blood in his veins. Only later, much later, did it become clear to me that she was not remarking on his color as much as on his islandness. Later, I regretted keeping them apart, because if I had allowed them to mingle, he might have brought her own islandness more to the fore; he might have brought something out in her that I had never seen before. I might have gained, through him, some understanding of her. But by the time I was mature enough to understand this, it was too late. Far too late.

Marcus didn't get his law degree. But he got enough experience to know something about the law. And after several years together, he left me suddenly. He tried to explain that he had to go back to his "homeland"—a word he had never used before—that the political winds were changing and there was opportunity to do something big, something important for his "people." Another word he had never used before. I could see that he was taking sides in something. Not just something in the world, but something inside of himself. His "people." As light skinned as he was, he was still island, enough island, enough colored, that he was more of them than of me. He was more of them than of us. He said he'd send for me. But he didn't. If he had, I would not have gone. The idea of an island, to me, was a place you left. For something bigger, better. For something more. Funny, I live on an island now. An island I have refused to leave. It's not bigger, not better. Just more crowded. With people, sure, but also with promises.

After he'd gone, I went to visit my mother, to tell her. I thought she might harrumph, give me a knowing look, somehow communicate that she had tried to warn me. But she didn't. She made tea. She rested her hand over mine. She said little and the silence was soothing.

Finally, when I was getting up to leave, she said, "Margaret, race has nothing to do with skin color."

I looked at her and made much the same expression I did when Marcus asked me to go to city hall with him. I had no idea what she was referring to.

Then she added, "The island. It is within me. It is within you. You don't need to have it any other way."

I was tired and drained, raw with the feelings of rejection his departure had left me with. I didn't understand what she was talking about. Or maybe I didn't care or just wasn't ready to know what she was talking about. Maybe I just pretended not to know. But looking back, it was simple, really. She had left the island behind and she wanted to make sure I did, too. She didn't want me going back there for him or any other reason. She preferred straight lines, one-way streets, doors closed and never reopened. She wasn't one for circles, rearview mirrors, or returns. I wasn't either back then. I was young and wanted nothing but to keep moving forward. It would be a long time before I realized that sometimes to move forward, you have to go backward first.

Now, these many years that have grown into decades later, her words come back to me and I find myself wondering: If the island is within me, where is it? I sit in my overstuffed, upholstered chair, a cup of tea growing cold in my hands, listening to the buses haul themselves forward from the stop on the corner, the barks of dogs and hollers of children drifting up from the street below, and I assess my various body parts: Is it in the pit of my stomach? That knot that stiffens my shoulder? Has it found a home in some small, dark chamber of my heart?

I don't look out the window. I am afraid that seeing the dark street, the sooty buildings, the sliver of charcoal sky would only hamper my effort to conjure memories of a warm, green place. I am afraid that whatever images I do conjure are a function of my imagination and not my experience. Or even worse, the imagination or experience of some writer, that they are culled from a book I read. I close my eyes and try to go back in time. I was young when we left. I am not even sure how young, because we never discussed our departure, never explained it, never wondered why. At least not out loud. We didn't share stories of the past. We rarely shared stories of the present. They were both challenging topics. They were both painful in some way to our mother. I can't even step back in time grade by grade as one might do now. Our education was informal when we were there, as was typical, and once we were here, we were placed into a grade through some alchemy of age, tests, available space, and administrator whim. Then we moved frequently, changed schools often, and sometimes my grade shifted again.

I think I was about eleven or twelve, maybe thirteen when we left. We were all so close in age, five children in six or maybe seven years. I see us all as one mass of children, like caterpillars in a web. I clawed my way free as the eldest, the girl, the responsible one; James was separate in his own way, of course. But the other three might as well have been triplets. I close my eyes and try to bring back something from my early years. I see an undifferentiated wall of green, a hundred shades of green, layered by leaves, some as big as umbrellas, and punctuated by the still, bright spots of flowers, the flittering, bright spots of birds. Or maybe butterflies. I see a porch of some kind, a hammock, a small table with some sort of device on it. Yes, I recall the childish feeling of desperately wanting to touch that metal and glass thing and simultaneously being afraid to touch it, scared of adult reprimand, but also that it might come to life under my hand and do something terrifying and unexpected.

The air was damp, thick, still and heavy like a washcloth on my face, stoppering my nose as I tried to breathe. But a scent made its way through. Prickly, sweet, and sour all at once. A cigar. Then a laugh, a deep rumble of a sound, like rocks tumbling over one another in a stream. My father. There he was, coming through the house, his steps rattling the floorboards. He was a big man. Not tall or fat so much as substantive. *Broad in the beam* is the phrase I have heard people use. He was coming for me, yes, for me. I felt delight swelling in my child's chest. He barged through the louvered doors, feigned surprise at finding me there, scooped me up under my arms, lifted me into the air, buried his salt-and-pepper whiskers against my neck. I squealed in delight.

God, when was the last time I ever squealed in delight? When was the last time I even had a hearty laugh? These are things I lost the habit of when we moved to New York. These are the things that drained out of me, then shriveled up with lack of use. But I did laugh and squeal and play as a child. Yes, I know that to be true. This was something that my father knew how to do, something he showed us how to do. He, unlike my mother, had a gift for happiness, I think. Or at least I'd like to think of him that way. If he is within me, as my mother told me the island is, maybe I can regain that gift as well.

Sometimes, when I sit here on an empty Sunday afternoon trying to remember, these retrospections take me into sleep. When I wake up, the apartment and world outside darkened around me, my limbs and neck stiffened and my body confused by the shape of the chair beneath me, I remember a dream that recurs, a dream that forms a blurry line between my waking and sleeping, my reminiscing and imagining mind. In this dream, the wall of pulsating greenery that I recalled opens, the leaves part, like a hand placed in a slow-moving stream, and a man emerges, impossibly, from the foliage. He stands askance to me, staring at me with interest, as if I am the strange apparition, not him. There are only the two of us. This man in my dream is unreal and yet very much alive. He is not my father—he is slender where my father was burly, well kept where my father was rough around the edges, clean shaven instead of bearded, wispy, ginger-haired instead of thickly maned. I don't know who this man is. But in my dream, he is hauntingly familiar to me. Seeing him is like looking in a mirror. It is like seeing a shadow part of my self.

Apparently, I was a sleepwalker as a child. It's not just that I remember my father and my brothers making fun of me for it. Although I do. The ribbing still stings a bit. Not just for the sleepwalking. They teased me about so many things. My red hair, my freckles, my seriousness, my very sensitivity to being teased. I remember the sleepwalking itself. Not just waking from the spell, but lifting my head from the pillow, sliding my legs from under the sheets, the cool, hard floor underfoot—it was as if I was observing myself from a perch where the wall met the ceiling, as if I were a bat or a goblin watching some other, human form of myself. I also remember finding myself standing in the middle of the kitchen or on the veranda or even in the middle of the yard, surrounded by the dark air of night. I remember the step-by-step, hand-over-hand process of slowly regaining my connection to the physical world, feeling the damp of the ground seeping into my feet and the dirt working its way up between my toes, wiggling my fingers where they hung from my hands at the ends of my arms, the moist thick air of the night filling my lungs.

These nighttime excursions never frightened me. In fact, I loved the sensation of waking up in a new place while the rest of the world still slept. I loved the feeling of unseen insects and bats making the air move over my face. I loved feeling that the world, for a few moments in that darkness, belonged to me and only me. There was mystery in the night that I longed for. When we moved to New York, this darkness was no longer available to me. I still walked, but now there was nowhere to go. The rooms were small, the doors were locked, there was no outdoors. I found myself waking up with an unwilling doorknob in my hand. More than once, I also had tears running down my face.

Of course, there were no locks in our island home. Doors and windows were often open, the interior and exterior worlds separated by no more than a gossamer curtain blowing in the breeze. I remember now that birds flew through the house, and we ate from the trees. I think, no, I know, that I walked in the night not because I was trying to flee something, not because there was somewhere else I wanted to be, but because I wanted only to be more fully, more deeply a part of that world. I wanted to be a bat fluttering through the night, a vine twirling its way up through the trees toward the light. I would have been happy to be even a chicken scratching in the yard. I wanted that air, those smells. I wanted to take it all inside of myself, to fill all the empty parts of myself with it. Then we moved, and that world was lost to me. I now realize that some part of myself was lost as well.

I did date a little after Marcus left. A few friends fixed me up with an older brother or a cousin. There was the rare male teacher at school with whom I might share a quiet lunch, careful the straws in our milk cartons did not poke us in the eye or go up our noses. Male teachers never lasted long, their motives always suspect, the pay not enough to support a family. Sometimes a mother of a student would invite me to an afternoon party, often enough a child's birthday party, where the rooms of her home would be filled with couples and one single man who would be enlisted to bring me a glass of punch. All of these men were perfectly nice. But they lacked the energy, the feeling of taking a risk that had drawn me to Marcus. I was perfectly nice. I suppose I was looking for someone different from myself.

The last man I dated was lovely. A truly pleasant man. Smart. Intense. A square-jawed, full-head-of-dark-hair lawyer. A real lawyer. One who had gone to school and graduated. The father of a student. All the teachers had a crush on him. His wife had died, I know not what of, and he was regularly late picking up his son, who often waited out the minutes that sometimes turned into a half an hour or more in the library with me. The father was always apologetic. Honestly appreciative of my time waiting with his son as he sheepishly tried to explain to me the struggle to balance fatherhood with commitments to the office. I said I understood, which of course I didn't, and said it was fine, which of course it was. After the fifth or sixth time it happened, he asked if he could take me to dinner. To thank me. I thought, "Fair enough." I said I'd be delighted.

We went to a small Italian place. He asked polite questions that didn't dig too deep about my work and life. I did the same. He was a gentlemanly lawyer, wills, estates, contracts. No criminals, he said. He didn't say how his wife died, only mentioned that she had, and that her family was nearby and helpful. His family was in the Midwest. He hoped to move back sometime before too long so his son would know his cousins. His sister and mother could, would love to babysit he said. It all sounded terribly wholesome to me. I imagined blonde women with frilled aprons at their waists waving from the front porch of a white farmhouse in the midst of a cornfield. I saw his thick hair slowly thinning as he sat behind a big dark desk at the little bright office on some downtown Main Street lined with wide sidewalks, brick buildings, and iron benches, where he greeted neighbors and welcomed farmers with manure still on their boots. It made me, perversely and totally unlike me, want to swear.

After dinner, he walked me home and I invited him up to my apartment for a drink. I only had tea, I apologized. He shrugged acquiescence. Somehow the whole thing, even with only tea for fortification, felt vaguely dangerous, a strange sensation for me. I wanted, inexplicably, to mess up his hair. He wandered my small living space, teacup and saucer in hand, and approached a little end table with a few family photos perched there. I wondered when I had last dusted.

"Who is this?"

He was pointing at a photograph tucked behind a lamp. His mouth was open in an eager smile, like he'd just laid eyes on a piece of chocolate cake discovered in the back of the icebox.

I started to answer, but before I could, he said, "Your sister?"

His tone was an accusation. As if he'd been cheated of something. As if he discovered I'd hidden the chocolate cake on purpose. He moved toward the photograph, bent over to look at it more closely, picked up the small frame and ran his index finger over the image there like it was a magic lamp and he could conjure the person pictured there. In the small, empty pause he created with this action, I felt anger flood my face with heat. Not anger at him so much as a vague anger at life, at fate, at circumstance. I made a strange decision, decided on an odd experiment.

"Yes," I said. "That is my sister."

He stared at the picture, and I stared at him. In that moment, I warmed to the deception I had created.

"She's younger. Pretty, isn't she?" I said. "Full of life and optimism," I continued.

I imagined myself as Jane Austen, creating a character.

"She was light and I dark; she cheerful, me pensive. And yet we were close. We understood one another."

"Where is she now?" he asked, his question not idle curiosity but filled with an almost palpable desire.

"She died," I said.

I suppose, in many ways, this was true. The earlier version of myself, the one he held in his hands, was like a twin, she the sun and I the shadow. She was younger, held herself taller, had longer hair, wore bright-red lipstick. She was someone who remembered how to turn her hip, push out her chin, and smile when someone pointed a camera in her direction. She knew how to attract a man's eyes and carefully divert her own in a way that made sure he saw it. After Marcus I had given up on her and she on me. I chose to keep us both in the darkness, and without the light, she eventually shriveled up and blew away.

I know that my life now appears to resemble my mother's: a single woman in middle age, a small apartment filled with only what is necessary and little that is comforting. But we are not the same woman. I didn't choose to be alone; I just didn't choose to share my life with anyone. She embraced her solitude; mine has simply descended upon me. She sought hers; I seem to have stumbled into mine.

Which is not the same thing. Not the same thing at all.

My mother wrapped herself in her solitude like a protective and comfortable cloak. For me, being alone has just become a bad habit I can't or won't bother fighting my way around, like biting my nails.

They are all gone, my family. Father, mother, four brothers, all dead. I am the only one left of my generation. The individual losses made their own small wounds on my soul. But now these insults are merging into a single scar, one large place on my heart where the nerves have been cut, leaving a blanched spot devoid of feeling.

I remember being told of my father's death. I loved him. I loved the memory of the man he was, but was strangely unaffected by his passing. I was in the thick of my post-Marcus pain and I suppose that was all the pain I had the space or time to feel. When my mother died, there was relief because she had been suffering with cancer. She had a long life. She lived it, it seems, as she wanted to, in her own quirky sort of way, unaffected as she appeared to be by things others would characterize as hardship. With her too I was strangely unaffected. Maybe it was just that her time had come, but maybe it was something innate to her personality. My mother was, to me, a presence more than a person. Maybe this is true of all mothers, and maybe this says more about their children's inability to see them as full people, and less about whatever is in their characters. But my mother maintained a moat of self-containment that kept us all at a distance. It is not that she was unaffectionate, although she was; it is not that she was undemonstrative, although she was. It was that she seemed to have no need of us. She was a good mother and showed her love and care for us by always putting our needs first. Of course there was little to go around, but even of that, we went first: we were fed first, our clothes mended first, we got the beds and she took the sofa. But she held these sacrifices so lightly, they affected her so little, it was as if they were no renunciation at all.

She never spoke of her past or of herself. She listened to us, whatever we had to offer of our lives, and asked small questions to flesh out the story. It was as if her sole intent in life was to take up as little space and use as few resources as possible. I think she found comfort in that. After she died, there was almost nothing to clean out of her apartment. The few things she had were completely used up: some dishes with the patterns worn off, a single chair, bed, table, all threadbare from long use, all seeming to echo the shape of her small body in their sagging springs and well-worn surfaces. No jewelry save her slim wedding band. There were a few hairpins, a cracked bar of soap, some shapeless dresses, and downtrodden shoes. It is not as if I had not seen her this way, wearing those same sack-like clothes and eating off those same last-century pieces of china, but I suppose some part of me harbored a dim fantasy that she had some sort of a rich past that would make itself known to me as I opened her drawers, wiped out her refrigerator, shone the flashlight into the far corners of her closet.

None of my brothers left much behind, either. A couple of widows, a handful of scattered children who came to whoever's funeral was taking place, daubed at their eyes, took a memento and went back to the youth, energy, and prospects of their own lives. My brothers Eddie and Percy, like our mother, lived in apartments filled with musty furniture, worn linoleum, and faded drapes. Tom had a little row house in Queens, but his wife never invited us in. Fussy, that one. Wanted to keep him from us. I imagine that house might not have been too different than the apartments Eddie and Percy kept. Well, barely kept.

James was once again different from us in this regard. No small apartments for him. No sofas with sagging springs. Nothing hand-me-down or picked up on the corner. No not James, the outlier, the black sheep, or should I say green sheep, the only one of us with a real education, with real money. He lived in sunny Southern California. In a house with large windows, white carpeting, blond wood, a tidy lawn, a picket fence even, shrubs and trees that bloomed profusely and fragrantly. Enough to make you sick, almost. I visited once. A friend convinced me to take a trip with her. She kept saying how fun it would be and set me up to think I was doing her a favor, accompanying her to a relative's wedding she didn't want to attend on her own. It was maybe a year after Marcus had left, I was still gloomy, not yet accepting of my single state, still looking over my shoulder as if waiting for him to turn up any day now, and I think she was trying to get me to enjoy a change of scenery. She was trying to be kind, helpful, to cheer me up.

I am not much for cheering up. I guess my mother and I have that much in common.

It was summer, school was out, and we took the train. The long days of staring out the window at the huge expanses of golden wheat and green corn did little to improve my humor, as it left me too much time to contemplate my losses. My friend was patient with me. We read books. Ate in the café car. I watched her flirt with a few passengers, a bellboy or two. An older couple tried taking us under their wing, talking to us about our "plans," our "futures," and telling us stories of their youth. We giggled at them back in our room, not appreciating how large and grand the feat of staying together and happy for many decades truly was. When we got to California, we stayed in a tiny pink motel with paper-thin walls and had to listen to a couple who spent the nights arguing and then making up from their arguments. The day of the wedding was unseasonably warm and we hung around the reception and fanned ourselves in the heat, she smiling and batting her eyelashes at the young men who passed by. I fear my presence created a sense of gloom that surrounded us both—the boys were drawn to the brighter lights of the West Coast girls.

My mother had told James I was coming. Left to my own devices, I might have told him of my trip, but I might not have. That is probably why she did. James and I were not close. The other boys and I had lived for more years with each other and with our mother. We were a tribe, a bit wild, untamed, quite literally running in the streets, but fiercely loyal to each other. James arrived among us deeply muscled from shoveling coal on the steamer to gain his passage, with slicked-back hair, thin but pressed shirts, and old shoes that had been much polished. He carried himself like a man, even though he was still a teenager, but we believed his bravado. He was disciplined and polite, holding his knife and fork properly, cutting and chewing his meat carefully, washing his own plate. He knew how to win at cards. He knew how to shake hands and slap someone on the back. He had plans. Big plans. Make some money. Get a better job. Finish high school. Go to college. Make things. Big, audacious things. Ships, buildings, airplanes. He stopped with us for a short time, just long enough to get a job and find rooms of his own. Then he came for meals only once a week, on Sundays. He told us he was scrimping and saving money by laundering his own clothes in the sink and patching his shoes with a needle and thread and a piece of cardboard smeared with shoe polish to blend in. He was always writing letters to people, making inquiries. I never really understood about what. Getting a better job must have been one line of his letter writing, because eventually he went upstate somewhere to work with a dentist. He stopped coming home then, but wrote letters telling us about the fine holidays spent in the dentist's grand house. Sometimes there were checks with the letters. I read the letters aloud to everyone and deposited the checks for my mother.

My brothers and I didn't care about the checks or the parties. Or the job or the grand plans. We looked at him and his ambitions as if they were traitorous. We didn't understand why he felt he needed to do so much better, so much more than us. We felt his self-control and goal setting was too showy, that it was somehow a put-down to us and the way we lived. His checks felt too much like charity. Like pity. These feelings only got stronger when he went off to that college in Boston, the Massachusetts Institute of Technology—even the name, the location, was an affectation, an affront. Then he studied some engineering something or other that was exotic and unknowable to us, who had all barely made it through high school, what with the constant moving and switching schools. The fact that he put himself through college, that he lived at the YMCA and ate the cheapest meals possible at some lunch counter, made it all that much worse to us. He was not just showing off his self-control and self-discipline, he was showing up, showing off our inadequacies. He was suggesting, by the mere fact of his accomplishment, that we could have made something more of ourselves, too. If we'd only tried just a bit harder.

It's unfair of us, I know. Small-minded and jealous. But there it is. The feelings stuck.

But once he knew I was coming, he did write and invite my friend and me to come to his house for lunch while we were in town. He picked us up in a comfortable car, wearing pressed khakis and a tidy shirt. When we got to his house, he took off his shoes and replaced them with brown leather slippers lined in red felt. Then insisted we leave our shoes on. As if we had any other choice. His wife had on fresh lipstick, a belted dress, and smelled of powder. His children were brought out for show, the comb marks fresh in his son's dark, damp hair, the ribbon still crisp in his daughter's. They were beautiful children, but there was a palpable tension in the atmosphere of the home. The wedding-present china and silver, the bright white of the tablecloth, the brilliant hues of the fresh fruit, the scrubbed skin of everyone's cheeks, the stiff table manners and the polite, almost formal questions about my day-to-day life back in New York. None of them ever made eye contact with each other. I felt like they were all playing parts they had been coached in. I felt as if I was on a television set.

His wife had made huge trays of food—we barely made a dent in any of them—and multiple courses with multiple options in each. A garden salad and a sweet salad, ham and roast beef, mashed and baked potatoes, three kinds of vegetables, two kinds of pie and four choices of ice cream. I wondered if nervousness had made her indecisive, but then I looked around at everything they had achieved—the wall-to-wall carpeting, the two children, the big car, the new clothes, the shiny shoes, the large radio, and well-appointed kitchen—and knew that she was trying to make a statement. That their choices, their marriage even, must have been made as part of an effort to tick things off some mental list they both carried of what success would look like. I had heard that she'd grown up poor on a hardscrabble farm with a completely fanciful and impractical mother. Perhaps someone not dissimilar to our father. I knew that we'd never had any money growing up either.

It seemed they were both trying to prove to someone, anyone, that they'd left that poverty, that privation, behind for good.

We ate as much as we could, and without asking us to move to the living room for coffee or take a walk in the neighborhood to settle the meal, James put us back in the car and took us back to our picture-postcard-kitschy motel, kicking up gravel and waving his arm out the window as he pulled away. It was the last I saw of them. The last I saw of him.

Then, more than twenty years later, almost a year after she found him dead of a massive heart attack in his sleep, his wife sent me two boxes, each the size of a ream of paper, neatly wrapped, carefully sealed, placed inside another, larger box, the whole thing wrapped in butcher's paper, an envelope with my address on it taped to the front, then the entire package tied with a piece of twine for extra security. Inside the envelope was a small, folded notecard with these two brief sentences in my sister-in-law's efficient, businesslike hand: "Dear Margaret, I found these boxes of papers and correspondence between James and his father, your father. I have never seen it before and have not gone through it all, but thought you would want to have it."

I opened the box carefully, untying rather than cutting the twine, peeling back the tape and folding rather than tearing the brown paper, taking the lid off the top box, lifting papers gently, riffling through it all as if I were running my hands through a pile of dead leaves. Papers and correspondence. Yes, indeed. There were envelopes still fat with letters, stacks of business cards, loose newspaper clippings, folded legal documents...and a stack of yellowed onionskin sheets filled with writing in brown ink. I saw an island address. I saw my father's signature. I let the papers drop. I replaced the top of the box. I couldn't bear it. It was too much to take in. I was filled with a sense of foreboding. I didn't know what was in there. But I knew these papers must be important or

James would not have kept them. I knew they must include secrets, or he wouldn't have kept them boxed away. I didn't know how I knew these things, but I did. I also knew I was not ready to have everything or even anything I thought I knew about my family reordered. None of them were alive to help me understand, to explain whatever these boxes had to tell me. I was afraid to tackle them by myself. And yet, if I didn't, who would?

I have never needed much space. I have never had, nor have I craved, large rooms, long views, expansive vistas. But I have always needed the space I have to be clear and free of clutter. I am impatient with visual distractions. If I take something out, I need to put it away again. A useful habit for a school librarian.

There was no place to put the two boxes. They didn't find anywhere to settle or hide in my apartment. I tried tucking them atop some books on the shelf, but they seemed always about to topple over. My desk drawers were full, but even if I emptied one, the boxes were just a bit too large to fit. I couldn't turn them sideways and put them in the file cabinet. The shelf above the coats in the closet was stacked with hats, gloves, umbrellas—gear for the weather. My kitchen cabinets were full of dishes, pots, pans, mixing bowls for cakes I used to bake for students. The plastic storage containers under the bed housed sweaters and winter boots, which were replaced by sandals and tank tops when the season changed. So the boxes rested on my tin-top kitchen table. I tiptoed around them like they were sleeping babies. Or sleeping monsters. I took to eating my dinner on my lap in the living room. The awkward position gave me a stitch in my neck. Every time I went to make a cup of tea, the boxes stared at me in silent reproach. I covered them with a towel to ensure nothing spilled or splattered on them. Or perhaps to disguise them from view. Of course, I only succeeded in making them more prominent, more obvious. Like a child who hides by covering his own eyes.

Sometimes I braved the boxes, peeled back the cloth, hazarded a peek at what was there. I found a 1938 newspaper clipping showing off a shiny new plane that the caption told me my brother designed. I saw a photo of my brother's daughter as a toddler, cheek to cheek with his kneeling wife. There was a business card that gave title to some long-forgotten job he once held, a piece of paper with notations on blood pressure and pulse rates, a place card with an unknown woman's name embossed on it. There was no cohesion to these fragments. Other than my understanding that they all belonged to my brother. That everything was important enough to him that he kept it, held onto it, protected it for many years. Decades, even. I treated each remnant of my brother's life like one of the books in the library—it was only on loan to me, so I handled it gently, read it closely, and then returned it to its place. The problem was I kept relooking at the same items, those few things that made up the top layer or two of several dense inches of documents. These layers seemed the most superficial in content, the least substantial in meaning. I could see that the boxes were filled with a rich pastry of many kinds of paper. But I was afraid to dig deep. I was not getting to the bottom of anything.

I finally gave up, temporarily, on the first box. As a means of avoiding it, I pulled back the top of the second box. Once I opened that one, I was done for. The contents of that box I couldn't dance around or ignore. That one was filled with a bunch of letters. Small envelopes, old envelopes, addressed in a hand that was achingly familiar, even though it took me a moment to recognize it as my own childish scrawl. Memories of bending over the table, pen in hand, carefully, oh-so-carefully addressing each of these envelopes flooded my mind. This was what we did on so many Sunday nights during my childhood years: after the dishes had been cleared, but before she took out the evening's sewing and mending, my mother would gather my brothers and me around whatever rough table we had and pull out strange scraps of paper, commandeered from a grocery package or wrapper for some cloth, cut down and then ironed flat, and tell us to pull out our stubs of pencils and write to our father.

"Tell him about school, tell him about your friends," she'd say as we balked at the chore she had given us.

Our father, by then already a distant memory, already an irrelevance in our day-to-day lives filled with trying to get to school, trying to avoid the bullies and the cool kids, trying to get our homework done so we could go back out on the street, into the lot, play stickball, jacks, or marbles. Well, my brothers played; I watched. We didn't know what to tell our father, that faraway man. We didn't know what he cared about, and we could barely recall his face. But this writing-letters thing was important. Our mother made it clear. He was our father and wanted to hear from us, to know about us. She asked us for so little. We should, we could, and we would indulge her this one small task. And then after all the writing was done, after we'd scribbled our small news, sometimes each of us putting down a line or two one after the other on the same sheet of paper, then came my job, the big-sister task. I was the girl, the one with the neat and tidy handwriting, and therefore it was up to me to address the envelope. Sometimes the envelope was just a fold of the same paper we'd written on, sealed with a piece of tape; sometimes it was a real envelope with the bitter-tasting adhesive on the flap. I remembered the care I took writing that address. I remembered wanting him to be proud of me.

And here they were in front of me again, dozens of these letters. I picked up one after another, expecting nostalgic joy at the simple act of sliding the letters free and rereading them. I had that first moment of excitement, thinking of the pleasures of returning to all those childhood memories so foggy from this distance of years, yet brought back with sudden clarity as I read what we'd written to our father of our lives back then. My heart leaped with appreciation for my father, who I assumed had held on to and protected these letters, precious talismans from his long-lost children, and then to James, thinking he must have retrieved the letters after our father's death, and now here they were, returned to me after passing back and forth across so many miles of ocean and time. I turned one over, ready to free the letter and its memories. It was still sealed. I picked up another one. Also still sealed. One after another I examined them. All the same. All still sealed. I was slapped with the same insult over and over. Not one had been stamped. Not one had been opened. They had never been sent, never read. Our father never saw them. I gaped, disbelieving. Unstamped, still sealed. She never sent them.

Somehow James came upon them. He, who was never there with us when we gathered around and hunched over our pieces of paper, got ahold of these letters and kept them, never forwarding them, never opening them. I knew my mother and James fought. Maybe that is too strong a word. A few times I recall hearing the strangled whispers of two people in a small room deep into a heated and oppositional discussion they do not want those on the other side of the door to hear. I could rarely make out any specific words. But I knew it was always about our father. She must have given him these letters during one of those confrontations. By then our father must already have been dead. I wonder if James kept them so he could keep the wounds our mother caused our father alive. I wonder if he had that much of a streak of malice in him. I certainly never saw any signs of nostalgia, which might otherwise offer a different explanation.

As I let the letters sift through my fingers, I was hit with a wave of anger, a very rare emotion for me. I kept thinking: She had us sit and go through this charade for who knows how many Sunday nights over the years, and then never sent the letters to him? Why,

why, why? Was this an intentional deceit? Did she want to keep him alive for us by having us write to him, but then punish him by making us effectively dead to him? But if so, why keep the letters, the evidence? Why give them to James? Did she intend to send the letters and then not bother? Was there some other explanation, something obvious or simple that escaped me? I found myself furious at her.

Then, a sentence that had been as much a part of my childhood as the concrete sidewalks of the city were came back to me and repeated itself over and over: "We left the island so you could be educated." I don't know who told me this—the sentence shows up without attribution, without an accompanying voice. It was something known, something never questioned, never elaborated upon. Something accepted as simply as my love for my brothers, without explanation, without even stating out loud. Like love, within those few words about her reasons why were whole worlds of understanding and assumptions. That the choice was made by both my parents. That he supported her move and had reasons to stay behind. That there was sacrifice on both their parts. That in the night after we'd gone to bed, she wrote to him herself, longer letters than we children were able to conjure, pages filled with adult themes and adult longings. Where these presumptions came from I could not say, but they were with me my entire life.

And then these letters arrived and destroyed the very emotional fabric that held together my image of my parents. Because in the presence of those ancient pieces of paper, I felt nothing but hostility from my mother to my father. I felt that she was purposefully keeping the letters from him, keeping news of his children from him. Which made me think, further, that he might not have been a willing participant in her departure, perhaps her fleeing, from the island. I was suddenly desperately trying to recall if we received letters from him, what they might have said, if we ripped them open, eager for news. But I could not recall. Surely he wrote. Yes, I remembered opening the onionskin. I thought I recalled that act. Or was it just the sight of his letters to James that I displaced onto manufactured memories of my own? Did she keep his letters from us, too? There suddenly seemed to be whole worlds of animosity and bitterness that must have once bubbled below my mother's calm surface and that I was just seeing for the first time. From a great distance. I was desperate to understand what game she was playing, but I had almost nothing to go on.

This much I knew: our father adored us with abandon. The contents of the boxes caused me to consider, for the first time, just how incredibly painful being apart from us must have been for him. Almost unbearably so. I was stabbed with a ricochet of agony for what he had been deprived of. I was equally stabbed with anger for what she did to him. Not what she did to us. Children are resilient and learn to live with whatever life they have in front of them. She did the best she could by us. And truthfully, I don't know that we missed our father terribly. Children are also selfish, completely absorbed in the pettiness of their own lives. He was not with us, and our new lives quickly closed over the gap where he had once been. But our absence must have left a yawning hole in his soul. Especially since she didn't just take his children away from him physically, she kept them from him emotionally. She ensured he went through his last years isolated, alone, lonely in an irreparable way. As all these realizations swept over me, a wail escaped from my lips—the magnitude of her betrayal of him seemed staggering.

As all my firmly established ideas and notions begin to be rearranged, some new and unexpected thoughts and ideas started to shake loose and fall around me. I was reminded of an article I once read about a man who decided in his sixties to learn to read and write. The first hurdle was not the education itself, but the telling of his friends, family, and colleagues, none of whom had any idea that he was illiterate. He was a man who worked with his hands, a machinist, as I recall. The family was poor—there would not have been money for books. News and entertainment could be had on the radio. He had developed surprisingly simple mechanisms to hide his disability from even his family members. He pretended to skim a menu and then ordered what someone else had. If he needed to read something, he would say he forgot his glasses and thereby got others to read and write things out for him. He ran his life with cash instead of checks. He read cues and shapes instead of words. A stop sign, after all, always looks the same. He said it was easy to pass because no one ever suspected illiteracy in the first place. He could hide behind everyone else's assumptions. It was when he had grandchildren who asked him to read them bedtime stories that he was both shamed and motivated to learn.

This story came back to me in a flash as I sat at my kitchen table, the envelopes to my father spread out in front of me. I stared blankly at my childish scrawl, the misspelled words, the poorly formed letters. My mother's voice rose up from across the ages.

"Oh, honey, my hands are full of soapsuds; could you write that out for me?"

"Maggie, I am busy with my stitching, could you take down a note?"

"You have such nice handwriting—why don't you fill that out instead of me?"

My mother rarely praised us for anything. My girlish handwriting was, in fact, not at all nice; my writing did not improve until much later when I went to get my teaching certificate. Then, my writing had to be neat and tidy and so I worked at it, practiced it. My mother didn't help us with our homework, always busy as she was with taking in sewing, cooking great stews to improve a poor cut of meat. We did not have books at home, although she always encouraged us to spend time in the library, advice I followed and my brothers did not. I don't recall seeing her read a newspaper, even though she followed the news closely. On the radio. She always paid in cash. Once we were adults and she was aging, my brothers and I took care of her finances, paid her rent, made sure she got a real lease, a proper will.

I began to wonder, was she illiterate? Was it possible? It was true that I sometimes saw her scribble a few words here and there. A brief note excusing a brother who stayed home from school sick. A simple list of a few things she needed us to pick up at the store. But a letter? No. Read us a book? Never. My father told us stories of studying at Oxford. He bragged about the school his parents started. He was proud of his multilingual mother. He rattled off poems and quoted entire Shakespearean soliloquies at dinner. How did he end up with a woman who appears to have been largely illiterate?

It was these questions—and so many others that suddenly seemed out there waiting for me—that finally compelled me to open the other box, to remove the layers of accumulated, almost meaningless detritus of my brother James's life, and to read, one by one, what I found buried at the bottom: more than a dozen letters from father to son, several officially sanctioned documents, an occasional note from a long-ago neighbor or friend, a heartbreaking newspaper clipping.

I thought my father was a gentleman, all high collars, cigar smoke, challenging words. But then I read this from an unnamed correspondent: *About Dr. Ford. He has a housekeeper with whom he seems to be living more intimately than necessary. She is, of course, colored. The old gentleman is a very genial-appearing chap, but living in a rather squalid way. We think he would do better living with his son because then he would return to his former habits and finer feelings would govern him. He appears to have sunk considerably. I am sorry to have to report in this manner, but I am sure his son would want me to say just what I discovered.*

I thought my father was a professional, a highly successful medical man. Then I read this from the same letter: *His practice is small and not remunerative.* And this, from a letter from him to James: *You see, I am all alone here and it would be a comfort to have one of you at least with me to cheer up the old man...but I cannot afford the money to send passage, which at present is about $100...*

I thought my father brilliant, magical almost with his strange equipment, exotic contraptions, grand thoughts, notebooks filled with scribbles, his pragmatic ability to fix a person's teeth. Apparently, his preoccupations were much more fanciful. *In my idle time I work on my great fly machine. Have not yet got those engines and the wings have not yet sprouted, so you need not expect to see me fly over to New York before next summer.*

I thought he loved the island. I recalled his backslapping joviality with everyone he met, his joyful plucking of flowers for the dinner table, his enjoyment of the breezes that caressed the veranda. And yet he wrote to James, *I have had no word from you, I am very lonely without you and am only hoping to save just enough to clear out of this beastly yellow dog hole; in no place that I have been have I ever met such a beastly lot of swine.*

I thought him a business-minded man, entrepreneurial, credible. But it seems he was full of strange notions and quixotic schemes. In letter after letter, he wrote of unsuccessful attempts to get patents and gain the attention of officials; he fixated on the absurd notion of panama hats.

My dear son,

I am glad you found out for yourself that the stomach out of order is the source of most illness, mental or physical. In fact, "a dose of salts would in many cases prevent a suicide."...I sent a plan and drawing to the Admiralty for the destruction of submarines. I got a letter thanking me and stating that it was under investigation and they would write if more information or my further assistance would be required so something may come of it.

Your affectionate father,

Henry

P.S. How about Panama hats? Anything to be done in that line? Have you sold those I sent you? I think there ought to be something in that line if you attend to it.

I remembered my father as vigorous, striding boldly out on the veranda, walking briskly into town, tossing us children in the air. Sadly, his letters were filled with statements like this: *I have been suffering with Rheumatism in the arm—very painful...*And, more ominously: *I am still bothered by that pain in the chest when I walk, but not so much as before...*

I thought my father knew so much about our lives. I thought he got our letters, approved of our lives, and yet over and over I read remarks like this: *I long to see you again dear son. I do not suppose the children care a snap for me and as I am not in a position to send them money they no doubt despise me all the more for they perhaps are not aware that most of my present troubles are due to their mother. Try to raise them far and above the influences that surround them. It is very sad at my age to be entirely alone. I suffer but there is no use complaining for I can, at present, do nothing to change things. Write me all you can about them and speak to them about their father.*

I thought James was devoted to him and wrote to him regularly. I thought they were working on projects together. I thought James's intention was to return to the island. Or bring our father here. But there is this letter, dated 3 January 1922, the very last letter in the stack:

My dear son,

What is the matter? Are you getting out of touch with your old father? Do not do that. You have not written me, you owe me two letters answers. I would like your idea of a velontepede. Of course, not practical with the present principle of aeroplanes. You have told me nothing about your engagement. I certainly was surprised after what you said in your last letter when I quizzed you about the girl. What are you doing now in engineering? Find time to write me a long letter.

I return herewith the photo you desire. She sent me a card at Xmas for which please thank her for me as I have not her address I could not send her one as I would have done.

Your loving father,
Henry

I thought my father was lauded in life and admired in death for his grand intellect and inspiring accomplishments. But his obituary was very brief and contained only a whiff of warmth, the sense of stretching for something to say:

We regret to record the death of Dr. Henry Benjamin Ford. Dr. Ford was a well-known dental surgeon and his manners and courtesy were those of the old school. He was a lively conversationalist and a well-read man particularly interested in mechanical inventions and the development of aerial locomotion.

I thought my father so proper, so attuned to the forms of things, always aware of how things should be done. In fact, insistent on it. The table had to be properly set, even though our silverware and china were mismatched. We had to thoroughly scrub our faces and hands before we sat down to eat. We were dressed up before heading into town. He corrected our grammar all the time.

Yet at the very bottom of the box of James's documents, I found one that upended my assumptions more than all the letters combined. It seemed benign at first. I almost didn't give it any notice, almost passed over it as just some paperwork of little consequence, something that mattered only in the fact of its recording what was already known, done, complete. It was a fat piece of paper, thick in the way of official recordings. It was oddly sized, folded several times and for so long that it kept springing closed under my hands. I had to remove books from my shelves and weigh down the ends in order to read it properly. It was a marriage certificate. Two names, two single-word descriptions appeared there. Henry Benjamin Ford, widower. Rachel Gilks, spinster. Yes, that's right, I thought, I had almost forgotten that my father was married before Rachel. I knew he was quite a bit older, it was somehow part of the fantasy charm in which I regarded them as a couple, perhaps their only charm as a couple, that he was so much older. I had forgotten this earlier tragedy. I seemed to remember there was a baby involved, that maybe the wife's death was in childbirth.

I winced a bit at the depiction of Rachel. Spinster. Such an old-fashioned pejorative, conjuring an image of a crone bent over a spinning wheel, doling out yarn through hands gnarled with age and work. Bachelors are seen as romantic, spinsters to be pitied. Or worse, something to be frightened of. She was quite young when she had us, I knew. All of us before she was out of her twenties, I seemed to recall. I wondered how she could qualify as a spinster when she married him. Perhaps it was merely a formal, literal use of the word, as simply a never-married woman? It was this wondering about nomenclature that led me to look at the actual date on the certificate. I was seeking some sense of her age when she married. We had so little documentation of even our own ages, I was looking forward to being able to place something hard and fast onto a timeline. My eyes latched on to the numbers printed there, and I stared and stared, trying to understand what I was seeing, confusion growing by leaps and bounds in my mind and my gut. I studied the archaic, formal writing to see if I had misread the numbers. The math was stupidly slow in coming. I did the calculations several times in my head and then wrote them out on a scrap of paper to be sure.

Finally, there was no avoiding what the numbers told me. Their marriage was six years after my birth, five after James's, four after Eddie's, two after Percy's, a year before Tom was born. Even if we had our own birthdays wrong by a year or even two—which was possible, I realized that record keeping was spottier in those years, in that place—still only Tom was "legitimate." *Legitimate.* A silly word. Full of judgment and formality. Another old-fashioned pejorative. But a descriptive word, a word with an unequivocal meaning.

This news was stunning and confusing enough. It also led me to wonder if we all shared the same father. She was not married before—the "spinster" moniker makes that clear. Was it possible that one or another of us were bastards? Was there a feminine word for bastard? I was letting the terminology distract me. I felt quite confident that Henry was our father. The boys all looked like him. I resembled my mother more, but I felt the long reach of Henry's paternity in every fiber of my being. And yet this news rattled me in a way I could not fully explain or understand. *Truly,* I said to myself, *what difference does it make whether they were married? Who cares as to the "why"?* Maybe customs were different on the island and in that time in ways I didn't know. I told myself I could do some research. I should do some research. I was a librarian. It would not be hard. I should set aside the novels that filled my evenings and read some history. Read something real. I should try to understand the milieu of which my parents were a part. I should take less for granted. Yes, I would get right on this. Even as I told myself these words, I doubted my intentions. The contents of these boxes were more real than any book, nonfiction, historic, or otherwise. The documents in front of me were telling me a vast story about real people, people I thought I knew. This was the book I needed to read. This was the research I needed to do.

The room had grown dark around me. I had been there, working at my excavations, for hours. The doorway and windows were black except for a single streetlight that dissipated the darkness of a single kitchen pane and cast a diffuse glow over my table. I heard a car screech to a stop at the intersection below. I heard two cats shriek at one another in the alley at the side of the building. I reached for my cup, but it was emptied a long time ago. There was a fistful of ache between my shoulder blades. My feet, shoveled free from my shoes, had become cold. I reassembled the documents. I restacked the papers. I closed the box. I couldn't take any more. Such a small package to contain such large revelations. It would take some time to adjust, to realign. As I folded down the flaps, I wondered: If we get our own parents so hopelessly wrong, how can we be sure of what we think we know of ourselves?

It was now time for me to revisit the central story of our lives, the one that I accepted as easily as the nose on my face. Perhaps even more so; after all, who doesn't wish for a slightly different nose?

This was the story "they" told: she took us, all of us, it was said, or understood, to the United States because our father, dentist, inventor, dreamer, spent everything on his so-called inventions and couldn't or wouldn't or didn't see the need to send us to school. She wanted to bring us to America, where education was free. She left James behind, the eldest, because he and our father were so close. She didn't want to separate them.

Who was this unseen "they"? I could not conjure even a single memory of actually hearing this tale of our coming to the States pass a certain person's lips. It must have come from our mother, as no other source was possible. Did she sit down and tell us? In the house as we packed, silently, secretively placing our very few belongings into a single wooden box? Was it in the cart that took us to the quay? In the bowels of the belching boat that brought us here? Or was it once we had found lodgings? Did she line us up for one of our ritual scrubdowns with a rag and a bucket of water and tell us as she soaped our armpits, feet, hands, and faces, handing us the cloth and turning her face away when it was time to wash our private parts? Or did the story come out bit by bit, made up as she went along and tried to supply us with a reason for our being in New York without James or our father, an explanation that we could understand and accept, something simple and unobjectionable that provided sufficient cover for whatever her deeper, more complex, more adult reasons were? However it came to us, it seems to have been something simply known, an apocryphal tale perhaps, that became part of family lore, accepted, repeated, never questioned or amplified. I certainly never questioned this story, never tried to square it up with my own memories or bothered to reconcile its internal inconsistencies.

But then, sitting among the piles of paper, one after the other telling me a story that challenged the one I had taken at face value for decades, for the first time, I was searching for and grabbing onto memories long scattered. I was asking myself those questions long left unasked. I was wondering who my mother was, who my father was. And not quite yet, because I was not quite ready, who this new information made me.

Our education. Well, yes, I suppose we did go to school. But we jumped from one school to another as we moved from one apartment to another. The boys skipped classes regularly and, as the years went on, attended less and less, opting increasingly for work. She did little to encourage our studies other than occasionally asking after homework, and she did even less when confronted with my brothers' abysmal attendance records. The teachers did little too, assuming, I imagine, that poor people were ill suited for and not in need of educating. I was diligent because I was serious. I made good grades because I cared what others thought of me. I wanted to find a way to support myself, to be self-sufficient, so I clawed my way through high school and went to teachers' college. I did the work, because, if I am honest with myself, I was conventional. Even more than that, given the disordered nature of our upbringing, I actually craved convention. Rule breaking was for the men in my life.

Truly, the only one of us who was properly educated was the one she left behind. James came to the States for the same reason we allegedly did. But he came on his own, a few years after us. And he really did focus on his education, both the quantity and quality of it. He did it all by himself, without any help or even encouragement from us. I suppose we seemed a bit of a mess to him. He had a serious and exacting nature and clearly found our somewhat miserly existence, which was natural enough to us by then, distasteful. It was nothing he said; it was just his way of being in the same space as us. He held himself stiffly and apart, as if he was afraid of getting dirty. The boys slept ajumble in one bed and my mother and I shared the other, we all slapped water across our faces in the morning, jacked up our ill-fitting clothes with belts and safety pins, and grabbed a slice of bread to chew on as we ran out the door in the morning. But he combed his hair carefully, mended his own clothing assiduously, washed his dishes and the table meticulously, folded the blanket he slept under on the sofa neatly. He tried not to resent us and we tried to not resent him. But we were not successful in these pursuits. The boys, they did make fun of him, mocking his grooming habits, making him out for a dandy. He caught them at it once, and his face set up with a very hard edge. We were all used to teasing and being teased—we gave as good as we got—and we were surprised by his primness. It seemed a new, unwelcome, distasteful thing to him, the rough-and-tumble of family life. He was like a visitor, a distant cousin, more than a brother. He clearly had his sights set on bigger things. We should have been happy for him. We should have been proud of him. We didn't know how to do that. Pride was nothing we had any experience with. We had so little for ourselves; there was none to spare for him.

JAMES

EVERYONE THINKS THAT I WAS HURT, DEVASTATED EVEN, BY HER departure. They say she "left me behind," and that I turned inward after she was gone. Stupidity. Untruth. Blatant silliness. I was always an inward-looking person. I was glad to be left behind. In fact, I asked for it. You see, I found the tickets. I was a nosy, suspicious youngster, I admit it. I still am these things, I am not embarrassed to say. These two qualities are essential to what makes me a good engineer. I saw my mother whispering with Vea on several closely spaced occasions and noticed the furtive looking about between them, so I started to pay close attention. Then one day, I saw them exchange some official-looking papers that my mother quickly stuffed into her apron. I kept watching and saw her dash into the kitchen, move a chair, and hide these papers in the back of a tall kitchen cabinet. Her choice of cache spot made it clear exactly whom she was hiding them from. Father never did any kitchen chores. Would not even get himself a glass of water, if it wasn't on the sideboard. There was no chance of him finding something there, so it was clear to me that he was the one who was being duped in some way. I loved my father, was deeply loyal to him, but already, at that young age, had need and reason to dupe him myself a few times. I knew what I was seeing.

After she left the room and got herself occupied making beds and such, I moved the same chair again and discovered the tickets. Then she found me finding them. I understood instantly what she was up to. I mean, I understood why she had the tickets—not just that she was leaving, but why she wanted to leave. Like I said, I was nosy. For this quality to be effective instead of just intrusive, it also required me to be observant. I could see what she didn't need to say, which was that she had wanted to leave the island for years. And that there was no way Father would go, or let her go without him. Here was her literal and figurative ticket to a new life. Of course, she was going to bring her children with her. There were six tickets.

Before she said a thing, when the shock and terror were still fresh on her face as she looked at me and considered the multitude of implications of my discovery, I said I would not tell as long as she did not make me go. She nodded. She relaxed. I said I would not leave Father. She nodded again. I told her to sell my ticket. She said she would. That was all. We never required many words between us. We both understood Henry, and what it took to live with him, better than anyone. She returned my ticket and she gave me the money. Which I used to help secure my own getaway some years later. A scheme I am sure she understood right then, in that moment of dual discovery, without any further explanation from me.

That story about leaving me behind? She made that up as a cover for me. Otherwise he would have known that I knew what she was up to and didn't tell him. Which would have hurt him even more than what she did. Because his loyalty to me was even deeper and certainly more blind than was my loyalty to him. I even tried to detain him on the day of their departure by insisting on attending a polo game after our morning sail to ensure they had ample time for a clean retreat. This was nothing my mother asked for, she never asked for even incidental things of me and would certainly never ask for treachery, but I had my own reasons for wanting to be sure they got away. I was, of course, concocting my own escape. I was too young to be fully aware of it, but already I had my sights on bigger things. I knew my father had his limits. I didn't know exactly what they were, but I could sense the taint of ridicule in others' assessments of him. He was well loved, but he was not taken very seriously.

She hurt him terribly. I know that. But did she hurt me? No, not at all. That's just another story people made up. There is no reason for me to bother correcting them. It wouldn't serve them, nor would having them know the truth serve me. Because they seem to want to believe this tale, because it seems to entertain them, or expiate some guilt of their own, I let them feel sorry for me, patronize me, be nice to me. And to my father. He always enjoyed the extra attention.

My father and I had work to do. In her presence, he was nervous, unsure of himself. He wanted some kind of approval or regard from her that was not forthcoming. In its absence, he stammered. No, not literally—he was an eloquent man—but emotionally he faltered. The uncertainty she elicited in him got in the way of his focus, his intellect. Thank goodness I have never let a woman cause me to stumble in that way. And the children, the other children, were a distraction. He set out to teach them, all of us. He was so much more than a schoolteacher. That kind of a role was a waste of his time. I know he enjoyed it, being up on stage in that way, in front of the adoring eyes and rapt minds of his children, filling their heads with facts, figures, literature, love of nature. But he should have left that task to some simple spinster and focused his entire efforts on our inventions. Even more than teaching—and the two often bled together—he loved playing with the children. I know that I was not much older, I was still a child myself of course, but I was never much of one for play. I had ideas that needed to be made real. That's what I wanted to do. Always.

My mother thought it bothered me to discover my black or part-black or whatever she was grandmother, who abandoned her when she was just a girl and then disappeared forever. My father thought I didn't want to use my middle name, Benjamin, because I didn't want to claim my Jewish grandmother, who converted to Christianity. They both thought, conventional and rigid in their own ways as they were, that I was a racist and an anti-Semite. My daughter, who married two different Jewish men, both of whom had changed their last names to something benign and decidedly unethnic sounding, accused me of anti-Semitism as well. Me, the anti-Semite? What of her name-changing husbands? What of my religion-changing grandmother? What of my child-abandoning grandmother? What of my mother who never spoke of her past, of my father who impregnated her before marriage and then tried to hide her spotty pedigree? These people, who have kept so much of their own pasts and their own poor conduct behind closed doors, who have tried to paper over so much of themselves, they accuse me? I who can stand tall behind every part of my conduct throughout my whole life? It is infuriating. I am not the things they accuse me of. Not one bit. But I am painfully aware that others are racists, bigots, misogynists. There are so many ways to be intolerant, so many ways to define various sorts of hatred, so many reasons to deny someone a promotion, a job, or a place at the table. That is why, it is in fact the one and only reason I do not want my mixed heritage known, why my daughter's choices anger me so. I don't want others to have any single thing they can use against me.

Both my parents adored their mothers. My father expressed it clearly and robustly whenever he spoke of the woman who raised him, as was his nature; my mother expressed it in the softening of her expression when she described the woman who left her behind. I admire their feelings even though I don't share them. It's not that I didn't adore my mother, although I am aware it might seem that way; it's just that adoration is not in my nature, which is ever fixed toward pragmatism and philosophy. I suppose I came close to adoring my father. Closer than to anyone. Our minds were aligned in many ways. He thought we were aligned in all ways. In this I have to disagree. I never shared this with him, no, it would have been far too devastating, but I do not believe our emotions were aligned. I can be cold and calculating, I am aware. These are helpful qualities to one as ambitious as I. My father, on the other hand, was sentimental. He wanted approval and adoration. When those were not forthcoming, he turned increasingly to nostalgia. A particularly unattractive emotion, in my estimation.

My dear Son,

I got your letter and was very glad to hear from you and to learn that you have been so successful. That is indeed a comfort for the reverse has been my fate for a very long time. However I suppose that is natural as one gets on and mistakes one made can never otherwise than produce their consequences. Hence, never make mistakes.

Well my boy I do not want to write you a lot of old man's babble, for whatsoever I feel my lot seems cast down here and I must make the best of it. You are young and hence have much to write about to your father that you know must feel happy in every success that you make and that longs to get news from you. I, on the contrary, old and living in a pigsty, have nothing to write about except my thoughts which so far do not seem to have led me to any successful actions as engine, no patent, fly machine, no money to complete. I just make a living at teeth, work on a lot of locals and yellow bellies at low prices, so you see I have no interesting news to send you.

I know this, I am longing to see you again, however that seems impossible just now for I have not the price of a trip worth, so you see I am trusting to your coming to see me as you will no doubt have enough to spare for it when you get through with your aerial engagement with the US. I hope the US won't send you to drop bombs on your father's head.

I note that you had your mother out to your commencement services. I suppose she has entirely forgotten me and cares less. I have never had a letter from her.

And now with the most heartfelt congratulations to you on the attainment of your BS degree and the feeling that you have worked hard to truly deserve it.

I remain ever my dearest son your affectionate father,

Henry

P.S. What does ROTC mean?

I am sorry, in some ways, that I moved beyond him so quickly. Well, for his sake, not my own, I am sorry, as my successes made his own disappointments and failures so much more manifest. It was inevitable. His education was medical; mine was engineering. He learned to fix things that were broken; I learned to turn abstract ideas into real things. He was a dreamer. His reach always exceeded his grasp. His ideas started out in the right place but then far too quickly went off too far afield. Because he did not know what could be done or what could not be done, he had no boundaries, no discipline. One minute it was a human-powered airplane, the next it was exporting panama hats. Neither had a chance of success. Not that any of that bothered him as much as it might, as much as it probably should have. Not enough to make him learn focus and follow-through. He was always in it for the hope itself—he fed on hope like a hummingbird to nectar. His dreams and schemes encouraged me, and for that I will always be deeply grateful to him, but my education made him into a bit of a fool to me. It was a large price to pay for my education. But a necessary one.

My dear son James,

Your very loving letter duly received and your well-meant proposition to send me an allowance, but my dear boy you have misunderstood me. If I sometimes feel downhearted and depressed it is not because I want money, for my immediate needs are small. The cause of my being sometimes downhearted is that fact that I have absolutely made a wonderful advance in the steam engine practice for economy in fuel and cannot further it and truly I feel too old to go through promoting it. I had hoped that you would be in a position to take the matter up and put it through because I look upon it as far more than if I had been able to leave you a fortune and you, my eldest son, would be carrying on your father's work, on which I have spent so much time and labour. But I also realize that now is the time when you should be making money. I think I sent you all the papers relating to my engine. See about the possibility of obtaining a patent and you may be able to make money off of it. Whatever I should make would be yours. I trust you will think as well of it as I do.

There is another thing that has made me sometimes despondent and that is my flying machine. I have made several attempts to make a model but have so far only produced scrap. I suppose that was necessary to learn for I had not till very lately got the true principle of flight by man from his own power sufficiently defined to produce working drawings on definite geometrical proportions. I have done work on this for forty years and hope to perfect it with your help now. Am making plans for the "Volantepede" which I expect to fly as its name indicates by my feet on pedals. You are not to suppose that it will be capable of making more than perhaps 50 miles an hour, probably only 26 or 30. I have already designed the type of motor, which would have to be reciprocating and abnormally simple in construction. If I can fly with my own power (1 man and an old fellow at that) that will be about 360th part of the power required for the present forms of aeroplanes. Of course this seems absurd looking at it from our present knowledge of aeronautical engineering, but in the flight of birds there is a principle that has never been discovered, hence the mass of nonsense that has been written about the flight of birds. You might find out about that metal that is I think a mixture of magnesium and aluminum—it is I believe lighter than aluminum and tough as steel. It might suit me to get a few pounds of it to make some castings.

Well my dear boy, you see why I get fits of disheartenment and feel that I am too old to work out these things that I feel so certain about. After all my life may be a barren waste while others with less work who have done nothing to further science and benefit to humanity at least have left money and happiness to their children. I hope to accomplish something before I die.

Your affectionate father,
Henry

I loved my father. I loved him like no other person I have ever had in my life. Not my own wife, not even my own children. Not my mother, no, certainly not my mother. I understand how deep and natural was our bond, as father and son—and first and eldest son to boot—but there was more to it than that. It is impossible to put into words. I respected him, too. Yes, I saw his limitations in all their maddening glory. I saw them perhaps more clearly than any other, as I saw, with the benefit of my own interests and education, just how absurd so many of his ideas were. Ideas that made his face alight with joy and optimism for some kind of beautiful, productive, vastly improved future. Not just for himself and his family, but for all of mankind. Yes, he wanted to bask in the glory he anticipated for himself. But he also wanted to make the world a better place. As silly as that sounds, it was true. More true for him than for any person I have ever met. It makes me sorry, so deeply sorry, to know that his wish, all his wishes really, remained unfulfilled. A sad ending for such a well-meaning old man. I never saw him again after leaving the island. He remained unreconciled to his wife and other children. He never got that patent, any patents. His engine never produced power. His plane never flew.

MARGARET

I never much considered my parents together. To me, they were always set apart from one another. Even when they were physically together, they were moving at separate speeds, in different directions. But it was hard to recall. It was so hard to see past our years in New York. It was as if the tall buildings were a shield, not just against a long view, but also to distant memories. Mother never spoke of her past, of our past. Following her lead, we never asked questions. I was focused, as it seems she was, on making it through the dozens of small dramas of our days. Then when I had some ease in my life, I suppose I became more interested in other people's pasts, expressed to me in the thousands of books I have stuffed my nose into over so many hours of so many of my days.

What did I see, hear, smell in those years before I came here? The feel of the sun. So strong it was like a weight against my skin. My mother's voice telling me to come in from the yard. The scrutiny in her eyes as she assessed a tan line on my arm, a bloom of freckles across my nose. The lament in her voice as she muttered, "Henry's not going to like to see that." The local women at the market, the bright colors and patterns of their clothes a boisterous clash against one another and their own darker skin. We were white; we wore white. They were a million shades of darker-than-me brown and wore a kaleidoscope of hues. They also talked loudly, slapping at one another for emphasis, cackling with laughter. I was told to "act like a lady," which I somehow knew without being told meant to keep my eyes down, my mouth closed, my hands to myself. These differences, they are a cliché, a stereotype, are they not? Yes, but they are also true. The truth of them was also a kind of glass wall through which I could look but never step or speak. The smell of the sea. Seeing boats coming and going from the quay—this was an excursion that we were taken on—"Let's go watch the boats! It will be fun!"—an adult holding my hand, squatting at my side, pointing at ships, as I wondered where they were going, where there was to go to, if one might take me someplace someday.

I raked my mind for more recollections. Soft dust that lifted in small clouds around my feet when I walked down the road. The breeze I made for myself when I swung back and forth in the hammock on the veranda. Finding a still-warm egg in a pile of dead grass under the porch and bringing it inside, setting it on a blue plate. Baby chicks that appeared, like some small delight that had drifted down from outer space, and then disappeared one by one, day after day, no doubt carried away in the sharp teeth of some other animal to feed some other baby. Mother asking Father for a henhouse, and him saying no, he didn't want the damn birds anyway. Waking in the gray half-light just before sunrise to the sound of the rooster's incessant crowing, followed immediately by Father's passionate cursing of the bird.

Dinner. That meal came back to me. Father sitting with us at the table while Mother hovered around, serving, filling dishes, taking them away, clucking at the boys to eat more, a nervous bird who would not sit or eat from a plate, but merely picked at the scraps we left on ours. At dinner, that's where Father told us stories. He described big cities full of buildings. He talked about flat fields of wildflowers that stretched as far as the eyes could see. He told us about ladies dressed in jewels so dazzling they glittered in the lamplight so that you had to turn your eyes away. He told us of his patients, making them the butt of many a joke, which, even if I didn't understand the humor, I recognized as something I would later call wit. He sang songs, recited poetry, stood up and delivered soliloquies, while my mother banged pots and cleaned the kitchen.

We gave him our rapt attention. He was our father, but also our teacher and our entertainer. She did not begrudge him our attention; it just seemed that she was having none of it herself. Or maybe she'd given his tall tales more than enough attention already. They did not touch one another. They moved around each other, made room for one another, water finding its way around a stone. But they wanted something from each other. Something the other was unwilling to give. Perhaps unable. Yes, this is something I could not understand or even see until I was old enough to have wanted something from a man myself. So many things that happen between adults are invisible, incomprehensible, when you are a child. Whatever it was they wanted from each other clearly left the other feeling undervalued, unworthy.

Was I making these memories up as I went along, or was I pulling them from some recess within myself? They felt fresh with reality. Or was it fresh with fabrication? Perhaps some of both. Because I was trying to find explanations as much as recollections.

I remembered a cart piled high with us, and a boat piled high with bananas. I remembered feeling sick and staying belowdecks in the dark, while my brothers came and went and told me stories of everything from fish that flew through the air above the waves to fires that roared in the bowels of the boat as they were fed enormous shovelfuls of coal by huge men blackened with soot. I remembered the feeling of us all lying together in a small, dark space, like a pile of puppies. Was this on the boat? It could have been. It also could have been any of our many apartments.

I didn't switch to my mother's bed until I blossomed into my early womanhood, but I was a late bloomer. When I moved out of our home, into my own apartment, I hardly knew how to sleep alone. My single bed, tiny as it was, seemed enormous, stretching away from me in all directions, as if I'd been set adrift. I slept fitfully, huddled along one edge, afraid to reach my limbs outward in the dark. Then, as if in some kind of strange rebalancing for all those years of shared beds, I became unable to sleep with anyone at all. I spent many a wakeful night listening to a boyfriend snore beside me; I left confused lovers behind in the middle of the night to return to my own bed; I waited until I heard my husband breathing deeply beside me and then crept to the sofa. The sofa. That was where my mother often slept as well. I went to bed before her, I would feel the weight of the bed shift as she joined me in the dark of night, and then again a few hours later when she left to creep to the living room. The sound of the rocking chair moving back and forth or of the floorboards creaking as she paced. Her form of sleepwalking. Insomniacs, us both.

I remembered my first sense of New York. Dark, damp stairwells, stone stoops, dirty buildings, laundry coming back off the line with fresh dirt on it, smells acrid in the nose, the people hurrying by, heads bent always against some unseen force. I remember being cold, so cold, so frightened by the way the chill seemed to seep into my bones, took away the feeling in my fingers and toes. I was afraid my body would seize up with the cold, that I'd stop moving and crack into a million pieces, like a piece of ice hit with a hammer. I was afraid I'd never be warm again. In New York, all the shades of island green had been replaced by an equal number of grays, the dense trees and shrubbery replaced with concrete and stone. The menace was still there as well, the sense of dangerous possibility should you stray out of known byways, should you linger too long, should you move from light to dark. Of course, this is

New York still, my memories constantly repopulated with a repetition of experience.

Did I miss the island? The thick heat, the dense greenery, the slow swaying of bodies as they walked in time to some silent island rhythm? How do you miss something known so thinly, so shortly, so incompletely, to only the unformed nature of your childhood self? Missing something is a luxury, the emotional luxury of an adult. I was busy, always busy. We were poor, but I recalled a time of being less poor, and it seems I was trying to make up for all that was gone, trying to polish what was left. I was also a big sister in a house full of brothers, always picking up what they dropped, wiping at dirt they would never notice, giving cautionary looks for the bad language the boys love. I cleaned because our living space was too full of people and I refused to live in dirt or among accumulated detritus; I mended because we had no money to buy new clothes and I didn't want us to go out in tatters; I sewed because it helped bring in extra money; I cooked long hours because it softened poor cuts of meat and made edible almost gone-by potatoes. There was no space or time to think about the island, to recall the island, much less to miss it.

As a mature, solitary woman, I had the time. But I didn't know if I had the memories to fuel my longed-for nostalgia.

Whereas it seemed the island gave us plenty of room to roam, seeking our own education and entertainments from nature herself, who also supplied us with a certain fecund abundance that allowed us to pluck our lunch from a nearby tree, we lived cheek by jowl in New York, like some cluster of half-feral things grappling for the small scraps life held out to us. Were we a family? Well, there are so many ways to be a family. I fussed over the boys. *Fretted* is perhaps a better word. I watched from just enough of a distance that I could intervene if necessary as they played jacks and stickball, smoked cigarettes and played cards, got in fights and made up in a moment, the way boys do. They tolerated my ministrations just barely, pushing me away after I'd broken up a fight, rolling their eyes when I plucked a lit cigarette butt from their mouths. Mother worried about them little. Not enough in my estimation. She had seen plenty of people from rougher backgrounds turn out just fine, I suppose. And plenty of people from finer backgrounds turn out far worse. Still, it was her lap they sought for comfort those few times they needed it. It was her they picked dandelions from the sidewalk cracks for. It was to her they showed off their occasional accomplishments at school. Even though she had little patience for or interest in such demonstrations of affection or sentiment. Our mother managed somehow to hold herself apart from us even as she kept us together.

Well, other than James. She left him behind. She said, or somehow we were given to understand, that she did it for him. That parting him and Henry would have been a strong blow for them both. I wonder if James was upset by her abandonment. I wonder that we were not more obviously hurt by the implication that he and he alone was of greater value to our father than we were. I wonder if we held this against him—our father and James—when we should more rightly have held it against her. Easier of course to resent the parent with whom you do not have to live. Easier too to idealize them. No day-to-day reality to interfere with whatever parental fantasy you need to create to assuage your own bruised psyche. I know James sent her money. I helped deposit his checks. Sometimes there was a note she asked me to read to her while she scrubbed vegetables or stitched a hem, but they were short and formal. He told his news and asked after ours. Did he send money because he loved her? Because he felt he should? He sent checks even when he must have had little enough to spare, when he was in school upstate and then paying his way through college. It must have given him a twisted sense of power to be able to help the woman who left him behind. After all, James was not someone naturally given over to charity. He was a self-made man who wore quite obvious pride at his accomplishments along with impatience at others' lack of thrift or determination.

Of course, I also saw them together, James and Rachel. Neither of them was naturally warm, but I saw her reach for him from time to time, to touch his shoulder or hand. I recall that he flinched. I remembered this quite distinctly, the way he moved away from her. The shadow of sorrow or regret I saw cross her face. At the time I assumed he was pained at being left behind. But that action on her part also made him special, better than the rest of us, something I think was not lost to him. After reading these letters from Father, it was clear James must have been carrying resentment for two. After looking through these boxes, it was also clear that James was looking for something. Something made him dig into her life and then keep all the evidence. He was not one for idle curiosity. Which makes me wonder if he was doing it out of spite.

In James's box there was a photo of Henry and one also of Rachel, neither framed, just loose, stuck among the other papers, not together, two singular portraits, buried in different places. Our father's picture showed him from the shoulders up, his body and face at slightly different angles, thick waves of salt-and-pepper hair cresting over his head, his graying beard trimmed close to his square jaw, sitting atop his high collar. He looked avuncular and well bred, while his rounded eyes, fringed with creases, were simultaneously gentle and just a bit pompous in their expression. Our mother's picture showed her standing, one arm hanging down at her side, the other resting on the back of a severe chair. Her hair was piled on top of her head in the style of the day, her dress covered her from chin to floor, and she was free of adornment. Her features were as they always were—there was no effort to suck up to the camera—her expression was serious, unsmiling. Some might have called her pensive, but I thought her simply dark tempered. I noticed her hands. They were well muscled, with thick fingers. These hands were familiar to me. I watched them many a time moving swiftly with needle and thread, surprisingly deft for such apparently rough instruments. She had hands not unaccustomed to hard work. In spite of the dour expression, which made her look older than her years, the dress she wore in the photo was finely made, elaborately embroidered, and her hair was fashionably styled. The photo must have been taken when she was a young woman—there was no money for such things as we grew older and certainly not after we came to New York. And yet her hands betrayed something of her. A woman of Henry's class would not have hands like that. They would have been smooth, soft, and ringed. These were hands already familiar with manual work. I wondered if she was some sort of housekeeper or maid. Did he fall for the help? Even a governess would not appear so world-weary already, I thought. How did they end up together, with so many children, yet unmarried? Perhaps she worked in his house, the one he once shared with his first wife. Maybe she was a mistress as well as a hired hand. Maybe she was never really intended to be a wife. Clearly, it was a role for which she was both reluctant and ill suited.

This was a strange endeavor, trying, for the first time in my life, to come to a more thorough and nuanced understanding of who my parents were, trying to see them in the fullness of who they were, not as parents, but as adults trying to navigate their own lives. I had my ideas about my parents made up, settled into the grooves of my mind and emotions like the ruts in a road used only during the dank and muddy seasons. Don't we all think we know those who made us? Understand what made them? And yet, we are doomed, I suppose, to see them forever and only as our parents through the fun house mirrors of having been their children. I wondered why it had taken me so long. A simple answer, I guess, one to which we are all mostly doomed: I was too busy seeking my own life to consider the life I had been born into. I was too confounded by what was in front of me to look back.

Of course, like most parents, my mother and father did not leave themselves open to much investigation, as they never revealed their other-than-parents sides of themselves. Perhaps it is not even possible to see to see one's parents as anything other than caricature. Henry was the romantic figure, brilliant, irresponsible, loving, kind, impractical, getting by on charm and brains. Rachel his opposite, dour, serious, pragmatic, dogged, a shadow of a person focused on making do, without the luxury of or interest in dreams, passion, an inner life. I never considered that caring for me and my brothers, the daily drudgery of poverty, and the lack of a partner who valued her and provided her with adult-to-adult affection might have subsumed whatever fancies she may have once harbored for herself. I never considered that she might have had her own dark secrets, that life might have been cruel to her long before we arrived, or that her character was not natural, but was shaped by whatever bad luck her life had given her. A cur raised in a junkyard can rarely be turned into a lapdog.

Maybe that was a romantic fabrication, too. I considered myself. I was without the excuse of children, of poverty. I had a husband who loved me, and after he left, I could have found another man. And yet I looked at the image of my younger self and all I felt was wonder at how much she tried, and yet how easy it was for her to stop trying. To give in to the little tasks of life and stop noticing the days, weeks, years rushing by. Maybe Rachel wanted more. But then again, maybe poverty and children provided her with a welcome excuse from wanting more. I was not sure what my excuse was. I was not sure I needed one, either.

For many evenings over several weeks, I combed through James's boxes. Everything I read was relatively easy to keep at a comfortable distance from myself. The pieces of paper I plucked up and scrutinized over and over were about other people. Sure, they caused me to wonder about family members and what alchemy of character and luck, both good and bad, had combined to make them who they were. I contrived to explain to myself the choices they had made. It was like a parlor game, a puzzle I was putting together, knowing many pieces were missing, while hoping I had the necessary parts to create enough of a picture that my rusty imagination could fill in the rest.

Then I found the letter that ripped me out of my comfortable, cocky, arm's-length complacency. I don't know how I missed it for so long. It must have been tucked between the folds of some document and only after many rearrangings of the paperwork did it make itself manifest. When I came across the small folds of notepaper with the black borders, I was frankly excited to find something new, something unexamined. Little did I know this modest letter would lead me to reexamine everything I thought I knew about everyone I had ever loved. But even more than that, to reexamine everything I thought I knew about myself.

Dear Miss Rachel,

I am telling this letter to my son Carell, and he is writing it to you. I just want you to know that our Mr. George has passed. I know when you saw him last, he was pretty poorly. Well, he took his time with his illness, he got better for a long time—you know how tough he was—but he is gone now. He did die alone. His girls did not make it back in time, but they back now, cleaning out the house and selling the plantation and all. Spoiled girls. Nothing but complaining about the heat and the state of things. Well, where was they this whole time after their mama died? Couldn't be bothered to leave that damn place England. Couldn't be bothered to look in on their papa, but they got here quick enough after he was gone.

Anyway, that's not what I want to write you about. Here's what I want you to know: at the very end, he was asking about you. Asking if I knew if you was ok. And asking after his girl Margaret. He said he wished he'd done right by her, wished he'd claimed her as his own because he always felt in his heart how very much she was his own. Maybe seeing the way his other girls turned out made him regretful. Anyway, I thought you might like to know that. I thought it might give you some comfort. Did you know he came to see her once? Your marketing day, so as not to bother you, he came up to the house just to look, just to lay eyes on her. Töld me she was a beautiful child. Which of course I knew. More beautiful child, he said, by far, than his other daughters.

He told me also to be sure to tell you that if you was ever to come back to the island, you should look in at a lawyer's office. He didn't say why, but gave me this card and asked me to send it to you. Said you should write and tell them your address. So that is what I am doing. It seemed very important to him, but he did not know how to reach you. Or if you would want reaching by him.

He did leave me a bit at the end. Enough to get me started with a business. I have a little store and café now, on the mountain road, just above the house your Henry left to me. My son and I live in the house. Keep it up just the way it was should you ever want to come back. There is room for you. Always a room for you, here. Rightly, I feel it is still your house and I am just keeping it for you.

I do hope you and the other children are getting on OK. You know how fond I have always been of both you and your children.

Vea

His girl Margaret? His girl Margaret? His daughter Margaret?

I said these words out loud over and over. I tried to imagine for a moment if she was referring to some other Margaret, if there could be some other Margaret. But it was impossible, in this context, for this to be about anyone other than me. This one short letter, undated, buried at the bottom of the box, an envelope almost in miniature, a scrap of paper inside, had in a moment upended everything I thought I knew about myself. My mother, yes, her, too. This letter said so much about her. But myself, mostly. And yes, my father. My fathers. My God. Who was this man, Mr. George? What was the relationship between them? How old was I when I became Henry's daughter? Why was I never told about this other man, this ghost that has visited me not just in my dreams, but apparently in my life?

This box, these documents, these letters filled my head with innumerable questions, and also helped me answer many of them. I was outraged, amazed, wrung raw by this information. And yet. And yet. Yes, it answered so many unasked questions, too. My hair, my freckles, my differences from my brothers...not just gender, but paternity. It also asked and answered so many questions about my mother. Her secrecy, her unwillingness to look backward, her disinterest in the past. She had much to regret, that I knew. I didn't realize how much she had to hide. I wondered how much she had to run from. It seemed she fled more than one man. And in the process kept me not just from one father, but from two.

RACHEL

"Shh. You got tuh stay quiet, you got tuh be still. Shh. Don't want to disturb no one."

My mother's refrain. It is what I remember most from my earliest years of life. It is all I have left of her. Her voice so soft, so close to my ear, it was as if the words were not even coming from her, but were being released from inside of me. These few sentences, said so often that even when they became unnecessary, when silence was no longer even a habit, but so much a part of me it seemed even my heart would beat without noise, she kept saying these phrases, over and over, a little song she sang to comfort herself, a lullaby she hummed to me when she put me to sleep in our shared, narrow cot, and she whispered again, later, when she crawled in with me, her flesh still warm from her time with him. She sang this song to me again the day she pulled my soft-from-long-wearing-and-much-laundering dress over my head and stuffed my limbs, rigid with resistance at knowing what I could not know but did know anyway, into that new, stiff, just-bought dress, and lifted me up into the carriage. She was biting her lip so hard against her own sadness that it leaked blood just as her eyes leaked tears. The drops of one glistened in the sunshine, dappling her toasted skin; the drops of the other bloomed like precious flowers against those dark lips that muttered over her bright-white teeth to be good, to be quiet, to be thankful, to be good, to do well, to be quiet, to watch and listen and learn, to be still. All of which I did. Because her words never left me. Her singsong was forever in my mind.

I remember kissing her soft, pillowy lips—lips like chocolate cake frosting, no wonder he couldn't resist them—one last time. And the surprise as the taste of her blood hit my tongue, bitter and sweet, metallic and warm.

I was told I was a guest. In this new house, with these new people, I was told I should feel "like family." I was told I was welcome, that I was home. But I was none of these. Nor was I a servant or a hired hand or a governess. I was not in bondage, nor was I paid. I was not white, I was not black, I was not colored, I was not Creole. No one knew what I was, and while some were curious, most seemed not to care. Nor did I. I lived not with the family, nor with the servants, but in a small room off a back hallway, equidistant from the kitchen and the living quarters. My skin had a warm hue to it that faded in bright sun, but showed up somewhat suspiciously after dark, especially in the dim out of doors and in candlelight.

Because no one knew where I belonged, I was allowed anywhere. Because I didn't know where I belonged, I went everywhere. Sometimes I ate in the dining room with family. Sometimes even with guests. Other times in the kitchen with the help. I even regularly brought my plate out to the barn and ate with the animals, in the company of their quiet, sweet, contented warmth, to the sound of the steady grinding of their large teeth. Sometimes I was dressed up and brought out when there was company, my affiliation explained away with some vague title such as "George's charge." Sometimes they said I was his ward. A few times I was a cousin. Everyone, it seemed, had an innumerable number of cousins of varying degrees of relatedness and closeness. It was a catchall term that tended to stop further questions.

Once introduced, I was generally ignored. Because no one knew quite where to place me, I was left to place myself. Which was usually in a nook or a window seat, partially obscured behind a curtain, slowly turning the pages of a book in my lap to make myself seem occupied. But in truth, I listened instead of read. I paid attention as they recited passages of Shakespeare or the poetry of Shelley, my lips moving silently along with their words, trying to make the sentences and phrases stick in my mind. I listened as they talked about slaves who wouldn't work, freedmen who would, importing labor from East India, the price of sugar, the laws of England, the mutterings of rebellion, their surety that the inherent laziness of blacks would protect them from their organizing and uprising. I took note and kept track as the weeks and months went by of all the ways they were right, which were few, and all the ways they were wrong, which were many.

Sometimes I spent hours in the kitchen, watching the women they had just called lazy work up a sweat to prep the meals they'd be stuffing into their fat stomachs. Their strength and stamina was staggering as they heaved dead animals onto a huge table to be plucked and cleaned and chopped and seared and basted and simmered into submission. I watched as the men they called lazy, their muscles hard and creased from their long labors in the fields, come to the back door for a cup of water, a plate of milk-soaked bread, a pan of the leftovers the people in the parlor deemed unworthy, but these working men and women knew to have the greatest flavor, the most richness and nutrition.

The household help and the field hands treated me no differently than one of the plantation cats, indulged because they kept the rats away—I was small, asked for nothing, and was sometimes useful. I might be handed a succulent morsel to nibble on, a bird to pluck, potatoes to peel, or other times a bowl filled with something dry and something wet that needed to be mixed together, the ingredients resisting each other turn after turn after turn, until proximity and gentle agitation broke down their boundaries and they became one.

In the great heat of the suffocating kitchen, the women's hair would be hidden behind colored kerchiefs, their skirts hitched up to reveal their dark, glossy legs, so sturdy and shapely they looked like long polished wood. Sometimes they took off their undergarments because this made things so much cooler, more bearable, and rolled them into their waistbands or stuffed them into a pocket. As long as no white person was within earshot, the women talked and gossiped and told tales and myths of people and gods, and those dead, alive, and somewhere in between.

Sometimes I heard stories of myself. They were brief. They were always the same. "Poor child" was usually the preface. Then some suggestion of who my mother might be. Mr. George's mistress was the usual guess. An Italian. A Jew. A Spaniard. Someone with the passion his wife was lacking. Someone he met while traveling on plantation business. Someone who begged him to care for me on her deathbed. In this, the kitchen talk and parlor talk was in agreement. The only difference was that in the parlor, there was a faint tone of superiority, in the kitchen a soft tone of indulgence. None of this was true, of course. But I never heard Mr. George answer or explain. I wasn't about to either.

As I grew into a woman and began to understand desire, I also began to wonder why those church ladies ever thought of giving a man like my father a woman like my mother. I was young when I got sent to the George household, yes, but I have my memories of him: pinched and glowering, serious and chastising up there in the front of the classroom or in the pulpit. His skin was always angry, red and peeling, never accustoming itself to the brutality of the sun no matter how many creams he applied to his cheeks and nose or how wide the brim on the hat covering his thinly haired head.

Friendliness did not come naturally to him. He seemed uncomfortable with people, even as he went through the required motions of shaking hands, squeezing shoulders, and ruffling hair as his parishioners left the church. He was harried by the effort, always had his eyes on the next person in line, was always hurrying the process along so he could get back to his dark office, his dusty books.

And she? Where he was all angles, she was all rounded curves. His rocky edges to her ripe fruit. His pale pallor to her warm, mulatto glow. Her easy laugh to his nervous glances. She cooked for him, she cleaned for him—this is why she had been given to him. She was not a slave—those days were over—but she was a present, nonetheless, her meager salary paid by a few wealthy ladies who pooled bits of their pin money. She also picked up his empty teacup and wiped the droplets he had spilled onto the table; she took the open book from his chest when he fell asleep in his chair, marked the page and set it on his desk; she adjusted his robes before he went into the church. It was she who applied soothing balms to his sunburned skin and it was she who filled the dark and empty spaces that collected around him with her songs. It was she who shared his bed, smoothing his scowls with the rhythms of her body, until he was spent and asleep. Only then did she return to her own, and then our, bed.

She didn't see him as others did. She was in love, so his coldness was only a defense to being needed by so many, his sensitive skin a reason for her to touch him, his hard edges were something for her to smooth over.

No one but me knew about any of these other, more personal services. And neither of them knew, of course, that I knew. My mother had taught me the value of staying in the shadows, of casting down your glance, of keeping your own counsel. This too was why she was given to him. People thought her timid and shy. They thought she would not bother the serious young preacher who seemed to have no time for anything but his school and his church. They mistook him, thinking his passions could only bend in one direction, toward God and service. They mistook her as well. It was from her that I learned there can be great power in a deferential stance.

It was clear to me, even as a small child kept mostly hidden, that he was respected by both the locals and the whites. There is always an open window, a hole in a curtain, a crack in a door to peer through. These things are easy to ascertain, especially when you are a child left too much alone and the noises of a crowd or a couple are frequently close by, providing cover for a small child's bare footfall as it pads against a stone floor. But I could also see he was not loved. Except by her. Her eyes glowed when they landed on him. Her touches to his shoulder, his face, his hand were full of the restraint and gentleness reserved for precious things. I also know that she must have loved him, desperately loved him, because she gave me up at his request. I know she loved me, certainly she loved me; she just must have loved him more.

My mother said it was for a better life. She told me that I wouldn't need to hide anymore. She said I'd learn to be a lady. She said they'd send for me once I was educated and proper. All these things whispered hurriedly to me as she changed my clothes from what I was comfortable and accustomed to into something stiff and foreign against my skin. I don't know if she believed what she said, or just wanted me to believe it. I don't know if what she said was true, in any sense of the word. I can't say if my life was better because I never saw or heard from my parents again, so I don't know what kind of life they had and therefore I might have had if they'd taken me with them. I don't even know if they had life at all, or died on the road, at sea, or from fever in some small town. I can say that I still had to hide, just in a different sort of way. I had to hide where I came from. I had to hide what my heart was made of. But by then, there was no effort to hiding these things—it was already simply who I was.

As to what I learned? It was clear that I would never be a lady. Not only was I not cut out for it, but no one was especially interested in turning me into one. Nor was I interested in becoming one. To me ladies were silly and useless, merely froth to be spooned away from the top of a bubbling stock. As for my formal education, that was left aside as well. I suppose Mr. George thought I had gotten some kind of education at the mission school. Enough to suit my needs and future, which he undoubtedly thought were rather slim. Forgetting that since I was not supposed to exist, I could not rightly show up in a classroom of any kind, but especially not my father's classroom. I suppose my father expected Mr. George would educate me. I did learn something, spotty as it was, in my own listening-behind-closed-doors sort of way. My father also did take the time in the evenings to give me some very basics of reading and writing. He taught my mother and me side by side, as she was largely illiterate. I, being younger, learned more quickly, outpacing her so fast and far that I began to help her sound out words and work out sums. But these lessons were few and far between. My father always had someone in great and desperate need of his ministrations—a sick child, a labor gone wrong, a head bashed in by a beast. Or a man. In the George house, because I was quiet, because I listened, I could take what I heard someone else saying and stick it to my brain in such a way that it didn't leave me. So when someone would start spouting Shakespeare or quoting the Bible, I could murmur the rest of the passage after they stopped. I suppose that's part of why no one bothered much to advance my book learning. They thought someone else had done it; they thought I had enough already.

Before Mrs. George got sick in the body, she got sick in the head. And the heart. Her eyes, once so bright blue, got dark, like a storm was brewing inside of her. She stopped inviting people over, stopped taking care with her clothes and hair. It happens to some people. They so badly want things to be different than they are. But they don't know or can't make the change they seek. Then, further, they can't let go of the way they wish things would be, and when this won't happen, they give up on themselves and everything around them. For a bit, people felt sorry for her, tried hard to help her, tiptoed around trying to make things nice for her. Even Mr. George did. But then she got mean. She picked fights. She clawed at Mr. George's face once, and he had to tell people that it was a dog that got him when he tried to break up a fight. I don't know that anyone believed him. She threw things. She broke many a piece of beautiful china and sparkly crystal. Things that could have kept a local family fed for a month or more if she'd sold them. People who work for their way in the world hate to see that kind of waste. Of things and of a person. So everyone started to leave her. Left a lot of work for me and Vea, as we were the only ones she didn't bother. And there was Sarah. She was pretty useless for work, but could take care of a small and simple chore. Mrs. George was bad to Sarah, but I guess she, like me, didn't have anywhere else to go. Sarah was more frightened of me than she was of Mrs. G—we called her that among ourselves, not as an affectionate nickname but because she didn't seem deserving of the respect of her full name—even though Mrs. G beat her. Beatings Sarah understood, beatings she took in silence; I suppose she had beatings growing up. As to Sarah's fears of me? I never touched her, but she thought I had obeah in me and that was scarier to her than anything Mrs. G could dole out.

Mrs. G did not beat me. Almost, once. But not even then. This is what happened: one day when I was about twelve years of age and a cow in my keeping got loose from its stake and ravaged a corner of the garden, she came upon the mess the animal had made, which I was trying to mend, and she raised her hand as if to strike me. The domestic animals were often in my care. I liked them and they seemed to like me. Mr. George noticed and encouraged me. So Mrs. G was sure this small disaster was my fault. Which I suppose it was, even though cows getting themselves untied or through a fence was not an uncommon thing. Not that she would know anything about such things. In any case, her hand was up, and I was watching it, a dark silhouette against the harsh sun, expecting it to come down against my head or face, getting ready to duck my way out of the impending pain, but she paused for a moment, the bright light causing her to squint at me. She seemed to be considering her actions, something that was growing more rare even back then. She held her arm up and then murmured, almost too low for me to hear, that her hand would leave a mark on my fair skin. She didn't say anything more, just lowered her arm and walked away. We both knew that a mark on my face would have to be explained to her husband. Perhaps to the guests expected that evening. That was more than she wanted to take on.

Maybe she thought, like everyone else, that I was Mr. George's daughter and she didn't want to face his anger—he didn't have many soft spots, and the ones he did have were not very soft, but even I could see he had a very small one, such as it was, for me. And this soft spot was one of respect, not sentiment. I don't know what Mrs. G knew of my provenance. Maybe the possibility that I was something her husband cared for was what stopped her hand then and then kept her from raising it again. I don't know. I do know that she cared for me little. In either a good or bad way. We were simply polite toward one another, cordial, formal. I knew she had no use for me, other than as an object to show her friends from time to time, living, breathing evidence of her supposed generosity and charity. I had no reason to disabuse people of this fantasy of hers. She was the one who told people I was "like a daughter" to her. Of course, her daughters never worked in the garden or kitchen. Her daughters never scrubbed the floors. Her daughters lived with rich aunts in London, not in a small corner off the kitchen. Of course, it was also true that I never wanted more or different than what I had. I preferred the garden to the drawing room, the livestock to the ladies, my compact room to a canopied bed.

Unfortunately, everything that was simple and neutral between Mrs. G and me changed in one day, one moment. I knew she was getting sicker in her mind, but I never expected her to go so far. It never occurred to me that her hatred of this place, this island her husband had brought her to, would cause her to do the worst thing she could to the man who was responsible for her fate. Like most women, of her class anyway, she had little or no power over her own life. She couldn't even find a way to have power over her own house, because she was a bad manager, with no sense or skills. She chewed on this grievance and whatever others she concocted. Then she found a spiteful, hateful way to act out, to show off some of her white-woman power.

I could hardly blame Sam, Sarah's sweetheart. He was a field hand, no more, no less. He was good with horses, good with mending tack, too, so he sometimes worked in the barn. That's where I found them. It was during that quiet hour when the morning chores are done, lunch is put away, the kitchen cleaned, and the preparations for dinner have not yet started. I went down to the barn because there was a new litter of kittens there and I liked playing with them, their fur so soft, their mouths warm and sticky with mother's milk. I stepped from the bright day into the dark cavern of the barn and stopped to let my eyes adjust. I stood there listening for the kittens' mewling. Instead, I heard groans from a pile of straw. I saw a broad, dark back moving rhythmically and started to turn away, wanting to give Sam and Sarah privacy, understanding there were few enough places where they could find it. But then there was the flash of bright white in front of my eyes, the scalloped and lace hem of a fine dress a shocking contrast to the dirt floor. I froze in place. I watched in horror as a pale arm was suddenly thrust over that black, muscular back and a familiar face appeared over his shoulder, brushing the loosened hair off her brow. Her eyes, shut in her evil ecstasy, slowly opened and met mine. The shock in them was perhaps equal to the shock in mine. No, hers must have been worse, for I was doing no wrong. I stood there only a moment more, just long enough to see her passion turn cold, and then I left.

From then on, whatever politeness she suffered toward me changed to raw terror. Which she was forced to suppress. Sam must never have known what I saw, and she must not have told him, because he never changed in his dealings with me. But she did. She glared daggers at me, her eyes danced in suspicion toward me, she avoided me. And yet she did not stop. I would see her slipping out from the barn, pinning her hair back in place. I saw Sam slip from the doors that led into back corridors of the house. In fact, she grew more reckless in her hunger for him, and he grew bold in whatever power he felt her taste for him conferred. I held my breath and waited for her to get caught, for Sam to get sent away. Or worse, for him to be accused of some crazy charge as an excuse to beat or jail him. Or kill him.

Instead, he and Sarah also became more bold with their affair. Perhaps he truly loved her, or perhaps he was using her for cover in his escapades with Mrs. G. Maybe he wanted Mrs. G to be jealous, and in that, have even more control over her. Maybe he was hoping for money. In any case, Sarah started singing while she worked, and Sam started hanging around the kitchen door. There was talk of them getting married and moving into a house of their own. Mr. G joked about the romance between Sam and Sarah once to his wife, but he was so busy with some paperwork that he didn't see the clouds his teasing brought to her face. By then the Georges had pretty much stopped paying any attention to each other, in any case. Mrs. G started keeping to her room and got a scowl on her face, a bitter darkness in her eyes that was terrifying to see. She also abused everyone she could with unreasonable demands and coarse insults. The Georges had already started entertaining less and less, but on the rare occasion when they had company, she got dolled up to an extreme and insisted on Sam waiting at the table, a job he was unsuited for. I saw her upset a cauldron of hot soup he was serving so it spilled all over his groin and legs. She tried to make it look an accident, like it was his own clumsiness, but I was watching. I saw what she did. And she saw me seeing.

Still, I never figured her for such violence. Of course, I never figured on any of the evil that woman did. I wasn't there to see what started her off, specifically, but we all noticed that Sarah had started to show, was even exaggerating her pregnancy walk, so full of herself for being full of Sam was she. It was the screams that got me coming. At first I thought it was some animal, a cow caught in a fence, a horse being gelded, a pig slaughtered. Then I realized there was a human voice inside all that noise. I ran toward the sound and saw Mrs. G's back bent over, her hand flying up over her head and then down again onto a broken pile of black skin, red blood, and a torn dress at her feet. Sarah's eyes were rolling as Mrs. G beat her with a piece of cane, not just raining blows down on the girl's head and shoulders, but thrusting the cane up between her legs over and over again. Sarah tried to crawl away, but Mrs. G, with some sort of strength fueled with rage and jealousy and a lifetime of accumulated disappointment, kept grabbing an arm or a leg and pulling that poor girl back.

I was shorter and smaller than Mrs. G. But where she had only anger and bitterness coursing through limbs that wealth had made weak, I had the fortitude that came from years of work in the house and yard and among the animals. I did not think. I did not choose. I simply moved. I wrapped my arms around her entire body in an embrace she could not escape and yanked her backward. We both fell into the dirt, her locked into my lap. Shocked into stillness, she let me rip the piece of cane from her hands, and I shoved her onto the ground next to the girl she had torn apart. Then I knelt down next to her and I hissed into her ear that if she did not stop now, if she did not stop forever, if she ever raised a hand to Sarah or Vea or any animal or anyone, ever again, I would tell. I said it over and over. *I will tell. I will tell. I will tell. I will ruin you because I will tell.* Now it was her turn to crawl through the dust of the yard in shame and fear. Finally she lifted herself and, totally defeated, walked away, her fury spent and replaced by loss and emptiness. Along with the impotency of wanting what you can never have, can never even admit you want: a different man, a different life, with no way to get either.

After that, Sarah kept to her room for a few weeks to heal and Sam went away for good. He went of his own accord, at least, or that's how it seemed, without trouble or a stain on his name. Told Mr. G he had a better offer. Mr. G never knew the truth and did not seem to care whether Sam came or went. There were other Sams. That's the way he saw it, I think. Vea patched Sarah up as only Vea could. There would be no scars—at least none to see. The girl bled for a few days and her belly went back to flat. Mrs. G went to her room and her real sicknesses started. The house grew quieter, social life dried up to nothing, the rantings, ravings, and beatings stopped.

Vea told me that when Sarah was in bed those days, feverish and scared, she told her she'd heard me curse Mrs. G. I don't think that poor, dumb, lovestruck girl ever knew that Sam was two-timing her with the lady of the house. When Sarah got better, she was even more convinced of the power of my curses. She was sure it was my doing that made Mrs. G so sick. She said she watched the way my mouth moved against the woman's ear and swore it was obeah. This was not something Sarah was thankful for—obeah was strong and scary magic to her, and gave me a power, so she thought, that was worse than a hundred lashes with a piece of cane.

Mrs. G had a cruel heart, that is for certain, as well as debased proclivities, and while I would not wish her sufferings on anyone, she did bring them upon herself. It was not me. I might have cursed her if I knew how, having seen her abuse Sarah and Vea and every other woman who was in her employ. But not like that, not that kind of drawn-out, ugly agony. Besides, curses are beyond my powers. Vea and I let Sarah and others believe what they wanted because it served us both to have people be frightened of me. It made them leave me alone, and Vea knew how much that meant to me. She also knew better, of course. She knew obeah had nothing to do with Mrs. G's illness. Vea saw all and knew everything that happened in that house, on that plantation, and even much farther afield. One day she told me that she had had a visit from her people on the other side of the island, where Sam had gone to live. He was sick, too. Same sickness, she said, as Mrs. G. Lucky, Sarah is, she said, that she got away with just a beating. She didn't mention that baby she lost. But we both knew that was a lucky thing as well.

MRS. GEORGE

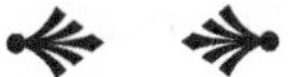

I MADE THEM TAKE AWAY ALL THE MIRRORS. I COULDN'T STAND the sight of my own face. All I see all day are black faces. Working in the yard, chopping vegetables in the kitchen, walking in the streets, talking to my husband, bringing me my meals, wiping away the dust. The dust. It is everywhere. Like them. Black skin and pale dust everywhere I look. Then I pass a mirror in the hall or come into my own room and am shocked by the white moon that stares back at me from the glass. I don't recognize it. I can't stand it. I don't know who that person in the mirror is. I don't know who I am anymore.

I loved my husband. It was not necessary, nor was it expected. In fact, it was viewed as almost unseemly. This was an arrangement. Our marriage, our union, being bound together in law and under God and as a part of the society we kept was no more than another business transaction in the long line of them between him and my father. My father invested in his plantation with cash infusions. And then with his daughter. With me. He traded me.

I was to look pretty, create social settings that were useful to his business pursuits, and provide sons. In exchange, I would be cared for. I would have a house to tend, staff to manage. In a location I was told was beautiful and exotic with abundant sunshine and stunning scenery. Some of this was true. Some of this came to pass. I was pretty and tried to stay that way. I arranged parties. I had children. This island is something to behold. He does keep a roof attached to a large and well-appointed home over my head. However, the island has many shadows as well as sunshine. He cared for me, but only from a distance. I had girls, but no sons.

I did love him. I think he even loved me. At first. For a while. I remember what that felt like, that loving him. Now, in the mornings, I lie in bed and try to remember. Who I was. What life used to be like. I was a girl. I was pretty. I was happy. Now I am a woman. An old woman. Well, a not quite old woman. Not yet. I was pretty for a long time, deep into my womanhood. Some cannot say that, but I can. I don't know what I look like anymore. I made them take away all the mirrors.

I lie here, safe behind the curtains of my canopied bed, full of dread. I do not want to leave this close space, so I lie here and remember. My whole life, I did what I was told to do. My days were, for so many years, completely structured. I went to the parties I was supposed to and talked to the people my mother said I should. I learned to embroider, to speak French, to read poetry. I had my hair pinned up, my jewelry assembled, and my body dressed by my maids. My plate was filled by hands attached to silent servants with food cooked in rooms I never entered. I learned to make a guest list, that rugs and beds were to be aired out twice a year, the proper placement of forks and knives. That I should stay out of the sun and never question my husband.

I did not learn how to speak patois or read the expression of a black face. I did not learn what to do when my husband stopped coming to my bedroom. I did not know what to do when my heart began to pound in my chest like a cleaver against meat on the cutting board and my thoughts began to run to and fro like sheep in front of an untrained dog. My life rarely required much thought. But that did not stop my thoughts. Even though I have done and still do so little during my long, empty days, my mind never quieted with stillness and disuse. Instead the thoughts just piled up and piled up and piled up, and I have never figured out how to arrange them or let them out to run free.

I try to remember. Because I think if I remember who I was, I might be able to be that person again. A happy, simple, contented person. A person excited about what tomorrow might bring. A person who believed there would always be a thick rug underfoot, a soft cushion behind the head, a full pantry off the kitchen, a checkbook forever filled with funds. A man always nearby, either a father or a brother or a husband, who would look upon me with kindness and concern.

I was told to marry him. Loving him was not a part of the transaction. But love him I did. Or so it seems to me now. I had feelings for him and I called them love. Because my parents respected him and women admired him. Because he had the manners of a gentleman, but the experience of an adventurer. His face was already creased from the sun and wind. From direct connection with the world. My face was unlined, my skin kept smooth and moist with passivity and emollients. I was so young. A teenager still. Naive. Innocent. I knew nothing. I cared for nothing. My excitements revolved around a new hair ribbon, a piece of lace to adorn a dress, a litter of puppies. A piece of gossip that would increase my social standing at the expense of someone else's. This was all I was allowed. Trifles. Absurdities. I was so stupid. So exceedingly stupid. Dumb enough to think that what I wanted was experiences! Adventures! I had never had any of either, so how could I think I wanted them? I had no understanding of what I was asking for. No concept about the price one pays for such things. I had no way to know that such things would ruin me.

My husband has always had so many occupations. He has his broad fields to stride through, his many staff asking him for guidance and direction all day long, his meetings with lawyers and accountants, the animals to harness and care for, his ledger books to pore over in the evenings with a cigar and glass of scotch. What do I have? Another party to plan? The businessmen's wives bore me to tears. Go to a polo game? How many polo matches can one woman watch? How much garrison gossip can one person listen to? Write letters to my daughters? They have turned out to be superficial and dull, fretting over the women wearing dresses that show off their ankles and whether they should follow the trend and bob their hair. Of course, we trained them to be dull, we raised them to be superficial. We can expect no more of them. I wish I had the luxury of dullness—like I once did, those many years ago—but my insides churn with desire for I know not what. I used to take long walks through the benign countryside at home. But here? I don't dare. The outdoors has been ruined for me by the presence of snakes, spiders, centipedes. Even the frogs are full of poisons. Everything is so beautiful, so colorful. Yet so terrifyingly dangerous. These dangers. I have brought them inside myself, so now they are within me. My hands tremble with the excesses of my anxiety. I used to do delicate watercolors and fine needlepoint. Now I could not hold a brush or a needle, even if I wanted to.

I have, for so many long years now, wanted something for myself. I have no idea what it is, but something. Something I have not been unable to create or conjure, something that is beyond my skills and resources. Something more. That is all I know. Something more. That has been as far as my atrophied imagination can take me.

The people who were supposed to be my friends merely attended our parties to soften up my husband for business deals. They cared no more for me than they did a lapdog. Something to pet politely and make a wee fuss over on the way in. I am sure the help mocked me because I have never properly known how to manage a menu.

I can't help it. There are so many unfamiliar ingredients. My husband. He seeks his pleasures with the maids and cooks. Perhaps he has always done so. But now he abuses them exclusively. I suppose I should be grateful. That I am relieved of him. I am grateful. We hardly speak. What can we have to say to each other anymore? I tell him the trivial news of his daughters. He nods without listening. He used to share his triumphs and frustrations. He spared me the details, thinking the feminine mind incapable of wrapping itself around the intricacies of business concerns. But he told me of himself, how he was within the context of his business. He does not even bother with the pretense of telling me anything, anymore. He passes more words with Vea about the qualities of her stew than he does with me about the quality of my life.

Vea is useful. He likes useful things.

Vea. How I hate her. Because I have always needed her. Everything that I could not do, everything that I was supposed to do but fumbled at, she did. I would make a marketing list. She would return with only half of what I asked for and many things I did not recognize. I would rail at her intransigence. She would keep her head down, wait me out, and then say, "Those things are not available." "Ma'am." Added that on. Of course. Adding the formality of insult to my injury. I would tell her the meal would be impossible. She would say nothing. I would storm away, cursing her. Then she would make the meal in spite of me, and my guests would heap compliments on my head. At my inventiveness. My skill and adaptability. I could say nothing. I could only nod and smile. And feel my hatred for them grow. Feel my rage at Vea and this place grow. Still, I smiled and nodded and went ahead and planned yet another party. Because it was the way things were done. Because we English always do things the way they have always been done.

Then there is that girl. She who has always hidden herself, behind a curtain or curled up in a corner. Once I found her sitting cross-legged under the table with a book. She is like some sort of a snake waiting to pounce on me. Her eyes are horrible. Gray and without expression, they seem to bear down on my very soul. I feel them always on me, even when she is not in the room. She is one of them, one of everybody else, the hordes of people who are against me, who defy and disrespect me. The help loves her; he admires her, defends her. She slinks around the house and pops up when I least expect it, startling me with her silent gray eyes. I don't know what they see in her. She has cast her spell on all of them. Spells. Another thing to be frightened of here. How can I live, how can I even walk and breathe, in a place where people cast spells on each other?

Ah, here it is. My wedding photo. I keep it in a drawer. So I can remember the person I used to be. Look at me! My gown was a beautiful shade of the softest dove gray—"gray, travel far away" went the rhyme. Look at the lovely lace at the hem, the neckline, the sleeves. A bustle was still in style then. Sleeves still followed the silhouette of the arm, before those absurd, oversized things began to adorn women's shoulders. My veil was made of lace my mother ordered from France. And there is my groom in his dark topcoat and doeskin trousers that match the shade of my dress. See the diamonds he gave me to wear around my neck. My skin was so pale the jewels were almost invisible against my throat. But how they sparkled in the candlelight. Now they look to me like nothing so much as huge teardrops foretelling my doom.

There was a long line of delicate buttons that followed my spine down the back of that dress. That night, our wedding night, he dismissed the maid and undid those buttons himself. At the release of each one, my trepidation and excitement grew; I wanted him, I wanted experiences, I wanted to be a woman, to be released from the confines of girldom. I was sure this was what marriage to him would give me. He began gently, slowly, deliciously. There were so many buttons. But his fingers were unaccustomed to delicate tasks.

He fumbled. Then he grew impatient. He became not just clumsy, but rough. This was who he was. A man who always began but did not stay long in patience. This is the way he loved me. Within an hour the dress was torn, the sheets were stained with blood, and he slept soundly beside me. And the panic that was to come to dominate my life began its distant trembling within my breast, a small spiderweb of terror being blown by a fitful breeze bringing bad weather.

Sam. Sam, Sam, Sam, Sam. He was so beautiful. He made me feel so beautiful. He made me feel. All that feeling again. It made me. It remade me. It ruined me.

They must blame Sam for my illness. But here is the truth: it was in me already. It may be that my husband got it first and then gave it to me. Picked it up from one of his liaisons. Although that is no doubt too kind a word, given as he has been to prodding his women where he finds them, with little more ceremony than a cur. If he had this horrible disease, he showed no outward signs of it. His body no doubt too hard and mean for even an illness to take hold.

I have not been intimate with him for more years than I can count, however, this sickness could have slept within me for all those same years. I was supposed to give him sons. But I miscarried son after son. Only the two girls grew inside of me and then came into the world whole, pink, screaming. Every time my husband came to me, and then a few weeks or months later, the bloody mess came to me, I lost a part of myself. And yet, every time my body rejected one of his sons, I felt a small victory against him, too. It was something. It was some miniature defiance. I was so angry at him. I had no place to put that anger, nothing I could do with it. My body found something to do with it. My body did what my will could not. My body defied him.

I told him enough, no more. The doctor told him the same. So he left me alone. There were plenty of other women around, and he was not particular about race or status or even looks.

Sadly, those small and bloody revenges were not enough for me. Every hole a lost son left in me was filled with an evil rage. One day I saw a mulatto child running around the plantation, a child that had echoes of my husband's features in his face. Then there was another. And another. All boys. I thought, I will give him a son. Yes, I will give him a son of my own. I will raise it not out in the shacks that lined the edges of our fields, but in our house. Our very own house. I will nurse it from my own breast. He shall have a son from me, one he will be forced to recognize. A son he cannot turn away from and a son that will shame him as he has shamed me.

I found a hand laboring in some isolated cane field and dragged him down into the dirt with me. I fornicated with a stable boy who innocently agreed to show me some polo ponies. I drove away one of my husband's best clerks, but not until he succumbed to my unrepentant and aggressive advances. I braved a back alley, me, who was otherwise so afraid of so much, and allowed a dishwasher to have his way with me against a sooty wall. A huge appetite for dark flesh rose and consumed me. Yet the baby I wanted never came. Not even Sam, with all his pulsating virility, could penetrate my scarred womb.

Then Sam made Sarah pregnant. When I discovered that she had accomplished so easily what all my sordid efforts could not, every bit of my acrimony and bitterness collected like so many dark clouds coalescing into a single, swirling tornado. I don't care what I did to her. She is no more than a low animal to me. She healed. She is fine. She is back to work. The world does not need her ugly little baby. Another black baby. The world is full of them.

I am paying for my sins. My body is revolting against everything I have done. Everything I am. I am dying. A disgusting death this one will be. An ugly death in a beautiful place. It seems exactly what I deserve.

This gray-eyed girl. In her silence, she is like a specter. In her touch, she is terrifyingly real. How do her hands know just how much pressure to apply when she mops at my sores with those damp cloths saturated with some vile-smelling brew Vea makes? I used to fight her. I would thrash when she came into my room. But the sores grew, the rash began to spread, my hair began to fall out, pustules began to grow beneath my skin, and she was the only one whose touch I could tolerate. Further punishment. That it would be her. The one my husband favored above all others, respected as he did no one else. So his regard for her can put his disregard for me in a sharper light.

Vea made my medicines, but I could not have her in my room. She frightened me. Her eyes were so full of all she had seen, all she knew. Everything collected in her eyes, like layers of leaves, season after season, piling up at the bottom of a still pond, making her eyes black with terrible knowledge and understanding. The girl's eyes were like water. Everything passed by her, passed around her. She saw it all, she took note of it all, but then it was all carried away. Nothing collected in those foggy pools. Nothing touched her or stuck to her. Not even my rages, my abuses, my sickness.

Day after day, week after week, month after month, I lie in bed. I stare out the window at that endlessly sunlit world that once seemed so full of promise and joy. It is now beyond my reach. It is no longer my concern. I do not wish to go out there anymore. I wish I were in a castle on a dank moor back in England. I wish I were locked away in a dark tower with only a rough, rude hag to care for me. Anything other than this girl, with her quiet forbearance. Anything other than those eyes that see me, wash over me, and take me down their hidden stream, caught as I am within their terrifying current.

RACHEL

I DON'T WHEN OR HOW OR WHY THINGS STARTED TO CHANGE WITH Henry and me. Actually, that's not true. I do know. He had asked me from time to time about my background. I told him there was no point in discussing the past. What's done is done and over and I didn't care to look backward. He thought I was hiding something. He thought I was being secretive. He began to be suspicious that I had darkness in my past. Which I suppose I did. I just didn't know why he should care, what knowing would do for him or me. He liked me as I was, so what difference did it make how I got to who I was? But somehow he found out. Or found the right questions to ask so he could get me to tell. Maybe I just got tired of not telling. Maybe I figured if he wanted to know so badly, then he deserved the repercussions that knowing might bring. There was not one conversation. There must have been many small talks, each giving him one more piece of my past. But they all blurred together in my mind and memory into a single confrontation that started us down the road of being a lot less peaceful, a lot less nice to each other. Which was the whole reason I didn't want to go backward to begin with.

"Why didn't you tell me?" he'd start in.

"Tell you what?" I'd say, pretending I didn't understand what he was getting at, hoping he'd quit.

"Why didn't you tell me that this woman was your mother?"

This woman. This woman. She is not "this woman." She is my mother. No matter what she did. You can criticize your own parents; others may not. These were my thoughts, not my words.

"Yes, this woman, as you call her, was my mother," I'd say.

I fear I rather spit the words out. He probably thought it was because of anger at her. But no, it was because of anger at him.

"But she abandoned you."

Well, yes. But no. It's not like my father had nothing to do with it. My mother didn't know the Georges to speak to, just as a couple who came to church. It was nothing she could have brought to pass on her own.

"My father," I said, putting emphasis on the word. "*He* put me in what he thought was a safe place. A place where I could grow up as a lady. Instead of an outcast. She, they both, I guess, wanted to give me something. A place to be."

"And that didn't happen," Henry said.

He had a way of stating the obvious. As if I could not see it for myself.

"No. That did not happen," I replied. "Other things happened. Not the becoming the lady part."

I was afraid to say more. I did not want to be angry. He would misinterpret my emotion.

"Why? Why did this not happen?" He badgered me. "Why were you raised in this in-between, this vague sort of way, where your place was so uncertain, so ill defined?"

I could not understand why he had begun to care about this sort of thing. He knew the woman I was. What did it matter how I became that woman? Because he cared about this sort of thing, he assumed I did as well. Which, of course, I did not. He knew I did not, but could not understand it. So he chose not to believe it. He thought I only pretended not to care. He chose not to see me as I saw myself. As I truly was.

"You'd have to ask Mr. George about why I was raised the way I was," I said. "I don't hold any grudge against him. He did fine by me. He didn't have to take me in at all. But he did. He took care of me. In his own way."

"What about Mrs. George? Why did she not care for you better? Why did she accept you, but then hold you at a distance?"

There was no way for me to begin to explain the varieties and intensity and reasons for her dislike of me. There was no way I would betray her secrets. There was no point. There was nothing to be gained.

"She was not fond of me," I said. That was enough of an explanation. And then for good measure, "She was sick, always sick."

"I thought you were his daughter."

The obvious, the unimaginative answer.

"Many people thought that," I said. "I didn't see any need to correct that notion. Neither did the Georges, I guess."

"But your mother was a slave."

"No, she was a freedwoman."

I chewed the inside of my cheek to get rid of some of my anger. Told myself to be steady. Told myself to not let this questioning and everything it might mean get to me.

"You know as well as I that slavery was abolished on this island before she was even born," I reminded him.

That's what I said. But what I thought was that there were many ways to be enslaved when you are a woman. The wrong parents, the wrong husband, too little money, too many children, too much bad luck, too much evil gossip.

"Rachel, I am as open-minded as it is possible to be," he said, "but I must ask: Was she black?"

I almost asked what the two things, being open-minded and being black, had to do with one another, but I didn't. I didn't want his answer. It would just be one more thing for me to add to the things I was starting to dislike about him.

"These lines are not always so clear. As you know," I said.

"In other words, you do not know how much Negro blood she had?"

In other words, I do not care. This I said only to myself. I was trying to regain my silence, my quiet. I did not need this conversation. In truth, I did not need this man. I would have been fine without him. I would have found my way. I gave him a different answer, an answer to a question he had not asked.

"This is why I did not want to marry you," I said.

"What? Not marry me for this?" He sputtered. I saw the drops of spittle gather on his mustache. The sunlight touched them. He was not done yet. "But it is I who am trying to lift you and the children, to give you a good life, a good name, a decent life, to give you respectability. And you act as if marrying me was an act of goodwill on your part?"

He was mad now. So was I. I was mad at him, but I was even more mad at the absurd notion of "respectability." This is not England, I wanted to say. You are not even truly English, I wanted to remind him. You were born here, you were raised here. Your father came here with nothing but a few shillings in his pocket. For all your accents and airs, you are native, you are local. The rest you picked up at school, like some kind of cloak, some garment that is fine looking but has no weight, cannot keep you warm. Your precious England and your precious English. Those island ways have no place on this island. That island is gray and damp and dark and old. Our island is always new, everything growing and dying and blooming and raining and starting over again. Your island: potatoes and beer. Ours: mangoes, hibiscus, sugarcane. Why would anyone want to make over our land like yours? Women here have no need of this stupid thing you so admire, this respectability. They can grow vegetables, raise chickens, and fish for what they need. They can raise their children in a small house with a galvanized roof. They can make a little money bringing in some sewing, doing some cooking, working on a plantation as they need. Like Vea. Raising her little boy by herself. Happy and peaceful and no one telling her the way things should or are supposed to be. Respectability. What do I need that for? And if I did, it's not something you, with your chipped china and your worn shirts, could get for me.

I didn't say any of this. It just rattled around my head like nails in a coffee can. It got so I could almost never stop this noise, these things I wanted to say but could not.

What I said, trying to make my voice come out even and calm, was this: "I knew you'd care, I knew it would matter to you. Being married to a woman like me, a woman who came from what I came from. To me it did not matter. It does not matter."

"What of the children?"

"What of them?"

"You would have raised them on your own?"

"Yes."

"How?"

"Many women do this," I said.

I did not say that many women have men, have children, have work, and keep all the three things separate in their lives. They keep their children, keep their independence, keep their own money. I did not mention money, money being always such a sore subject for him.

"Black women, Creole women, mulatto women do this," he said.

I sighed big just then and said, "Which, as you have just pointed out, I am."

I perhaps should not have said this, in quite this way. He was always sensitive to contradiction or the inkling that he was being teased or fooled with.

"Yes, I know! I know that now," he said, his voice getting louder. "I did not know this before. I thought you were Mr. George's illegitimate daughter."

You are suggesting that was somehow better, I thought, to be a daughter of, what, a prostitute and a gentleman, than what I was, which was the daughter of two people who were completely mismatched according to so-called polite society, but who at least loved one another? Which they did. If I had had any experience of love in my life, it was through the gentle touches and warm glances I saw pass between them. But I did not say any of this. What I did say was much worse. For him anyway.

What slipped out was this: "No, I am not Mr. George's illegitimate daughter. That honor belongs to Margaret."

That bit of news, and I suppose everything else, all the other assumptions he now had to rearrange, the realities he had to make room for, well, that made him real quiet real fast. Maybe he knew it already. Knew it in his heart if not in his head. Maybe he was just sick of talking. But he shut up. He left me alone, then. It was not what I expected, but I was relieved to have it. The quiet, that is.

I had just sat down. The morning sun was high, beginning to beat on the flat, broad green leaves all around me, but it was not yet midday, and there was a patch of shade in the yard where I sometimes pulled a chair to rest after the early hours of getting the children fed, the kitchen cleaned, the cutlery and crockery put away, and made plans for the rest of the day and the evening meal. I was wondering whether I should walk into town today or tomorrow for marketing. Whether I should do laundry this afternoon or wait a few days. Whether there was enough bread for the week or if I needed to do some more baking. If Tom's shoes would last a few more months, if Percy could get a few more wearings out of James's hand-me-downs, if the tear Eddie got in his shirt could be mended or if it needed to be turned into rags, if Margaret would ever take to wearing proper girl's clothing. If Henry had any patients this week.

The chickens scratched and clucked, fluffing their feathers and beating their wings. I envied them the simplicity of their lives.

Sometimes I got so tired—tired of the chores that kept coming and the money that didn't—that I wished I could just sit in that spot for days on end. Sometimes, it's true, I did sit for a few days. In that chair, on the veranda, in bed. Henry called them my spells. Well, they were no such thing. I was just resting. I suppose part of me was also testing. Him, that is. To see what he would do, what might get done in my absence. Sometimes he called Vea over. She'd put things to rights. She never bothered me, knowing me as well as she did, knowing what life was like. Mostly, he and the children just waited me out. Let things pile up. So when I did rouse myself, there was twice as much to do. But still, the shutting things out for a few days always helped me. It always settled something down inside me that was threatening to boil over, to spill out of me.

I watched the chickens, looked at the garden and tried to ignore the weeds for the moment. I thought about the sewing I had in my basket and how much money it might bring in and then what percentage I could put aside and what percentage I could use to buy more fabric. I thought about all the things the children needed. They were growing so fast. So fast that they were outgrowing instead of wearing out their shoes and clothes. Henry's dentistry brought in barely enough to keep us in coffee and fish stew. He could do more, but he resisted. He needed time, he said, to work on his engine, his fly machine. Those things, he insisted, were the most important because those things could make us rich one day and dentistry never would. Dentistry was just to pay the bills. Which it barely did. Anything extra he used to buy piles of twisted metal that he promised would one day sprout wings and fly away, only to bring us back bushels of money. Yet everything remained firmly grounded in the dirt.

I tried to stop contemplating these things. I took a deep, fragrant breath. I pulled my skirts up over my knees as I sometimes did when no one was around, and let my bare legs stretch out past my patch of shade into the sunshine.

I do not recall where the children were that day. Sometimes Henry took them all to work with him, letting them play with his tools and entertain his patients as they waited. The children's antics took the patients' minds off the impending pain. It was a treat for the children. And also for me. He knew how I craved peace and quiet and a few moments of uninterrupted thought. He also did it in the hopes that my demeanor would be more soft and willing at the end of the day when he returned. That some gentler version of me, some phantom, brighter self that he fancied was hiding within the shadows of my darker self would peer out, wave at him, invite him over for a quiet moment of tenderness. I tried. I did try to find that girl, the one he imagined me to be. Sometimes I could coax a smile to cross my face, a gentle caress to come from my hand. But this was not a natural yet repressed state for me, as he hoped. I was not a demonstrative person. His explanations for my reserve, that my heart had been hardened by my life and was wanting only his sympathies to return to an earlier state of softness, were, I fear, untrue. My constitution was not that of a willow, yielding to the breezes. Mine was of a harder wood, of sterner stuff. I did not become hard because of my experiences. I was born hard, and that is why the bad things that life had thrown at me did not leave dents in my soul. I was no more harmed by the events of my life than I was softened by the entreaties of my husband. I simply was who I was, and I was without any ability to pretend otherwise. It seemed to me that I was born with my personality fully formed and my experiences of life served only to reinforce my basic nature.

But I did enjoy those days when he took the children along with him. When the day stretched out in front of me without the constant interruption and noise and clamor of the boys tumbling through our small house and yard. I did appreciate Henry and his gentler, more natural, and indulgent love for the children. I did not love him the way he wanted, but I loved him in my way, in the ways that I could. And I kept loving him even when it became clear that my kind of love was unrecognizable to him.

The soft smack of footfalls on the dirt path to the house interrupted my reveries. I knew immediately who it was. That Sarah. She always did walk heavy and sloppy. It was only a mild surprise to see her. She did not come often, but she did come. Not of her own accord, but at Mr. G's behest. She would bring something special from his much-larger garden, some sticks of sugarcane from the plantation for the children, sometimes a pie if she had baked more than was necessary, sometimes an extra cut of meat. There were fewer and fewer guests there as Mr. George grew older and more frail, but he kept the house going—well, Vea did—and she often continued to cook and prep as if it were the old days when there were lots of ladies and gentlemen coming and going. She was always trying to fatten him up, which never worked. I am sure Vea also had a hand in making too much so there would be extra for us. Sometimes, in the basket, at the bottom, underneath the cloth, there would be a few bills, enough for a couple of pairs of new children's shoes. I could see Mr. George handing these to Vea with a nod, no words of explanation necessary.

"Miss Rachel?"

She called to me from the side yard.

"Over here, Sarah."

I was in no mood to get up. There was no need. She would have already stepped into the kitchen and deposited her basket there. Sometimes I didn't see her at all—she just dropped off what she had and slunk back from where she came. She had no use for me, was scared of me still. On this day, I expected she was looking for me to give me a message from Vea. How many new shirts she thought she could sell next month. But when she came around the corner, there was something different about her. Her eyes would not meet mine—this was not unusual—and her face was streaked with dark lines made by tears running rivulets through the street dust that had accumulated there.

"Sarah?"

She scuffed her feet in the dust, wiped her cheeks with the back of her hand, smudging tears and dirt together.

"What is it, Sarah?"

"It is Mr. George."

That name still had the power to make my insides tighten and turn. My feelings toward him were such a mix of things. He had given me some sort of a home, a life, a set of skills useful to a woman. He gave me just enough of these things, but just enough was an awful lot, compared to what I might have had. He gave me also a kind of love. At first it was just a kind of cool regard and respect, a touch of gentle affection from time to time. Then it did turn into that subverted thing that never should have taken place, but that did result in Margaret, which then turned him back to the man he had been to me. Someone capable of giving me some kind of small love that asked for little in return, which, truthfully, suited me better than most other kinds of love I had seen.

"Yes, Sarah, what of Mr. George? Is something wrong with Mr. George?"

Saying his name myself calmed the jumpiness in my stomach. But it was replaced with dread. I knew the answer to my question. It was all over her face.

"He wants to see you. He ask me to come get you."

"Now, Sarah? He wants to see me now?"

Mr. George had never asked for me before. From the day he caught me vomiting in the backyard and ascertained the father of the child growing in my belly, the child that became James, from the day that Margaret and I went away with Henry, he had not asked for me. So when I said "now" I did not mean now, as in this instant. I meant now as in why not ever before. All this was not meant for, was lost on, Sarah. She knew nothing of our history. All Sarah meant was now, as in this instant.

"Yes, now, Miss Rachel," she said. "Mr. George quite poorly."

The tears started down her face anew. Until that moment, I had not had any desire to see him. I rarely thought of him, except for those few passing instances when I saw traces of him in Margaret's face. I am not proud to say this, but when I saw him in her, I turned away. It would take a few moments, a few breaths, to calm myself. Then I would turn back to her and try to make up for my lapse with some attention or affection. Now, hearing he was ill, my body rose of its own avail, my skirts fell back down around my legs, and suddenly I was moving off down the road. Sarah's noisy step jogged a few feet behind me. I don't know what I expected to find, what I wanted or feared to find. We trotted on together and I tried to clear my head of everything other than listening to the rhythm of our footfalls counting down the distance between my small cottage and his expansive home, between my life as it was now, and what it had been then. I didn't know then that covering this distance between our houses would also take me into a completely different future. Sarah and I were silent on our journey. She led me through the back door, past the large, wooden table, stained and worn with years of chopping vegetables and meats in preparation for cooking. We moved down the familiar hall. Sarah stopped in front of the door that led to what had once been my room. I looked at her in question.

"He too weak to go upstairs no more," she said. "Nice breeze blows in here. He has fevers all the time now. Breeze gives him some comfort."

That was true, about the breezes. I remembered seeking refuge here on hot afternoons. Before those few times when my rest was interrupted by his visits, and my afternoon hours became tainted with memories that confused me with the conflict between my own desires for the warmth of bodily contact and my disgust with what I had to tolerate for a little touch of humanity. Sarah opened the door. I thought at first there was a sick child resting in my bed—he was that much diminished—and my misunderstanding softened the wide variety of my shocks. He had been in this bed before, of course, but as a different man, a man still strong even if somewhat broken. His eyelids fluttered open. The color of his eyes seemed to have been washed away by some strong soap, but he finally rested them on me, focused, and a shadow within him seemed to dissipate. He pushed himself up on his elbows. Sarah came around me, through the door, and helped him to sit upright, arranging the pillows behind him. He thanked her, squeezed her hand in a gesture that was unusually tender and appreciative for him, and then asked her to leave us alone. The sickness had softened him, I could see that. Softened his soul in all the right ways, even as it stripped his body of its strength. He gestured to a chair at the foot of the bed. I sat. He regarded me for a few moments, his face blank with assessment.

"Rachel," was all he said at first. A statement that was somehow full of thanks for my being there, for my having come.

I waited. Then he sighed. His voice when it came was stronger than I had expected given the condition of his body.

"I will not insult you with pleasantries or small talk," he said. He was always one for directness. "I know Henry barely keeps you and the children, but you make the most of what is in front of you." He coughed. "As you always have," he added, after catching his breath.

I dipped my chin in acknowledgment.

"Well, as you can see for yourself, I am dying," he went on.

I did see that, but hearing it so plainly stated still put a rock right in the middle of my throat.

"I am sorry to bring you here." He paused. "Especially here," he said, his eyes glancing around the room. "But for so many reasons, I obviously could not come to you."

There was no need for me to respond to that, knowing as I did that he knew he was perfectly understood. I kept quiet and waited for him to go on.

"I would like to do something for you," he said. He waited for this information to sink in. "As you must understand, I cannot make an open bequest. I am not afraid of whatever scandal it would bring on me, as I will be nothing but dust. I am not afraid of what my daughters may think, because they are spoiled and ungrateful, and thankfully are running up their husbands' accounts instead of mine. I cannot make an open bequest because I am afraid for the scandal it would bring on you. I am also afraid of Henry. Because he is now your lawful husband, anything that comes to you will rightfully belong to him. And I don't want him spending—nay, wasting—my money on his absurd inventions. But I would like to help you, and only you. I would like to set you up in some way, give you some independence, some security of your own."

That was a lot of talking and explaining for a sick man. Especially a sick man trying to make some kind of atonement, some kind of accounting. He closed his eyes for several moments and his breath wheezed in his chest. While we sat in the silence, my mind raced down paths that were both new and familiar. My thoughts took me places I must have already traveled in my few idle moments, finding fantasies I did not realize I must have entertained in my dreams.

He opened his eyes, coughed into a napkin, and said, "Is there something you would like to do? Something you have considered before? What can I do to give you some ease in life? I know how little you have had so far."

"Get me out of here."

The words surprised me as they came out of my mouth. They surprised Mr. George as well. I could tell by how startled he was that he had mistook my meaning. He began to motion toward the door, as if to call Sarah back.

"No, no," I quickly added. "Not here. Not this room. I don't want to get out of here. That's not what I meant."

I swallowed. What did I mean? This suddenly fervent desire had not been fully known to me, not even partially realized, until this moment. I struggled to understand the feelings his offer was releasing within me. I was so unused to wanting something. And now my wanting and the means were standing bold and bright in front of me. I was almost afraid to speak. As if stating it would make it real and also disappear all at once.

"I want to get off this island," I said, the words a hiss through clenched teeth. "I want, I want..." It seemed I had never spoken a want out loud. "I want to start somewhere new. I want to get away from this..." I gestured with an open hand. "All of this."

The oppressive heat, the oppressive gossip, the weight of my past. Henry's disappointment in me. The confines of our home. The dust. I saw it all disappearing behind me as I put a huge sea between what had been and what could be. Even the things I had favored about this place—the broad blue skies, the dark-green hills, the ever-present sunshine—it all flipped and sank within me, like a person exhausted from trying to stay afloat and giving in to drowning. As I asked, I knew I would not be getting what Mr. George wanted for me: ease. But ease was not what I wanted. A fresh start, that was it. A cliché—the biggest cliché possible—and yet, exactly and only and profoundly what I wanted.

"Please," I said, shaking a bit as I tried to control my voice. "What I want is passage away from here for me and the children. I want to go away. I want to go to America, to New York. I want to start anew."

Mr. George nodded. His eyes closed. He understood, completely. Of that, I was sure. And so it was done. Tickets were purchased and delivered to me. A cart arrived and exchanged our possessions for a few of the bills in the wallet full of American dollars that had been delivered to me along with the tickets. We didn't have much, but it would get us started in the new world, our new life. The children and I were taken away to the boat. Except for James, of course. That was by his request. I knew by leaving him people would say I betrayed him. It is one thing to betray a husband, quite another to betray a child. No one but he and I needed to know that it was he who betrayed me. I didn't choose the other children over him. He chose his father over me. Or perhaps himself over both of us. The knowledge of this, the secret of what he had done, of his manipulations, were to be my burden, and I bore it readily. I had long experience of bearing other people's secrets.

Mr. George didn't die. Not then, anyway. He recovered and regained his health. For a few years. I imagine that Henry suspected he had helped us. They were never friends after I left the George house. Perhaps they were not even friends before this. I imagine it could be construed that I left one man for the other. Even though romantic love was not involved, it was a betrayal of a sort, nonetheless. I imagine the knowledge of George's complicity gnawed at Henry. Maybe he felt Mr. George was getting back at him. As if this was something Mr. George did to him instead of for me. I guess it gave him an excuse to not consider what part he'd played in my leaving him. That's what I'd seen men do—their feelings, feelings they were unused to, got involved at times like this and they laid the blame on causes that made them feel more important than they really were. Easier than just hurting, I suppose. Men don't know how to hurt, having less experience of it than women do.

I don't remember much of the boat ride. I was so focused on where we were going I didn't spend any energy on the how of it. Just held my breath with wanting to get there. I recall being stuck in the stinking bowels of the ship, crammed up close with so many other people. Mr. George had wanted us to travel in a different class, but I insisted on the cheapest tickets. I knew I'd need money to get set up in New York and wanted whatever he was willing to give to go for that instead of for our passage. Which was of short duration, compared to the new life ahead of us. I knew we could manage it. The boys, of course, did not care at all, they were just full of excitement at everything new and different. They were always off exploring every place they were not supposed to be while Margaret and I stayed below with our hands clasped over our heaving stomachs. By the time we got to New York—I can't even recall how many days later, as they all run together in a blur—my clothes hung loose from my much-diminished frame. I think I ate no more than a few pieces of bread and sucked on some citrus I had brought with us.

Margaret tried to keep me down, belowdecks, always. A little girl still, yet somehow so serious, so much always the older sister, the fretful babysitter, even with me. She thought staying below would be better for our nausea. But she also was terrified of us being seen taking liberties, mixing with the upper classes. She was like me in her quiet and pensive nature, but she was more austere than I. She had more fears than I did. She actually said that we were not allowed up there. I don't know where she heard these things and, even if she did, why she cared. My children—how did they get to be so stubbornly conventional, so frozen into the forms of things? Well, she and James, at least. I suppose it is common enough among those with a haphazard upbringing to search for a certain kind of stability, the stability that sticking to rules others set forth for you confers. Or appears to confer. And even though that stability is just a house of cards ready to be blown down by one whispered meanness, one step outside the lines arbitrarily laid out and redrawn mindlessly for generations upon generations. Or perhaps they do know how fragile this supposed stability is and it is for this very reason that they cling to the edifice of convention in the hope of some kind of reward beyond the stiff walls of its own construction.

I did as Margaret wished during the day. She clung to my skirts and cried so pathetically, I had no choice. I did not want to leave her alone in that cramped space with so many men around, in any case. It was not safe. The boys were nowhere to be found. I had no friends there. But at night, surrounded by the chorus of snores, when I saw her tucked in between her brothers, who were finally exhausted from their adventures and escapades, then I would slip away and creep up one dark flight of stairs after another, sniffing at the scent of salt water strengthening with every step, until finally my face was fully met by a blast of sea air. Once out on deck, I looked out into nothingness, the black sky meeting the dark sea at some place in the distance indiscernible to me, the one above dusted with a scattering of stars, the other below flecked with the crests of an uncountable number of small waves. The breeze soothed my stomach and braced my constitution. I was weightless and alone in the cold and quiet emptiness of the night. I didn't recognize it at the time, the feeling being one wholly unfamiliar to me, but now I know: in those moments of solitude, where no one knew me or where I was, when I had nowhere I had to be, nowhere to go, and nothing I had to do, I was, quite simply, happy.

New York was a spectacle to see, the buildings rising up to impossible heights, the people shoving and pushing, living under each other's feet. I knew I was taking on a task that would stretch me to the edges of my abilities, my tolerances. That I was ready for; that I anticipated. What I was unprepared for was how hard everything was. Hard underfoot, hard under hand, painful to breathe, difficult to accomplish. The faces were hard, too. So much effort spent trying not to notice the dirt, the concrete, to not make eye contact with the constant sea of humanity that was pounding over and around you. The island was all soft. The dusty roads that cushioned every footfall. The fullness of the local women's figures. The greenery that parted at your touch and then took you in a moist embrace. Here, everything was in shades of gray and charcoal, there, all the bright colors of flowers and fabric.

The children didn't seem to notice. Or care. For them, the street was the same as a yard. They played with jacks and marbles instead of chickens and lizards. They were happy to have surfaces to bounce their balls against. They were happy to have so many other children close by. They came home covered in soot instead of dust. Sometimes with torn clothing, bloody noses, and black eyes, as well. That was new, but I knew not whether to blame that on them, their age, or this place. Maybe it would have been the same if we had stayed. I more than once found cigarette stubs in their pockets. Yes, they were too young to be smoking. But my chides meant nothing to them. They were boys. They learned, from a young age, to turn off the sound of women's voices.

Margaret always tried. She fussed over them like an animal mother, preening them one moment, cuffing them the next. They tolerated her more than they tolerated me. Although I think they loved her a little less, poor girl. She got no reward for her ministrations. I never knew what sustained her in her efforts. She fussed over whatever tiny apartment we were in at the moment, as well. She managed to create order from our meager possessions. Few as they are, they were still always too much to fit in. No wonder the boys stayed out in the streets. We never had the space to contain their energies. Sometimes Margaret even brought flowers. Pitiful things that she found thrown out by whatever florist might be within her walking range. They were wilted before she even got home. They were a poor excuse for the flowers we once had in abundance. She stuffed their limp stems in a jelly jar. And for some hours, we had a little color in our lives. Even when the petals dropped, they were lovely on the mean surface of our rough table.

Those letters were such a trial for me. I wanted the children to know their father; I wanted their father to know them. He would have been welcomed if he had come. Just because I had no use for him anymore does not mean I didn't recognize that the children did. I am sure I would have even gotten some pleasure from seeing him. If he could have, for even a moment, kept the disappointment and displeasure from his face when he looked at me. If he could have kept himself from nagging at me to be someone I was not and could never be. I asked them to write to him as much as I could. I tried to make it every Sunday night, but it was, truly, just whenever I could get the boys to sit still long enough to put themselves to the task. And whenever I could find something for them to write upon. It was never my intention to keep the letters. What good would they do me? I certainly never meant to hide them. I always told myself I'd get the stamps tomorrow. Or the next day. But then there was always something else that required that little bit of spare change. Then there they would be, cluttering up some corner of our always-tight accommodations, and I would put them in a drawer just to get them out of my way, out of my sight, and then another week would be gone by and the children, restless in those after-dinner hours of some Sunday night, would ask about writing to their father again, so I would drag out whatever scraps of paper I had that would do for stationery, and they would scribble their small news and words of love, and I would fold the pages neatly and set them aside, and there they would sit in their endless waiting for me to find something extra in my purse. Oh, from time to time I sent a few off. But never regularly. Never enough. The letters sat.

Accumulated. I wished and hoped forever to send them all. I knew how much they would mean to Henry. I could not bear to throw them away. I always thought I was just a day, a week, away from getting them to him. Eventually, just as the children fell into and then out of the habit of writing to him on a Sunday night, I fell into and out of the habit of thinking I would send them someday. For a while, they were in a cupboard, then in a drawer. At one time I wrapped them with some muslin, stuffed them in a case, and they became my pillow, the children's words infecting my dreams. And then he was dead. For want of a few coins, I deprived him of his children's letters. I am not proud of that fact. I am not sure how to get around it. I was faced with filling their stomachs or his heart. Always that seemed my choice. Of course, I know that a few coins are often all that stands between a child's life or death or a man and his happiness.

At least he had James. He always had James. When the children were young, Henry was attentive and playful. He was like a mother dog with puppies, letting them climb all over him, tug his whiskers, explore his equipment. As they got older, he became more, what can I say, *professorial* is a word for it, I suppose. He began to focus less on their happiness and more on their manners and their education. Instead of playing in the yard, he checked their fingernails for dirtiness; instead of letting them have free rein in his office, he asked them to sit for regular instruction from various books he had on hand; instead of plucking fruit from the trees, he made them sit upright at the table and learn the proper use of cutlery. The children naturally chafed at these restrictions. They seemed confused by this new and different father. Except for James. Where the others set their lips and wiggled in their chairs, waiting for the lesson to pass, James always gave Henry his complete attention. He was truly interested in the way things were supposed to be done. He liked order and rules. He frowned upon the rowdiness and freedoms the other children so enjoyed. When the others were crashing through the underbrush and coming home with torn clothes and bugs in their pockets, he was in the office in uncreased clothes studying nature, not right out the doors in front of him, but in the pages of books.

It was right that he stayed. He and Henry had work to do. He had much to learn from his father. Our irregular living arrangements and hands-off habits were distasteful to him. He did join us eventually. For a short while only, because he had his own plans and schemes. There was little I could do for him. Little he wanted from me. I fear he was poisoned to me for having left his father. I am sure his father railed against me. I betrayed Henry, it is true. He could not possibly feel any other way. I thought he might follow us. He had often talked about the United States in general and New York in specific. It is where he made his best money, and he spoke highly of the people he found here. But James made it clear to me that Henry had too much anger and not enough funds to come. Maybe the stories Henry told about his experiences here were not even true. There is no way for me to know.

James came not to be with us, but to pursue his education. We were simply a brief way station for him while he put aside some funds and found a situation where he could use his dentistry skills, live quietly, and finish high school so he could then go on to college. He came on a steamer, shoveling coal for his passage. So like him to do something so mulelike. I am sure he had money for the fare as he worked a variety of jobs on the island—everything from helping in the fields during harvest time to tutoring wealthy people's children. I know he kept money hidden from his father. As I had to do. I found a wad of bills under James's mattress one day when I was changing his sheets. If James had not secreted his savings in this way, Henry might have commandeered it to buy a pile of scrap to go into some earthbound contrivance. I admired James.

He was focused; he set goals and pursued them with dogged intensity. Though I did often wonder why he needed to be so calculating, so narrow sometimes in these pursuits.

Like his pursuit of my past. Maybe his father had hinted at things. Maybe he was motivated merely by his own fears, which were fed by the importance he placed on propriety. Perhaps he wanted to know so he could be aware of whatever it was he felt he might have to hide. In any case, he hounded me for information. He said this information was due to him. That my background was his background and I had to be forthcoming and forthright. The things children latch onto! As if knowing about my past would change anything about his future. Children. Always looking to use the sins of their parents as a means to excuse themselves from their own idiosyncrasies and from the assessments of the rest of the world. Even when no excuses are necessary.

James. From whence did he get such conventional and closed-minded sensibilities? Even his father, with all his blind love of the proper English way, and all his "one does this" and "one does not do that" posturing, was never this straitlaced. James was like his father in many ways, especially in the bent of his mind. But less so in his heart. There he seemed so much colder than he needed to be. He had his moments where he was full of good humor and sly wit, like his father. His smile was something to see, all the more beautiful for appearing so infrequently. Woman regularly turned toward him when he entered a room, what with his thick shock of black hair rising in a wave over his tall forehead, strong nose, full mouth. His confident bearing. Bordering on arrogance, I would have to say. I have seen him be downright charming when he chose to be. But he chose not often enough. For his own sake, I would say.

I should not have given in to his questions. I should not have asked him to read me that letter from Vea about Mr. George dying. I should have waited for Margaret to come home. She never asked questions. She seemed able to read the words in such a way that she gave each one to me without holding them for a moment herself. But I was tired after having spent so many hours on my feet and bent over a sewing machine. Worn out from having moved yet again, our few things still bundled and boxed. Worn down by his persistence. Tired from holding onto all this information for so long. But still. I should not have given in. It was unfair to burden him with it all. It was unfair to give him yet another reason to turn against his mother, Henry having given him plenty already. I suppose I had given him a few reasons myself. Maybe there was some part of me that thought the truth might help him understand my choices. Maybe I hoped I might find some empathy within him.

Of course, he needed documents to attend school. That was the start of it. He asked me for dates and places of birth and marriage so he could prove his own existence. And then Vea's letter came at around the same time. I was, also, if I am candid, a little frightened of his temper. None of my other children had a temper, but he did. At first it came up in his dark eyes, in tension between his thick eyebrows. Sometimes it boiled over into demands that came hissing through his teeth or flying out from his raised voice. More than once he began to rail at me loud enough that the upstairs neighbor banged on the floor for quiet. Once he threw his plate across the room, where it crashed in the sink. Another time he smashed his fist into a wall, which was already dented from who knows what abuse earlier tenants had rained upon it, so fortunately the landlord didn't notice. But James had to nurse bruised knuckles for that explosion. He did not bear contradiction well.

I didn't understand why it mattered to him so much that there were five years between his birth and our marriage. These things, after all, were common enough in the islands. He wanted to know why I eventually acquiesced to marrying Henry. So I told him about the possible legacy that Mr. George had discussed with me.

I thought this information would free him. He wanted to know so badly I thought knowing would give him some peace. I never anticipated that it would send him into a frenzy of letter writing and document requesting. He kept coming back to me for more and more. Tell me this information. Tell me this date. Tell me exactly what so-and-so said. I gave him what I could. But I cared little for dates, for papers made out in some government office and kept in some dank basement for no obvious reason. I told him to ask his father, but he didn't want to involve him. He said he wanted to surprise his father with the good news when he found it, but I suspect he feared his father would just waste away whatever legacy might be coming. I didn't believe the money was there, anywhere, in any dusty court in England, but I thought knowing would ease some distress he had within him. Instead, everything he learned seemed only to further feed some insatiable hunger within him.

The letters came and went, and he got facts and figures and dates, but he never got money. He never got answers. He never got peace of mind. Just like his father with his endless attempts to get contracts and patents. Or even mild interest in his inventions. They both came up completely empty-handed. All that effort for nothing.

I imagine what James really wanted, beyond money, was reasons. Reasons why I was who I was, why I did the things I did. As if people always have well-considered reasons for what they do. As if they take actions based on reason. And as if reasons somehow magically become resolution. I had no reasons to give to him, so I gave him stories instead. He asked and asked, and eventually I told and told every story I could think of about myself, my parents, my life, my children, the men who were the fathers of my children and even how my first pregnancies came about. I thought the stories might help him learn to love me a little. Instead I got his judgment and pity. I got his checks when he could spare something extra. I got his filial solicitude. But I never got his love. Oh well. Love, I had learned, came with its own burdens.

I made a life in New York. I used my skills with a needle and thread to bring in enough to keep us off the streets. It wasn't much, but it was enough. I had no one to answer to except my customers. I had no one who knew me, only people who knew my work. At first it was mostly mending. I would ask around at the various laundries within walking distance of my apartment and they would send things my way. First, just the torn clothing. Then the customers themselves. Before long I was making garments for everyday wear. I never saw anyone at my home of course, but I met people in their own apartments or at the laundry or not at all, simply communicating between the Chinese men and women who worked over steaming vats of wet clothes. Sometimes we were reduced to hand signals and motions, but it got the job done.

Then one day when I was making a delivery to a customer, she asked me if I knew how to make a fancy dress. She was a working-woman with not much means, but her daughter was getting married. She wanted something simple and elegant. She also wanted something more special than what could be bought in a store. We talked things through, and I drew something on a piece of paper. I surprised myself, actually, not realizing I could make someone's ideas real in that way. That I even had ideas of my own about how a dress might be cut to flatter a young woman's figure or how some unexpected thing I saw someone on the street wearing could be incorporated into a totally different kind of garment. It was a new thing to discover I had a talent that went beyond fixing things into imagining things.

So that's how that started. A couple of guests at the wedding eventually came to me as well. Some friends of the bride and the bride's mother sought me out. They all said my work was so fine that I should charge more. Perhaps. But, as I say, I had enough. With the work making dresses and the kids growing up and making their own money, I for the first time truly had more than enough. I often got invited to the weddings. The brides wanted me to see them in the finery I had helped create. But I never went. Seeing the girls in their dresses through the scrim of a mouthful of pins as I tugged and adjusted the fabric that hung from their nervous shoulders when I went to their homes for a fitting was more than enough for me. I was interested in the dresses because I was interested in making something. What the girls made of the dresses by getting married mattered nothing to me at all.

In spite of our troubles, I do have James to thank for showing me the library. It was where he spent much of his time. Research, he called it. For what, he couldn't be bothered explaining. His own inventions, I suppose. The first time I went there, I went wanting to know what it was that captured so much of his time and imagination. I actually followed him, at a distance, ducking behind stoops and carriages when I thought he might see me. I was unclear what the building was. I didn't follow him in for fear of being discovered. But I went back on my own, on another day.

I was there too early, before opening. I rested on the broad expanse of steps filled with the morning light. There were other people there as well. People of all sorts, it seemed, not just one class or another. When everyone is mingled and mashed together that way, you feel welcomed. At least I do. This is something Henry described and then I too found and loved in New York. For him this melting pot was an opportunity to become known for something; for me it was a chance to disappear. I sat among the others and let gravity sink my eyelids. Let the sunshine warm my face. Some time passed. When I reopened my eyes, blinking against the bright light, I saw one of the lions. So regal and powerful. Poised and thoughtful, even in stone. Then I noticed people climbing the stairs and going indoors. I followed.

Ah, books. Thousands of them. Enormous arched windows with light streaming in onto the rows of oak tables. A faraway ceiling. Chandeliers and desk lamps. I was brought back immediately to the George household. They had a library, too. Obviously much smaller, but a similar sort of room, all serious shelves, dark wood, somber books. And, best of all for me, silence. I heard Mrs. George many a time call that room a dreary, musty place. Yet more reasons for me to like it. At the George house, the library was a hideaway where I could be sure to be left alone. When I walked into this similar but far more grand space in New York, even though there were people scattered all over, their heads bent over books, I was instantly comforted. And I was drawn in, hand over hand, like a fisherman bringing in his nets. I kept to the outside edges, walking slowly, letting my fingers trail over the spines of the books. I took one gently off the shelf and let it open to random pages. Maps, charts, notes. I replaced it and tiptoed my way back outdoors. I had seen what drew James there. I understood it, too.

I didn't stay long that first day because I was a bit disoriented by the size of the room, the spectacle of it, the shared silence of so many people together—that was something I had never experienced before. I also did not know what was allowed. I didn't fully understand the idea of books for public consumption, having seen only a private library before. But the space drew me back again. It wasn't for a long time. Years, actually. I had no free time when the children were young, no time for such a thing as books or reading. I remembered, though. I remembered. Once they were gone and I had the luxury of hours of time to nothing else but myself, I returned. Each time I came back, I stepped a bit deeper into the room. I took books off the shelf. I sat down at a table and turned the pages. I tipped my head back and around to take it all in.

Then one day, while staring up at a wall of books, a slender woman stood next to me and whispered, "Can I help you?"

Her voice was so warm, her gray eyes so gentle. They implied a whole world of sympathy and understanding. I turned to them like an abused dog does to a soft hand.

"I am not sure where to begin," I said.

With a nod, she guided me to a different part of the library, a smaller, more intimate space. She pulled a few books from the shelves and sat with me at a table.

"Maybe one or another of these novels will be a good place to start," she said. "I think you'll like the stories."

She left me for a moment and then came back with a different, thicker book. There were little thumb-sized cutouts in the edge of the paper.

"A dictionary, in case you need help with understanding some of the words."

Then she smiled and left me.

This is how my education truly began. I was not very successful at educating my children. James and Margaret found their stubborn ways through high school and college, thankfully, but my other sons disliked school, had no affinity for books, were wired for action instead of contemplation. I eventually took for myself what I had hoped to give them. Yes, I had some education prior. To call it spotty would be generous. There were my father's minimal efforts. I had a tutor for a short while when I went to the George household. But Mrs. George begrudged the investment in me more than the expense itself, so this teacher didn't last long. However, I always loved books. Even when I could not parse out their content, I loved the physical objects. I could sit for hours turning the pages, running my fingers over the words there, trying out the few I knew. I tried to string them together into something resembling comprehension, but it was like trying to mend a piece of moth-eaten cloth—there were simply too many gaps to fill with too thin a thread. Still I tried. It must have looked like reading, which I knew was something to be valued, because whenever I was found with a book, I was left undisturbed. Another reason to love them.

In this new-to-me library, I was also left undisturbed. I was allowed to take as much time as I wanted or needed to unlock the tales within the pages. Occasionally the kind young woman would find me and press a favored volume on me. Sometimes she would direct me to a quiet corner where we could sit together and she would read sections out loud, but in a whisper meant for me alone. Then she would encourage me to read to her, helping me work through difficult words with an eternal patience. Finally, I had many empty hours in my life and I spent much of them at the library. I read about little women and orphaned children, a spurned governess and an island woman turned mad. I read about Jarndyce versus Jarndyce and thought of James. I read about Heidi and thought of Margaret. I read about the England Henry revered and saw little there but dark weather and a decaying culture. I even read his beloved Shakespeare, and while I didn't understand some of the language itself, I saw how expertly his plays captured how one betrayal can lead to another, until, in their efforts to ruin others, people merely ruin themselves.

I have little use for people anymore. My life has moved beyond all that pity and love, need and want, desire and hurt. It is like I live in a state that is beyond emotion, unfettered, a balloon that has freed itself from the clutches of a child. My children are grown, gone, making their own lives, their own mistakes. They are too old now for me to do anything for them. I know I did little enough for them when we lived together, but I also know I did everything that I could.

My days are filled with a pleasant emptiness. The hours stretch out in front of me uncommitted and undifferentiated. I take as long as I want over my morning pot of tea. Then my limbs begin to get restless and I go out for a walk. I have always been a walker.

Henry was forever exhorting me to stay out of the heat, to find a carriage, to learn to ride. But I have always been fond not just of the feeling of the ground beneath my feet, but also of the strength in my own legs, the freedom of being propelled forward by my own power. Horses make me nervous. Everything goes by too fast from the window of a car. I am too hemmed in by the metal and glass. My skin wants to feel the wind, the weather. So I walk.

Of course, there is little natural here. All seems man-made. The buildings either block or concentrate any and all weather conditions, so Mother Nature's moods are never left to run their course. On the island it was plants layered upon each other; here it is sidewalks, asphalt, buildings. Both places are crawling with life that is only minimally visible through windows or from behind leaves, but here it is all grays and charcoals and soot and there was all greens and blues and dust. Here it is concrete underfoot, there, soft dirt. Still, I walk. If it is not too cold, I may lose track of time, lose track of place, find myself in unfamiliar neighborhoods. I do not worry. I am not a target for anything. The grid of streets always gets me home.

I am slow now. My feet shuffle a bit. I have to rest regularly. There is fortunately always a bench or a coffee shop near enough, a stoop if nothing else. People do not mind an old woman sitting on their steps for a few moments. I am completely unthreatening, neutral, almost invisible. I am not complaining. This is a state I enjoy. This is the state of being I have spent much of my life wishing for. To be unknown. To have no one trying to figure out my background or read between my lines.

Sometimes I wander west until I am faced with the great expanse of the Hudson River. When I see the water flowing almost under my feet and the great boats chugging, sailing, drifting by, when I feel the moist air on my face and see the dark-green shore on the other side of the great flat river, when I smell the thin hint of salt from the not-so-distant sea, I am reminded: I left one island to come to another. This water in front of me flows out and away toward that other island. It flows out and away toward him and everything else that I left.

I am grounded here, the walls of buildings anchoring me in a way the mountains never could. But I am still on an island. I am still of the island. The island is within me, still.

My apartment is many flights up. The stairs don't bother me. I have been making my way up dark stairwells in this city for more than thirty-five years now. I take them slowly. The only thing I have in abundance, after all, is time. I am unsure of my age. Late sixties, I guess. My mother never recorded the year of my birth. The only thing I knew was the day. The last day of the month of September. She told me the numbers nine for the month and thirty for the day were auspicious. Of course that's not the word she used, a word of that many syllables being beyond her abilities. When I was born, she had someone do a reading, someone versed in the power of numbers. This reader, this clairvoyant, said I was to become practical and prudent, with a strong will and determined character. I am not given to extended bouts of self-reflection, but those predictions have stuck with me because they were true. It seems that the numbers witch who never even met me knew me better than people I have lived with for years.

This will be my last home. I will not move again, no matter how long it takes me to ascend to my little cave, with its well-worn furniture, cracked china, mismatched silverware, rubbed-raw tin-top table. Everything here has become shaped to fit my hand, my back, my life. I moved so many times with the children. What choice did I have when there was no money for rent and the landlord offered to forgive the debt if I gave him myself instead? I fled and then had to keep fleeing. I am done with all that.

I would have no more men, for any reason, good or ill, after Henry. My womb and everything that led to and from it was done.

A dry riverbed. The way I wanted it. The way I wished it. The way I asked Vea to make it. Full of stones made small and smooth by the tumble of so many lives now long gone by. Finally, I became too old for offers or even sideways glances of men. Yet another reason I am thankful for age. All my life, I wanted to be old. And now I am. I always sensed there would be freedom in advanced age: no more children, no husband, no one needing you, all your errors behind you, all your quirks forgiven, explained away by the years. I am anonymous now, another indistinguishable, wizened, somewhat stooped old woman shuffling along on the streets. This is what I came to America for. This is what was forbidden me on the island. Where so little is said, but so much whispered about. Where the suspicions of the locals combined with the formality of the English and the fractures of class and culture in a colony created messy piles of things not spoken but inferred. Where lies were well known, cover-ups well understood, and veneers of rites, rituals, and roles were layered, like the vegetation of the jungle, until there was no way to know where the real self began and the one created by your neighbors ended, any more than one could separate the tree from the vine that entangled it.

Here, I am free because I am unknown. I sit in a café and sip coffee and nibble at my piece of pie until I am forgotten by the waitress. I sit in the library and read until the cleaning people come in. In my own apartment, my tea grows cold before I empty the cup even halfway, the getting up to add more hot water to my wilted bag the only punctuation to my afternoon. I look down from my high window and watch the people in the street ebb and flow from the rush of lunchtime, which melds into the quiet afternoon, to the scurrying of children letting out of school, and on to the end of the day hurrying home by men in suits and women whose shoes click-clack along the pavement. There is only one small patch of sky visible to me from between the buildings. I watch it go from the thin gray of morning to the clear blue of day and then back to the thick charcoal of evening. The room goes dark around me. My body tightens around the emptiness of my stomach. My heart tightens around the emptiness of my days. It is a feeling I love, a feeling like sliding in between the comforting pressure of a well-made bed, the crisp sheets tucked tight in between the mattress.

My sons used to pay the rent. Now they are all gone, so Margaret does. I should be more sad at those losses. But they were grown men when they died. I hardly knew them anymore. They had little use for me for more years than I care to recall. They left me in so many ways, so long ago. The truth is that I am less sad they died young than that they were not more happy while they lived. I suppose I must take some of the blame for that as well. I took them from their father at too young an age. I did not give them the education I had hoped to. The many manifestations of my own poverty were in varying degrees transferred to them. I do not have the gift for happiness, so I could not pass it on to them.

Margaret calls every week. Just to make sure I am alive, I suppose. The sound of the phone always startles me so much I am afraid it may give me a heart attack. I have nothing to say to her, no news of my own to share, and I seem incapable of knowing what questions to ask her about her own life. She comes by every couple of weeks with food. Has even begun to parcel it out into individual containers of one meal each. Puts several into the freezer and a few in the refrigerator. Wonders every time why I have so little on the shelves. Some plain biscuits to go with the tea. A few cans of chicken noodle soup, a loaf of bread, a few slices of cheese—everything I eat is pale and plain, the diet of a child. She brings lasagna, chili, casseroles, things dark and rich and full of texture. I do try to eat some. For her sake. Because it matters to her. Because I didn't love her like I should have and here she is trying to love me as she should. Her face reminds me so much of Mr. George's. She was told that she looked like Henry, but it was not true—just something people said and I was never going to correct. He adored her, Henry did. That's what people saw, how he doted on her. Maybe the strength of his love, the way it washed over her for those years, messy, rambunctious, without boundaries, eventually rubbed off Mr. George's edges, those thin lips and sharp looks, and did cause her to resemble Henry more. But I can't help myself—I look at her and I see Mr. George.

I could love her better, even now. So I try. I eat what she brings. I try to enjoy it. I try to be thankful, appreciative. It may not be love, but it the best I can do. I am just no good at love, I guess.

Mr. George said he loved me. That he was ashamed, but that he loved me, that he did what he did out of love. My father said he loved me, and that was why he was sending me away. My mother, too.

The things people do and call it love.

I have never done anything for love or done something and called it love. I did the things I did because I did the only things that made sense to me at the time. People say I left the island for love of the children. As if children growing up on the island are not truly loved? That explanation makes no sense. But why correct them? People tell that kind of story because it makes sense to them, not to me. I'll let them hold on to it.

Truth is, my truth is that I left to get away from every knowing look, every comment whispered behind a hand as I walked by, every person who thought they knew where I came from, what I was made of, why I was who I was. This dark, dirty, difficult place was my version of a fresh start. Mr. George knew. He understood. He knew what I was leaving behind, having played his part in it. I could not have done it without him. Maybe there was some sort of love in that. But then again, maybe there would have been a whole lot less to run away from had I never met him and his kind of love.

Love. Is it ever without its own agenda, just something clean and simple and knowable, like a winter wind?

Henry did love me. He loved me, at least for a while, and he loved the children, always, abundantly. I have no doubt of that. I am sorry, I am so sorry that I could not love him better myself. He was a man made for loving. The children benefited from his love. Me? I am afraid I was too dry a patch of dirt by the time he came along—no matter how much you pour, water just rushes off the surface.

This is my curse. It is perhaps one of many. Some came to me unbidden. Others I brought onto myself. Or asked for. Vea cursed my womb because I asked her to. Sarah cursed my womb to exact revenge. She blamed me for Sam's leaving. She blamed me for Mrs. George's anger and sickness, which she believed led to Sam's leaving. She thought Mrs. George sent him away. I found Sarah's little obeah bundle in a corner of my room one day when I was sweeping. At first I thought it a dead mouse and I picked it up with the intention of flinging it in the yard. Then it disintegrated into a small pile of fur and feathers at my touch. Sitting in the palm of my hand were things benign on their own, but dangerous when combined by someone skilled in dark arts. A few white needle teeth. The heel spur of a chicken. A smattering of black dirt. I swept up the remnants that had fallen to the floor, combined everything together in a piece of muslin, and buried it in the family graveyard one night when no one could see me. I am not superstitious, but I am respectful of the powers of things I may not understand. I told no one, but when my palm flared up, scaly and red, oozing, Vea asked me simply if there was dirt in the bundle. I nodded yes. Graveyard dirt, she mumbled. I felt a chill then. She looked at me, all serious, and told me to hope for girls. Girls will live long for you, she said. Boys? She just shook her head.

I didn't know then what she could mean. I figured there was no reason to curse a girl, given how cursed they are by their gender alone. But now I know. All my boys died young. Even James, pickled and stubborn in his own bitterness, I suppose. All those vitamins and weight lifting. That upright carriage. Like he was always fighting to keep something at bay. He was afraid of something inside himself, afraid of his own heart, I suppose. Afraid it was no good. His father's heart killed him. Broken in so many ways. James tried to make his own heart too hard to be broken. But it busted up in the end, anyway.

I don't know whether it was Vea's or Sarah's curse that infected my womb late in my life. I felt the cancer growing in me. I didn't need a doctor to tell me what was there. Like a stranger in your unlit home, you know someone, something, is there without needing to see them. I also knew there was nothing to be done about it. No point in bothering the doctors or Margaret. I lay in the dark waiting for my own death to come lift me in its long arms, wrap me in its dark cloak, and take me away. I was ready. Perhaps I was simply tired. Life is long. Too long. I had been tired of the large things, the big insults for ages. Then I grew tired of the petty and necessary, too. Brushing my hair. Sweeping the floor. So I begged the thing inside me to grow, to consume me, to send its poison into the far reaches of my body. I embraced Sarah's curse, the one I didn't ask for, or maybe it was Vea's, the one I did, and in that way took the evil and energy out of it. In that way, I turned it away from them and made it my own.

Some might say I was cursed from the start because of my parents' illicit love. But I think not. Illicit or not, it was still love. Maybe it was a love made even more powerful because it was forbidden. They had to work for their love, my parents did. I was born of and born into a deep ocean of two sorts of loving that crashed into and caressed and strengthened each other. My wish, my only wish, my impossible wish, is that I could have done the same for my own children.

VEA

She didn't tell me there was a baby, but I knew. And I knew whose it was, too. She asked me to help her get rid of it, but I told her she should keep it. Babies are a blessing, even if the men that make them are not. I told her this. She was so young then, she didn't understand. I told her that if she kept it, he'd owe her something forever. She didn't understand this either. But I did. You never know when something like that might turn up useful.

The other girls, they were scared of Miss Rachel. They called her the white witch. But they were happy about what they think she did, what they think she brought on with a curse, because they had no love for Mrs. G. They got scars on their bodies and their souls from that one. She was the real white witch. Beat those girls in the meanest ways. On their feet. On their hands. So it wouldn't show or so she could say it was from the kitchen or the cane or walking barefoot. She didn't ever do it when Mr. G was around. He wouldn't stand for that. Not just because he took one of those girls for himself from time to time. Mrs. G didn't care about that. That's just the way it was. Half the time the girls didn't mind because if they get a baby or sometimes even if they don't, they think the rich white man will set them up with some money, a house, piece of land, ticket to go live someplace else. Which Mr. G did more than once. Mrs. G didn't care that Mr. G wanted that girl. She'd had enough of Mr. G herself—had separate rooms, those two, for years. And they didn't visit in the night. I know because I cleaned up those rooms. No, that's not what made her jam a piece of cane in between that girl's legs. Mrs. G wanted a different man, and that man wanted a different girl. Mrs. G had the same tastes that Mr. G did. Everyone expects it from a white man, but not from a white woman. Even though it's common enough. More common than anyone wants to admit.

But that man Sam, he was just after her money. Mrs. G fell in love, the old fool. Or thought she did. Sam always had his eye on Sarah. Course he did—why he want some old white woman when he could have a young girl full of sass? But that man Sam was a fool too and figured he could make some money if he went with Mrs. G. He thought he could get money from Mr. G by telling on her. Money he could use to set himself up in a house and a food stall with Sarah. Ha. Showed how little he knew. Mr. G would have just laughed at him. Mr. G cared as little for what his wife did as she cared for what he did. Ever since they sent their fancy daughters to England for school and husband finding, those two started to go their separate ways. Before long they didn't bother with parties or pretense anymore.

The house girls thought that after Rachel pulled Mrs. G off her beating of Sarah she put some curse right into Mrs. G's ear and that's why she came down with that slow sickness that ate her body and then her mind. But I knew better. First off, curses don't work like that; second, Rachel did not know any obeah. That I know. She didn't even believe in obeah. Even when she asked me to help her get rid of the baby, it wasn't obeah she was asking for. She wanted something she could count on, medicine, a certain kind of doctor, not curses. I also knew it wasn't any curse because once Sam left here, full of fear of how crazy with her sick love Mrs. G had become, scared of Sarah and her ruined self, too, he moved away someplace where I had relations. They told me. He got sick too. Just the same way as Mrs. G. He carried his sickness to Mrs. G and then back onto himself. Somehow Sarah escaped the sickness. Well, that sickness. She got her own sort of sickness. She didn't get off easy, that's for sure.

It was no matter that the girls thought Rachel was a witch. Made them respect her. Made them steer clear of her. Made them think twice about making messes of themselves around her. This whole mess was what got Mrs. G stuck up in her room where she couldn't do no one harm anymore. So it worked out in its own way. As usually happens.

I also told her not to marry him.

I told her, "Keep free. No need to marry just because you have children. Marrying is fine for those other white women. You look white, you are part white, but you are something else."

I told her that. More than once.

Oh, she looked white, with that fine, fine skin of hers. Everyone wanted to touch her skin. I saw that. I didn't know and I didn't care exactly what color she was on the outside. All I know is she had a heart that longed to be free. She had a soul that longed to keep its own company and no one else's. Not free to be wild or lazy like some, but free to be kept alone, apart, to hold its own secrets.

She kept saying no to him. She listened to me. Course, saying no was what she wanted. Easy to take advice when it's what you wish for yourself anyway. I watched from the kitchen as she shook her head, eyes down, looking at the ground like there's something in the dirt that will help her. That will help make him understand. But then the babies kept coming. And he went to town every day to pull people's rotten teeth and listen to them talk their gossip, even while he had his hands in their mouth. People pay too much attention to that kind of chatter. Gossip is just like a bee—it comes and it goes and it stops at every pretty flower, but it does no harm unless you stop it, try to catch it, and hold onto it. Then it stings you.

He kept asking me if I knew. He meant did I know she was planning to leave, to take all the children on that boat.

I said, "No," and that was the truthful answer to his question.

But like men do, he was asking the wrong question.

He should have been asking me, "Why?" Why did she want to run away like that? Run so far away where it was cold and she didn't know anybody. That question I had an answer to. But maybe it was an answer he didn't want to hear or wouldn't understand if he did hear. He thought, he was afraid, that she was running away from him. He was unhappy because he thought her leaving said something bad about him, about why he couldn't keep her. But that was not it. She wasn't running from him—he was not a bad man, he was far better than most, and she knew that. What he didn't see was that she wasn't running from much of anything. She was running toward something. She wanted a life that she could call her own. Maybe, probably, a worse life in all kinds of ways. But at least it was her own.

Of course, as Henry aged, and I tried to help him take care of himself, everyone talked about the two of us. Everyone had some stupid thing to say, some snickering to do behind the backs of their hands. Here we were: him an old man; his first wife, the good wife, dies young while trying to have his baby; second wife, bad wife, too young, born of bad blood, left him years ago, and he never got over it. Then he's living alone in a house that has seen a lot better days with no children, no woman, just his housekeeper. His housekeeper's son, all grown now, isn't even there anymore to keep things on the up-and-up. This son, which she had even though she was not married and had no man, had skin lighter than her own, a whole lot lighter, in fact. You can see how people might add things up. But in my case, the math did not work. They were adding the wrong things together. Silly talk. All just silly talk.

I cooked, I cleaned for Henry. He was a good man who needed someone to take care of him. He never was good at taking care of himself. I was getting old myself, so I moved slow. I made the garden grow again and sold my vegetables for good money. The chickens, her chickens, they came back from the hills and had babies over the years, so we had plenty of eggs for ourselves and to sell. I banged together a coop to keep them safe. Henry and I kept each other company. Sat in peace, without talking. He was so nice to my boy. Taught him to read and write. Showed him all his tools. Told him lots of history, all about England, America, other countries, always pointing at things on the globe.

Silly talk, that gossip about us.

It's not like he was a real man anymore, anyway. I saw that when I helped him into his bath. Henry was too old for that sort of thing. And I had enough of white men in that way, anyway. Mr. G took me too many times without my wanting him to and tore me up inside for good for that sort of thing.

Here she comes, across that tarmac. Margaret. Maggie as a girl. Now a woman, so Margaret again. Look at her. Tall, like him. No flesh on her bones, like him. She got that nose of her mama's. She got her freckles, too. But look at those eyes—they are Mr. G's, all right. Dark. Watching, watching, looking for something to go wrong. The way she walks, too. Striding forward like she needs to catch up with something. Which I suppose she does. I suppose it's why she came.

My boy has it, too. Like her, he is more his daddy than his mama. I wonder if she'll see it in him. If she'll see herself in my boy's face. If it will be a mirror to her the way it is so clearly to me. Or if it will be for me to tell her.

Ah, she sees me. Look at that smile—now I see her mama in her. Rachel smiled so seldom. But when she did, it was a thing of beauty. I think Margaret is like her in this way. Her father, Mr. G, he was a frowner, too. So she has it from both sides. Maybe she'll find more to smile about here. Now she's seen her husband. Her lips tighten up a bit, but in a good way. Like she's holding back a whole big wave of emotions she was not expecting to have and not sure what to do with. She's looking at my boy, my boy, Carell, grown into a man now. That smile of hers. It's changing again. Not so sure. Like she's has caught herself reflected in a store window. You see some version of yourself you didn't expect. You are a little unsure of yourself all of a sudden.

She came here thinking, wanting, hoping she'd find some part of her mother, her father—both of them—and of course some part of herself. She wants to find something she thinks she lost along the way. That is clear. But we, her husband and I, we have a few surprises for her. At least they are, finally for this family, good surprises. Real good surprises. Her husband? He found her a small fortune that was left to her a long time ago by a father she never knew and never knew she had. As for me? I have a son to give to her as a brother.

MARGARET

I CAME HERE WITH THE IDEA THAT IF I UNDERSTOOD MORE ABOUT my past, I would be able to have a better present. I never imagined I'd get an entirely new future.

Marcus and I did not reinstate our relationship; we fell in love afresh. It is a different kind of love than we had before, with none of the breathlessness and sharp edges of fear that you might lose something you desperately want, which so often goes along with a younger sort of love. We were no longer restless or wondering about ourselves, our places in the world. This new love we found was clean and fresh, like the breeze coming off the ocean.

Vea is like an auntie I never had, fretting over me as if I were a child, not a mature, middle-aged woman. She worries over whether I eat enough, eat well enough, take enough time away from my desk. I tell her to save her fussing for the children at the school we've started. It's an orphanage too, of course, but we don't call it that. Too Dickensian. We've made it into a home where kids who don't have one can come to live and learn not just about math and reading and science, but about how to be a part of a family. Even if it is an ersatz family. We all seem to know an awful lot about cobbling together a family from the people you find along the way.

We call it the George School. Some might wonder why we named it after a man who did so much bad to so many people in his life—not that there are any but us who know his full history. We named it after him not just because it's his money that made it possible; we named it after him because he is the reason we are all here, together. He is the man who knits together our history. And our blood, in its many manifestations. He caused our blood to run in us, and yes, in some cases out of us. All the more reason to do some good with what he left us. Left me, I know, but I don't look at the money like that. Seems he left it to all of us. They just needed me to release the funds from the legal limbo in which they'd been left. With plenty of help from Marcus.

The money also belongs to Carell. Vea chose the name because she liked the sound of it. But I looked it up. His name means happiness, and that is what he brings. Always smiling, always gentle. His is a face that brightens your own. His name also means warrior. If so, he is a warrior for peace. The way he separates fighting children, soothes their anxieties and hurts. Especially the hurts they carry inside. He gets his way from his mother. Vea says he is like his father—like my father, our father, I often remind myself—but I don't know. I see so much of her in him. They both, Vea and Carell, make my heart swell with a deep comfort.

Vea. My mother must have loved her so. What a calm, still island of peace and tranquility Vea must have been for my mother in the midst of the many dislocations of her life. Sometimes on a Sunday afternoon I take the quiet walk out of the busy streets of Royalton, up into the hills thick with greenery where she still lives in the house Henry left for her, the house of my childhood. It is like returning to your grammar school as an adult; all the rooms seem so much smaller, more modest than you remembered. We sit on the compact veranda—a space that in my memory was so vast the child I was had to run for many steps before she could find her father's lap—and we sip lemonade, our outstretched legs propped up on the railing. We don't talk much about the past. We chat about the school, strategize how to bring along various students who are stuck either academically or emotionally, dream big futures for Carell's teenage twin boys, who are doing so well on their own, scholar/athletes that they are, they hardly need our fantasies.

Sometimes she tells me something of Henry or Rachel. A small story, a wistful anecdote, a passing memory. She knew them both in the fullness of everything they were and were not. She gives them back to me, bit by bit, piece by piece, so I can have them not just as parents or memories or emotional baggage, but as complex, damaged, quirky individuals who were trying to do the best they could with the flawed, dinged, hand-me-down tools they had at hand. She sends me home with fresh empathy for them. She also sends me home with fresh eggs from the descendants of the chickens my mother once kept.

Some days, when I am at my desk working on a new lesson plan, the children's squeals as they are let into the courtyard for recess are a welcome distraction from my task. I watch them race around, skip rope, bounce balls, and I sometimes wonder if I'm trying too hard to make up for something, trying to fix somehow all the sadness and misdirection in my parents'—all my parents'—lives. And then I think, well, so what if I am? Does healing old wounds dilute whatever good we are doing for these children in the here and now? Of course not. It took many bad things to bring us all together, here on this island. But it is good things, only good things, that are keeping us here, that are keeping us together.

AUTHOR'S NOTE

DURING MY CHILDHOOD, THIS WAS THE STORY, THE ONLY STORY, anyone ever told about my great-grandparents: Henry and Rachel lived in Jamaica for reasons having to do with Henry's health. One day Henry and his eldest son, my grandfather James, came home to an empty house; Rachel had taken the rest of their children on a steamer to New York because Henry was so impractical, he spent their money on crazy inventions and there was never enough money for school or even shoes. She wanted them to be educated. She left James behind because he was so close to his father, she didn't want to split them up.

This tale, like much family lore, was told without elaboration or question. No one explored its internal inconsistencies. No one asked how Rachel pulled off this feat: a woman with no apparent means, in secrecy, cleaning out her house and taking five of her six children onto a boat from the Caribbean to New York City sometime in the early 1900s. By tone of voice, the teller of this story, who was most usually James's wife, my grandmother Daisy, made it clear that there was something heroic in Rachel's shrugging off her irresponsible husband and setting out on her own. The tale stuck with me. The idea of this woman named Rachel stuck with me. The question of her motivation, daring, and what the results of her bold move might have been stuck with me.

When I was in my late teens, I met Tom's eldest daughter, my mother's first cousin, and began hearing more Rachel stories. She was thought to be illiterate. Part mulatto. From a different class than Henry. She never sent the letters she had her children write to their father. Her children were never properly educated because she moved constantly to stay ahead of the rent. Then, when I was twenty years old, my mother was murdered. After cleaning out her house, my brother sent me a box of letters and documents that included dozens of letters Henry had written to James after James followed his mother and siblings to New York in 1914, up to Henry's death in 1922. My mother's cousin and I compared more notes and documents as we tried to piece together our shared history and I began doing the research that would inform my memoir of my mother's life and death, *Unraveling Anne.* When I discovered, by looking at Rachel's death certificate, that she and I shared the same birthday, I knew that someday I would write about her, too.

Because I could uncover almost no facts about Rachel's history, I eventually realized that the book I would write would have to be a novel. Let me be clear: all the characters in this book, even the ones inspired by family members, are complete products of my imagination. But this is a fiction that utilizes a series of facts, documents, and stories from real life within its invented universe. For instance, all of Henry's missives, other than the one where he refers to Margaret's parentage, are excerpts of the actual letters in that box my brother sent me when I was twenty years old. Many of the documents my completely made-up Margaret explores are the same ones the real me explored. Some of the details about Henry's life and parentage are documented truths. Other anecdotes from my research have been dropped in here and there where they fit my literary purposes: Rachel's eldest daughter had a father who was not Henry; there was apparently some sort of "kidnapping" of Tom when he was quite young; my grandfather James did finish high school and work with a dentist in Utica, New York, near where I lived when I wrote this book; James also did attend MIT, became an aircraft engineer, and designed, most notably, the legendary 1937 Spartan Executive, the first all-metal aircraft; the real-life Tom was a painter of Broadway sets; Rachel died of uterine cancer; some thought the family had been cursed.

This real-life woman, my great-grandmother Rachel, has occupied my imagination for many decades. The researching of this book allowed me to conjure who she might have been. The writing of it allowed me to create a much more complex and contradictory woman than I originally anticipated. My great-grandmother was an enigma, a puzzle of scattered pieces I wanted to put back together. In the process of creating my fictional Rachel, I also created a set of other characters who were striving to understand her just as much as I was.

ACKNOWLEDGMENTS

FOR INSPIRING AND INFORMING ME WITH THEIR OWN STORIES, travelogues, collections, research, and memoirs, I thank the following: Lady M. A. Barker, Eliot Bliss, Charlotte Brontë, Winifred James, Evelyn O'Callaghan, Mary Prince, Jean Rhys, and *The Routledge Reader in Caribbean Literature.*

For her *My Jamaican Family* blog, which provided so much information on Henry's family, I thank Dorothy Kew.

For always being a click away when I needed to check a geographic or historic point, I thank Wikipedia.

For being as interested in family lore as I am, I thank Linda Ford Blaikie.

For her excellent editorial insights, which added immeasurably to this book, I thank Charlotte Herscher.

For their exceptional care of my work and for being such lovely individuals overall, there are not enough thanks to extend to the entire team at Amazon Publishing, especially Victoria, Daphne, Brooke, Jessica, and most of all Terry, without whom I never would have had the deep personal, professional, and literary pleasures of your company.

And for making me feel brave, I thank Ned.

ABOUT THE AUTHOR

Photo © Hudson Photo, 2013

Laurel Saville is an award-winning writer. Her memoir, *Unraveling Anne*, originally published under the title *Postmortem*, won a Next Generation Indie Book Award and a Hollywood Book Festival Award in 2011. A graduate of New York University, she also holds a master of fine arts degree in creative writing and literature from Bennington College in Vermont.